GABRIEL'S BODY
Curt Siodmak

Dr. Patrick Cory had dedicated his entire life to science until an accident killed his trusted assistant and scarred him beyond repair. In constant pain, the biochemist turned to his work and found that, with the technology he had created, science could give him a new life. All Cory needed for his experiment to succeed was a living body. But with the body came hidden desires, and soon Cory realized that the brain-dead man he thought he would command like a remote-control toy had a deadly will of his own.

GABRIEL'S BODY

BODY

CURT SIODMAK

LEISURE BOOKS **NEW YORK CITY**

A LEISURE BOOK®

October 1992

Published by

Dorchester Publishing Co., Inc.
276 Fifth Avenue
New York, NY 10001

Printed in the United States of America.

For Henrietta,
with admiration for the patience
she needs to be married to a writer.

GABRIEL'S BODY

Preface

Gabriel's Body is the third part of a trilogy. It started with *Donovan's Brain,* followed 20 years later by *Hauser's Memory,* and after another 20 years by *Gabriel's Body.* All three have the same protagonist, Dr. Patrick Cory.

I found the name Cory on a street sign off Sunset Boulevard in Los Angeles. The year was 1940. That name attracted me. It was short, mysterious, and difficult to forget. *Gabriel's Body* had in its first version the title *Dr. Cory's Experiment.*

I mailed *Dr. Cory's Experiment* to my publisher in New York. He sent the manuscript back with a scathing letter. He had never heard of a more silly idea! I had written about microchips, which had not been discovered at that time! I still have that letter somewhere in my files. Should I find it, I will frame it.

Every idea that opens a still unknown face of science is frightening. I wrote *Skyport*, a novel about a satellite that circles the earth, just before Sputnik appeared in the sky, awakening the lethargic, smug American space scientists. To leave this earth and float above this mortal ken terrified the public. But as time went by, sending people to the moon and returning them safely became an accepted venture. So have the invention of microchips, semiconductors, microscopic miniaturization of electric conduits, and fiber optics—the technical possibilities of which have scarcely been explored.

In the Middle Ages, the Church discussed earnestly how many angels could stand on the head of a pin. Now we know: millions, with the help of microchips. That silly idea of microchips has changed the face of the scientific world and is intruding into our private lives.

But at the time I sent my novel to the publisher, I was so chastened by his criticism that I buried that manuscript among the unsalable material in my files. Dr. Cory, however, refused to be buried, and he soon found himself in scientific peril again—this time more successfully in *Donovan's Brain*.

Dr. Cory's Experiment remained in my files almost forgotten until my wife Henrietta found it years later. On her insistence, I took the book along on a trip to Europe and revised it. The book was immediately published in Germany under the title *Ich, Gabriel* (*I, Gabriel*).

The three novels about Dr. Cory—*Donovan's Brain, Hauser's Memory,* and now *Gabriel's Body*—seem to be a mirror of my life span. He was a young man in *Donovan's Brain,* middle-aged in *Hauser's Memory,* and now in his later years in *Gabriel's Body.*

America has a singular cult: staying young at all costs. Is it the fear of dying? In contrast to Europeans, people don't die in the United States. They pass away with the hope of being reborn in a better ken than this troubled earth. The German just die—they *sterben;* in French the word is *mourir.* Those languages have no substitute word for death.

But Americans don't easily face the termination of life or even aging. It seems to be a deep fear in them to enter that void for which religions have fairy-tale vision: believing souls are transported into a better world. But I cannot visualize what good that will do if we have no memory of our past lives to compare the next one with the former. The saved souls might be as discontent in another world as they were on this one if they are missing the memory of the tribulations they suffered on this planet.

But the earthly race is always searching for eternal youth. In 1513, Juan Ponce de Leon, who had been with Christopher Columbus on his second voyage, discovered Bimini. This fabulous island, which might have been present-day Florida, was believed to contain a miraculous fountain or spring whose waters would restore old people to their youth. The hope for regaining a youthful body, enjoying again those fleeting, short years is an obsession now helped by face-lifters, weight watchers, and youth worshippers. People hide their real age as though getting old were a crime looked down upon by the young.

The story of *Gabriel's Body* asks which is the more important objective for a scientist: to reveal to the world his discovery—or to gain in his declining years the power and exhilarating joy of youth, which he never had, but now craves to experience? The meaning of *Gabriel's Body*, for me, is a symbol of our time.

A new body would not change Cory's approach to living since his mind must also be recon-structed. Cory is a finely honed intellectual involved in scientific research, but he is devoid of any human empathy. He cannot change the ingrained pattern of his ego, which has always dominated his life. He does not know that he is a slave of a perception that arrogantly refuses change.

This state of mind also is the ailment of nations that cling to ingrained routines of life they do not want to give up. As a result, they lose their flexi-bility to change and decline. They are bypassed by other nations that willingly adjust themselves to the demands of this rapidly shifting world.

THE ARIZONA DESERT, 1988

Chapter One

The same dream has harassed me for more than two years—a nightmare that reels itself off like a motion picture, starting the same way, ending always with my involuntary scream. Though tortured by the dream, I continue to argue in my sleep about its origin, rationalizing that it is only a fantasy and that, as soon as I choose to wake up, the nightmare will be but a dull echo of a terror that could not stand the light of day. But while trying to uncover the etiology of my recurrent dream, I also am aware that waking will project the terror of the nightmare into my consciousness.

At night the incubus squats on my face. As long as the demon presses himself on me, the task of separating the psychic from the somatic dream stimulus is postponed. I am aware that I don't want to face the fact that the explosion, Malcolm's death, and my own disfigurement had, in reality, occurred.

In my dream I see myself in my laboratory. The image is imprinted in my memory as statically as a photograph. I watch myself as an onlooker. My eyes are shielded behind heavy goggles as I observe tiny electric circuits etched in plastic, conduits so infinitesimally small that they can only be seen through magnifying glasses. The laboratory is crowded with electronic equipment. Malcolm and I are working on miniature computers, which, activated by isotopes, are independent from outside power sources. It is the trend of the technics to develop machines toward the microscopically small.

In the corner Malcolm is lighting the needle-thin flame of a blowtorch. The sharp green flame's intensity is blinding.

Suddenly, in my dream, the room bursts into a cloud of crimson. I am catapulted against the wall, then the sound of the explosion echoes back from the room's ceiling. My face is on fire and flames are dancing on my hands like candles stuck to my knuckles. As I stagger to my feet, the cracked window reflects my face. But it is not a face anymore; it is a mass of raw flesh oozing blood. Where my mouth had been, a flame flickers. Only then do I hear my scream.

This is my recurrent dream. It starts with the picture of the laboratory and ends up with this maniacal cry, a cry that invariably forces me to wake up. At once the demon that had been squatting on my face vanishes. I find myself in bed, wet with perspiration. For a moment I don't dare touch my face, lest I find out the truth. But that dull pain at my temples and cheeks reminds me that the dream has been the repetition of reality.

Before I returned to Brentwood House, I would awaken to a reflection in the window staring at me: a horrible mask only faintly resembling a human face. The mouth had been grafted and supplied with artificial lips; the skin, melted to the bone and crisscrossed with red scars, was tightly pulled over the skull. Not a shred of flesh was left underneath. My features were immobile except for the eyes, which heavy glasses had protected from destruction. Every morning I looked at a face that was not mine—the caricature of a bloodless, pale death, as Brueghel or Bosch might have conceived in their eternal fear of the hereafter.

Outside my window a desert stretched, studded with saguaro cacti that reminded me of demons with upraised arms and tails. The sun, still below the horizon, sent a spectrum of light in colors of transparent greens and reds into the sky. Soon it would jump over the horizon and cause the air to vibrate with a heat that enclosed my house like a wall.

I liked to be walled in. This was my choice. The world behind the end of the desert did not interest me anymore. I had not left since I left Brentwood House, where I had undergone therapy to make me accept my new face, if it could be called a face. A weak spot in a small steel drum containing a highly volatile liquid had shunted my life onto a single track.

Every time I come across any new problem in my work, I think of Malcolm. There was an indefectibility in our collaboration. As a teacher at Berkeley, I at once sensed the genius in that young man who had become my assistant. Our different interests fused. He reminded me of part of a computation of which I knew some symbols; the missing ones he supplied. We worked together like two hands of the same body. Once we found a mutual satisfaction in our research, the outside world became dim and unattractive to us.

It might be that this devotion to our research was a flight from ourselves, but the best stimulus to run ahead is to have something to run from. It is the result that matters and not its compulsive force. Research into thought transfer became the predominant issue in our lives, the only avenue of our conversation. We constantly and passionately talked shop, as if we feared that time for the exchange of ideas might run out.

It has. Malcolm is dead. With his death the world moved even farther away from me. And since I did not communicate with people anymore, time had been added to my life—time that before had often been squandered on amenities, conversations, lectures, and conferences. I allowed no time to be stolen from me. My face was the barrier that kept people out of the house, and I hated to show myself with a black mask like that of an executioner. To be shut off from the diversions of the world helped me to discover my values. After leaving Brentwood House, I didn't come across a problem, however complex, that I could not solve. And my disfigurement had become a weapon for safeguarding my hermit's life. Still, in my dreams, when my guard was down, I heard that scream.

I didn't sleep much—three or four hours a night. Like the repetitious chores of every day living, sleep was time lost.

At six every morning, Kaweah's old ford truck would stop at the house. Kaweah was an Indian woman from the reservation. Every day she drove up in her boiling car to clean the house and to put food into the refigerator. She also brought the mail, letters from universities and hospitals with my name still on their lists for lectures and contributions. I never answered, and the one-sided correspondence had almost trickled out.

Kaweah moved noiselessly; she avoided me and I usually stayed in the laboratory as long as she was around. I would also put on that black piece of material with slits for my eyes in order not to scare her unnecessarily. We rarely spoke to each other. She followed her unvarying routine, which eliminated surprises. There was always enough money in the kitchen drawer for her wages and the household expenses. She put the receipts in the drawer, but I never looked at them and threw the bundle away when it became too large. Kaweah was a shy person, and I don't think she could have worked for anyone but me.

I wanted to use her for my experiment, but believed she might refuse. The morning I asked for her assistance, I knew I had to be careful not to frighten her, which was almost an impossible task.

I called her as she stopped in the door of the laboratory. Kaweah was in her late twenties, thin like a reed, her dark skin baked dry by the desert sun. Her hair was shiny black and pulled tautly over her narrow-boned head. Despite her youth, she was beyond her prime as a woman and had become a working machine. Behind her carved, unemotional face I sensed her alarm.

"Come in and sit down," I ordered her from behind my mask. I could hear my voice, a voice cracked due to my artificial mouth. When Kaweah did not move, I became impatient.

"Don't be afraid, damn it," I said with deliberate gruffness. Anger would make my demand seem less important. "I won't hurt you. I need your help." And to arouse her pride, I added, "Why are you frightened? All I want is to test this little gadget, and I can't without someone to help me. See how small it is? It couldn't do any harm."

I picked up the two tiny electrodes, small oblong capsules, the result of ten years work. They were receivers containing their own amplification.

"Now sit down, will you?" I said, calm now. "All I want to do is tape these two little things to your temples."

The mask and my rigid attitude must have frightened her even more. She wanted to run away but pride prevented her. Any deviation from her routine alarmed her. Changes are danger; the new is the menace, the unexpected the enemy.

"I won't scalp you," I joked and she sat down, her hands trembling in her lap.

"You've never seen anyone else in my house," I kept on, knowing that as long as I talked she had no time to think. "I depend on you to assist me. You won't even know. See—that's all!"

I fastened the electrodes to her brown skin and stepping back, continued as if soothing a child. "I know I look like a witch doctor to you. Whatever we don't understand looks like magic to us. There is no magic in this world, only a lack of information and superstition. Man's limitations are of his own making."

I inserted the tape into the small recorder, then slid the miniature circuits into the same case and connected the power. The pilots shone like tiny, moving pearls. The miniature transcorder flashed its coded message as I watched Kaweah's reactions.

She gripped the armrests of the chair. Her mouth half opened, turning out the lighter insides of her lips. She exposed her strong teeth and the muscles of her cheeks started to work as she vainly tried to suppress the compulsion to

23

talk. Her jaw moved, fighting the force she could not resist. The miniwattage of the output was stronger than her brain impulses. She became an automaton as she started to speak in very heavily accented French.

"Il est évident qu'il y a infiniment plus de saints obscurs que de saints publics. Nous savons de toutes parts qu'il y a eu d'innombrables saints secrets. Nous savons de certain qu'un très nombre peut, par une sortie d'affectation à Dieu, tourner sa maladie on martyre, faire sa maladie la manière même d'un martyre."

The tape ran out. Kaweah stopped talking and utter bewilderment covered her face. She lifted her hands to the electrodes on her temples. Quickly I walked over to her before she could take them off, and I removed them.

"You see," I said, "it didn't hurt at all. Or did you feel anything?"

"I heard a voice," she muttered. "Who was it?"

"Yours."

"Not mine," she insisted. "No, I didn't talk."

"You heard it, but didn't know that you talked."

"Did I really? What did I say?" She stared at me. The bottomless fear returned to her eyes. "What did you make me say?"

"It didn't hurt, did it?"

"No . . . but I talked . . . against my will!"

"All right." I wanted to end that conversation that could only disturb her. "Thank you. You helped me a great deal."

Shafts of pain suddenly attacked my skull, and my vision, as always during these seizures, blurred.

"Go home," I said. "Come back tomorrow."

She heard the agony in my voice and disappeared. A minute later I heard her Buick grind its gears.

I went to my bedroom and picked up the Demerol tablets. I held them in my hands just as a safeguard, but used them only as a hypnotic focus point, a kind of crutch. Knowing they were there helped me control my pain.

There is a delicate relationship between pain and illness, pain and personal existence. I can control my algophobia by hypnotic commands. Since the accident, as soon as my control relaxes, pain attacks me like a pack of wolves. Pain does not explain anything. Its role is merely to make us aware of any body ill by instantaneous sensation. But chronic pain, *la douleur-malaise,* is of its nature absolutely senseless. I finally made the pain retreat until it again was sheathed by the constant dull sensation of my mutilated nerve fibers.

Kaweah had spoken French, a language she had never heard in her life. It had been transmitted to her. I held an awesome discovery. If I were to die the secret would perish with me. I thought of Malcolm, and how his genius would spout out the possibilities of this discovery, expand its ramifications, compute its potentials and dissect them with his surgical mind. I knew I had to talk to somebody and decided to call James

O'Brian. He might be able to grasp the extent of this phenomenon. O'Brian was not creative, but analytic. He dealt with the past and not with the future. I had known O'Brian since he was a sophomore studying psychology at UCLA 25 years ago. Now he was the head of Brentwood House, a hospital primarily for the mentally retarded. Brentwood House was only 40 miles away. O'Brian was a link with the outside world.

As I picked up the telephone, it occurred to me that I had not really intended to cut all ties with the humdrum of civilization. For why should I have kept the telephone? It once had saved my life when I called for help after the explosion, dialing with my elbow since my fingers had been too raw to move the disk. Now again it served a purpose.

A girl at the Brentwood House switchboard answered. As I asked for James O'Brian I experienced a weird emotion; I couldn't tell if it was regret or pleasure at hearing a human voice.

"He's with a patient," the girl said. "Could you call later?"

She annoyed me. "It is important," I said and sensed her hesitation.

Then O'Brian was on the phone. "Patrick!" his voice expressed pleasure. "How nice of you to call. Yes, suh, what can I do for you?"

He faked that Southern accent, knowing it helped him by smoothing out harshness, producing confidence, and making things seem less important. But he did not need to put on that act for me. I know his professional mannerisms better than he does.

"I want you to come over right away," I said, hating myself for having called for help. His trained ear caught the urgency.

"I'd enjoy stoppin' by for a bourbon and branch, Patrick. You know in fact, Ah'll just come ovah." He hung up as though afraid I might change my mind.

I had been his patient for six months, first at the hospital, then at his home within Brentwood House's compound. He had insisted that the plastic surgery be performed at his hospital. I know he thought I needed mental therapy, a polite term for bringing disturbed people back to their senses. Brentwood House was well equipped for that phase of recuperation. At his home we discussed my case with a frankness that would have shocked any other psychiatrist. But he knew that I was as well equipped to judge my disturbances as he. His mind was slow, but he maintained that a man who thinks slowly had a chance to think more clearly. He smoked a pipe, believing that the unhurried puffing set the pace for his thoughts. I am sure the guards in a prison feel as shut in as the prisoners and that the doctors of an asylum are affected by the mental unbalance of their inmates. The borderline between sanity and insanity cannot be established. Psychiatry is supposed to deal with the mind, but no one has ever seen a mind not associated with a heart, a set of lungs, and other miscellaneous machinery that certainly influences the gray matter. In our discussions about myself, we usually ended by analyzing him and not me. I can handle my problems without the confusing thoughts of a psychiatrist.

Being around people more disturbed than I restored my equilibrium. I must have been his toughest case, partly since we had been friends for years, which impeded his authority as a doctor, and partly because he knows that my intellect surpasses his.

O'Brian would have liked me to have had a complete nervous breakdown instead of adjusting to fate with such ease. A nervous breakdown would have given him the opportunity to apply his cherished shock treatment, which impedes man's memory. He also would have had the chance to impose his therapies on me.

All geniuses are monomaniacs, he has said, and in his opinion I have never been normal. During my recovery, he pointed out that I showed unreasonable tendencies and interests in only one area of my life. After all, even Einstein had a hobby—playing the fiddle. How well, we did not discuss. He questioned the cause for my attachment to Malcolm Unwin, which he called an obsession. In his opinion Malcolm and I both had been unable to control the flow of associations, which moved us into abstract fields where O'Brian's knowledge ended. We had escaped into a realm where he could not follow. He never forgave me for that.

"You are trying to achieve complete concentration on your work to the exclusion of other thoughts. This is unhealthy. It creates, perforce, a constant struggle within you. Besides, your problems find their only expression in the intellectual sphere, and you deliberately detach yourself from every emotion. This is dangerous."

"Dangerous for whom?" I asked,

"For your sanity."

"Define sanity," I challenged him. He was working with patients whose IQs started near zero and went up to sixty. After that number they would be let loose on the public. "I think I must be insane to be able to live with my new face."

At once I knew that I had made a mistake and had given him an opening. I should never have brought up my concern about my face at all.

"You believe in the omnipotence of thought because it gives you a feeling of superiority over me, for example," he said, purposely not taking advantage of me. He was probing to find out how far he could go in his analysis of me. He even tried to arouse my anger.

I knew he considered me a compulsive neurotic, even paranoic. Compulsive neurotics are inhibited in the expression of their emotions. In my case he was right. Normal people are able to neutralize rising emotions of hatred. Compulsive neurotics are not. That makes them dangerous, and he was afraid of that. But he did not need to worry. I kept myself well in hand, so well that I left no opening for his professional aggression.

"When you have your new face, you're bound to change your outlook on life," O'Brian told me. He, the psychiatrist, made an unpardonable blunder with that remark. He should have taken into account that the plastic surgery might be unsuccessful, that it would create the mask of a monster, which any sensitive person would never be able to endure.

Dr. Vainhuus, whom I knew from UCLA, worked on my new face. If agonies could be turned into pleasure, I would have had the most enjoyable time of my life. Pain can be endured by anticipation; pain that arrives without forewarning, finding the mind unprepared, can destroy. Before Vainhuus started on me, he told me in detail the agonies I would have to go through. For him the operation was routine, for me an experience bolstered by curiosity. I accepted the accompanying tortures as such, knowing that one day they would be over and that I would have a face again. What it was going to be had been sketched out and left to my approval. I found it amusing to have a new face molded. None of my former acquaintances would be able to recognize me. I had chosen a Greek nose, a larger mouth with full lips. All in all, at the end of the napping out of the new face, I found to my surprise that the sketch resembled Malcolm! That might have been coincidence—or my wish to bring Malcolm back.

The work was done at Brentwood House. It seemed to go well. Vainhuus accompanied every step with a lecture, informing me about what he was doing and how pleased he was with his grafting of skin and shaping of tissues. I was not able to see myself and began to feel like the Invisible Man since my head was swathed in bandages. Vainhuus also warned me about the lengthy work he would have to do later removing the scar tissues. He showed me a motion picture of burn victims and the work that was done on them. Some of those men had been kept away from the public eye for 15 years or more. After what had happened to them, third-degree burns, reconstructive surgery was a job that took time.

Mine did not. One day, when Vainhuus removed my bandages for further work, I saw him pale. I felt my face become liquid, running, bending, caving in. The bones had been too weak to carry the new structure. Within a few minutes, in front of Vainhuus and the shocked nurse, my features changed into a mask of death—the mask I now wear. Vainhuus gave up his work on me. There was no chance of osteoplasty. O'Brian insisted that I stay on at Brentwood House. He would look after me.

I didn't need to be looked after, but I stayed on. The surrounding of misery had a stabilizing effect on me. If a man has the choice to look like a monster but to have a mind like mine—or to have the features of an angel and decayed gray matter—what would he choose?

O'Brian's concern amused me. He pronounced that I could save my sanity only by submerging myself in work. I had never done anything else.

The shape of my face did not make any difference to that obsession, as he called it. We talked about my supposed bipolarity, a bisexuality that had never become active, but had found its compensation in my friendship for Malcolm. This revelation did not shock me, though it surprised me for a moment. But then, why had my choice of a new face resembled Malcolm? I pondered that fact for days.

Malcolm had been too good-looking to be called rugged. His eyes had a peculiar brilliance, as though they could shine in the dark. His skin was smooth like a girl's. However, he was never effeminate, not even when he was excited. Excitement betrays the bisexual or homosexual male. Malcolm had an unbelievable success with women, which was not surprising since he did not cater to them. They ran after him like hypnotized hens. We talked about his adventures without a trace of jealousy on my part. On the contrary. I was highly amused by Malcolm's exploits. Or did I enjoy his experiences vicariously? I thought not.

O'Brian did not believe me, of course. I didn't care what he thought of my relations to Malcolm. I only knew that we had shut ourselves off more and more from other people as our work progressed. The nature of our experiment had been kept secret. Was this secrecy part of our attraction for each other? O'Brian wanted to know what we had been working on, and I did not tell him. He construed my refusal to talk about it as proof of my sexual affiliation with Malcolm.

Only if I were ready to talk about Malcolm and divorce myself mentally from him, would he consider that I had ended that morbid relationship. The word morbid was, of course, his.

Psychiatrists construct their own jungles. They start in primitively, relating every phase of their patient's behavior to sexual desires, and then add secret paths until they constrict themselves in their own maze, a labyrinth that thoroughly befuddles them and their patients too.

O'Brian asked me why I was not married. I put the same question to him. He, in his early forties, was still a bachelor. He excused this by saying that he could not take a young wife into a hospital for the mentally retarded. That couldn't make for future happiness, especially since 60 percent of his patients were children. How could a woman become a mother in such a surrounding? Wouldn't she be convinced that her child would be like one of those mentally deformed? The gentleman doth protest too much. O'Brian lived in one of the rows of separate houses occupied by doctors and technical personnel. Many of the others had their prolific wives with them. Not one had less than three children. Some had even adopted children. It was as though the mass of useless humans collected at Brentwood House, the refuse of nature, spurred the people who worked there into replacing the wasted humanity with a healthy new crop.

I was kind enough not to bring up that fact. I did not want to disturb O'Brian since his surroundings were not conducive to normal reactions. I told him that thoughts express themselves in microwaves, measurable emanations that impact on the brain. They wear down the brain's clarity and resistance to the warped, make it finally accept ideas created in diseased brain matter. At the end, exposed to irrational people, O'Brian himself would not be able to resist thinking like his inmates.

"Not a happy outlook," he consented, but I knew he did not believe me. Besides, he ran an asylum for the mentally retarded and not one for lunatics. But I don't know which would be worse. Lunatics are often highly intelligent people. They might stimulate even doctors.

My ears have become attuned to faraway noises. I heard O'Brian's car approach the house. Somehow I was happy that he was coming to see me. I was also anxious to watch his reaction to my work.

Chapter Two

"Glad you make old-fashioned house calls," I said as O'Brian entered, wearing a cap that had once been white, but now was yellowed by the desert sun. He was half a head shorter than I, stockily built, careless about his clothes. He always wore the same cashmere coat mended with leather at the elbows.

Throwing his driver's cap on a chair, he looked around with the envy of a collector. I had covered the house with Navajo rugs, hung them on the walls, where the elongated figures with their microcephalic heads looked like mystic gods. Years ago, when I still had time for hobbies, I had collected antique Indian artifacts, sculptures, pottery, and straw baskets—things that O'Brian admired. They had lost their appeal to me, but still cluttered up my house. As though they were aware that they were not loved anymore, they had taken on an air of abandonment.

"I was going to will all that stuff to you, Jimmy," I said, following his gaze. Take them now."

"No. I don't want you to live in an empty house. And you don't need to wear that Halloween mask when I'm around."

"I don't want to make you feel uncomfortable," I said, knowing that by trying to make fun of my face he wanted to minimize its importance.

"Where is Kaweah?"

"I gave her the day off. She will be back tomorrow, I guess. I shocked her."

"Shocked her?"

"Wait and see and you'll be surprised too. You wanted a drink."

His grin made his face boyish. "You know what I saw all the way over? A giant bottle of ninety-proof Jack Daniel's. Mellow, potent, and soothing to the palate."

Knowing where I kept my liquor, he stepped into the living room and opened the bar. He found ice and water in the small refigerator. As one observing a ritual, he took his time mixing his drink.

"Liquor for you is a repetition compulsion based on unsettled problems. You maintain there isn't such a thing as an alcoholic," I said and he laughed.

"You're almost as bad as I am, trying to find a meaning behind everything. The fact is that I just like that stuff. Besides it is the closest thing to a perpetuum mobile—anyhow, it is with me. Have one too."

"My problems are solved."

"To your solved problems!" He lifted his glass and I took the face mask off. Despite his control he winced.

"One never gets over it, does one?" I said. "Okay, I'm putting that rag back on my face."

"Don't bother, I'm over it now," he said. "What is that solved problem? I know you have been working on one for years. Is this the day of revelation? So far you have kept it a secret. You know my theory about you and Malcolm. Congratulations. I'm very curious to hear if it lives up to all that mystery."

"I'd like to play a tape for you," I said and heard to my surprise a high pitch of excitement in my voice. It did not escape O'Brian.

"A tape?" he said, taking his glass with him as he followed me into the lab.

"How's your French, Jimmy?"

"Three years Sorbonne and five years a French mistress. I'm practically a native."

I switched on the transcorder and at once Kaweah's voice talking in a heavy French accent came from the loudspeaker.

"Il est evident qu'il y a infiniment plus de saints obscurs que de saints publics."

O'Brian listened to the voice, the sound harsh, labored, and unknown to him. It was not a French voice, and the intonation had an accent he had never heard before.

37

"Why do you want me to listen to that?" he asked, baffled, as the voice continued.

"Le dernier des malades peut, par une sorte d'affection à Dieu tourner sa maladie en martyre." The last among the sick can, by the kind of aspiration to God, turn his sickness into martyrdom, make the sickness itself the selfsame substance of martyrdom . . . *"faire de sa maladie la manière même d'une martyre."*

The tape ran out. I shut off the recorder.

"It's all about martyrs," he said. "Why martyrs, and whose voice is it?"

"Kaweah's."

He looked dumbfounded. "You are kidding! You know, my drawback with you is that I can't see the expression on your face because you don't have a face. You always have the advantage. Kaweah, speaking French? That woman hasn't heard one French word in her life!"

"Precisely," I said. "That's why I used French for the experiment, a language my medium did not know. I put a few sentences from Péguy's *Basic Verities* on tape. I transmitted that tape to Kaweah, who received it through amplified impulses. She was forced to mouth the same words, sitting in that chair where you are sitting. I could've made her bark like a dog or hiss like a cat. Whatever was on that tape, she had to repeat."

I watched his shock and apprehension with delight.

"If I understand you, you transferred the French words to that Indian woman. You mean to say you could with this devilish contraption force anybody to say anything you wanted him to?"

"That covers the subject completely," I said. "I started these experiments about fifteen years ago. The last four years Malcolm assisted me. I think it was he who broke through many of the barriers. But we were never aware which one of us solved what question. Now the work has been partly concluded."

"Partly?" His alarm seemed to increase.

"My approach is still clumsy. It needs more tests. I will have to construct still more miniaturized transmitters and receivers. Since we can put a whole computer system into the size of a coin, the work to be done is empirical, and a question of patience."

"Amazing!" O'Brian gulped down his drink, I believe, to gain time to overcome his shock. "It's frightening in its potentials. It's terrifying!"

I had to laugh and the laughter hurt my face. "Right you are. Here goes man's last liberty!" I said.

"What are you going to do with it?"

"Turn it over to people who will use it. For example, to you. You could try it out on your schizos and vegetables. I don't know what the government would do with it. As everything of power can be used for good or evil, I guess it'll be applied for evil. Every dangerous discovery has always been used first against man."

"But how could you? You, a saint!"

O'Brian's answer startled me. "I'm no saint."

"Then why did you select those sentences from Péguy? There are more secret saints than known ones. The last among the sick can turn his sickness into martyrdom, make the sickness the substance for martyrdom. Doesn't that describe you? You the martyr, having the power to do good, turning your martyrdom into holiness. Correction: wanting to turn your pain into martyrdom and become a saint."

He annoyed me. "You with your constant analysis read intentions into my actions most convenient to you. You bore me, Jimmy!"

"Don't be so damn sorry for yourself," he said, seeing that he had hit home. "You've pitied yourself long enough. Face the facts! And by confronting the facts, face the world and not your daydreaming. You believe yourself super intelligent. And still you haven't got the guts to stand up against ordinary life. Hell, a man who can add two and two together can build that contraption of yours or the moon missile if he spends enough thought on it. You're only one of many. Relax, old man!"

"What's the lecture about?" I asked, startled by his outburst.

"Don't you see?" He leaned forward and stared at my death mask as though to read my thoughts. But you can't read the thoughts of a mask. "You are no martyr. Your intelligence and inventiveness are ample compensation. What you lack is tolerance. You could give so much to the world and you're shutting yourself in, because the world has done you wrong. You're a conceited bastard, Patrick. What do you want? Be yourself! Do something for mankind!"

"You're talking nonsense," I said, exasperated by his silly accusations. "If this is a performance for my benefit, you're a lousy actor."

"Now you are talking nonsense," he countered. "Even if it were a psychiatrist's trick, you know I'm right."

"All I want is to carry out my ideas and to transfer them from the drawing board into practice. I've given up listening to people. What can they tell me that is so much more to the point than what I've always known? All the mistakes in my life came from accepting advice. After all, I'm working near the limits of my capacity on these problems. Why would they know the right answers when they don't know even part of my subject? Now you, the master of the snake pit, tell me what I should do. How did you become that clever? By intuition? Certainly not by insight."

"My advice has nothing to do with your research, Patrick," he said. "I want to bring up something you might not have considered. And I know what I'm talking about. You are cracking up. But this seems to be the last thing you'd ever admit to yourself. You have told me that the insane ideas of my inmates will finally finish me off as a doctor, and that I wouldn't be able to distinguish between rational thinking and paranoid ideas. Let me tell you, as long as I'm not completely affected, that your mind which can think much more abstractly than any other human being I've come across, and which also has the technical know-how to convert those ideas into gadgets like this tape-thing here—your mind will snap if you don't live like a human being and mix with other human beings."

"And suffer their stupidity, ignorance—share their boredom?" I said, knowing well that he wanted to drag me down to his level.

"Right, absolutely right! That would counterbalance your work," he said as I expected.

"You need a drink!"

His propinquity bothered me and I got up. "I'd better get you another one. When you're sober you don't make much sense."

As I walked to the bar in the living room, he shouted after me, "You can run away from me but not from yourself, and you know it."

He followed me.

"Here is your drink," I said. I had made it stiff. I wanted to slow him down. This discussion bothered me more than I dared to admit to myself.

"I don't need it," he said and glared at me. Never did I have an argument with Malcolm like this. Now I was sure O'Brian considered me a paranoid, but he also should know that great ideas of mankind were conceived by paranoids.

"It took me years to cope with myself. Now you come along and try to kick over my defenses which you were so anxious to build up."

"The martyr again!" he sneered. "I once had a man at the hospital who was dying of spinal paralysis. He couldn't talk anymore; all he could do was point with one finger at an alphabet spread before him. That finger was the only thing he could move. You know what he did? He dictated a book letter for letter, a book about philosophy, and a damn good one!"

I asked him what that story had to do with me.

"Lots," he answered. "He wasn't sorry for himself for one second. Not one split second. But you are, or you wouldn't bury yourself in this place and keep all your work a mystery. Go out and contact men who are working on similar projects. Work with them, as you worked with Malcolm! Exchange ideas with them! Go out and lecture as you did before! If you don't want to show your face, hide it behind that piece of cloth. That'll make you even more interesting. Protect yourself, Patrick, before it is too late for you to do what I've asked you to do."

"You should've become a preacher instead of a medicine man in a home for idiots," I said. I was aware that I was excited. This proved that he had succeeded in cracking my shell. There it was exposed, the soft meat inside the nut.

"There is nothing wrong with preachers." Only now did he pick up the glass that I had put in front of him. "I want you to talk to a group of people at the City Hospital in Los Angeles about your work with thought transfer. I'll arrange that for you. You don't need to speak to big-shot scientists. Talk to the staff, the interns and nurses. Try yourself out on them."

"Why should I do that?" I said, suddenly afraid to leave the shell of my house. The house was the nut, I was the meat . . .

"In our friendly talks at Brentwood House, you asserted you had adjusted to your new personality. Of course you meant your new face. Put that assertion to the test! Or do you need more therapy?"

I slipped the cloth over my face to hide it, forgetting that I could not show any expression. O'Brian was clever. If he could not get people with logic, he got them by their pride, and if that did not work, he made them angry with themselves.

O'Brian walked out of the living room, leaving the half-filled glass behind, which he had never done before. He picked up his worn driver's cap. Suddenly I dreaded to be alone in the house. I hated him for putting me in that situation.

"I agree—but only if you come with me to Los Angeles," I said against my will.

"Of course. I'll be your chauffeur. I always wanted to change my profession for something solid." He grinned and put on the cap, pulling it at a rakish angle on his square skull. He was gloating at having won. "Next week, Patrick."

I panicked. "Today is Saturday, next week starts tomorrow," I said.

"That's what it is." He grinned broader and left. I returned to the laboratory.

Every journey into the unknown has its aspects of fear. But man so far has always been able to cope with his discoveries and has brought them under control. Though this has been the rule, one deviation from it would smash civilization and with it the world.

I looked out of the window. O'Brian's car moved quickly down the long stretch of desert highway. The yellow void looked eternal. But now man had come along and with it uncertainty. Nature had always been in balance. Even after holocausts it had regained its equilibrium. Was that a rule that could never broken?

An animal has its function; so has a tree, or a blade of grass. Each has its definite place in nature.

But man's brain is a cancerous growth. Lately it has burst through the walls of its limitations. It is not our business to fly into space, to crack the code of heredity, to create powers that are unlimited, to upset the balance of nature and destroy the equilibrium of every existence. That monstrous gray matter has begun to ooze out of its confines, destroying values and conceptions that have ruled man's existance for thousands of years. Man's brain has become nihilistic, without direction, except toward its own destruction.

When had the nightmare originated? With the discovery of the first antibiotic? The cracking of the atom? The conquest of that vacuum above us, in which we do not belong, as the fish do not belong on dry land? For thousands of years, man has governed his behavior with the help of taboos, calling them religions, morals, ethics. Now he is breaking them all apart, discarding them, without having any idea how to replace them with other values.

In my work I also was smashing up the established verities that hold the texture of society together. But there was no way of stopping. I knew that man had reached the point of no return; he could not put the genie back into the bottle from which he had called it.

I was aware that my discovery might change mankind into robots. But if I didn't follow the path that I had opened, someone else would have stumbled upon it.

If a man by adding two and two together could build a missile to the stars, as O'Brian said, he could also break the structure of the world apart. His cancerous brain, insensitive to dangers in its quest for knowledge and achievement, could not be restrained by common sense—that taboo man invented to imprison himself within artificial limitations.

Chapter Three

I felt at ease as we went down the corridor of the Los Angeles City Hospital. My face was hidden behind the black cloth. Here, among the sick, the maimed, the bandaged, and the bedridden, nobody took notice of my mummery. Even if I were covered with a plaster cast from head to foot and had peacock feathers sticking out of my back, nobody would have looked at me twice. I was accepted in the world of freaks, if aberration from the normal could be called freakish.

"I could make my living in a sideshow," I said to O'Brian. He did not answer. I had not talked much on the trip from Desert Rock. He could not sense my mood since he could not see my face and since my voice had no inflection. As

47

we walked along the tiled corridor, I regretted having come. Why should I give a speech to nurses and interns? What would be gained by it? O'Brian would then try the next step: wanting me to talk to research people, medical men, to collaborate with them as I had with Malcolm. But there could be no second Malcolm. Even if there were, how could I ever adjust myself to another human being? That adjustment had been possible only as long as I had looked human.

"Here is your room," O'Brian said and opened a door. He had parked my suitcases on a table. The small cases with their complicated contents were all my equipment. My next transcorder would go into a jeweler's case.

"What do I need a room for?" I asked defiantly. I believe anything O'Brian said would have angered me.

His patience too was on edge. "Quit fighting me," he said "For heaven's sake, act like a human being."

Like a human being—he drew the line between myself and other people.

"I'll have interns and nurses downstairs in the lecture room at seven. No experts in your line. It might interest you to get a reaction from laymen to your monster machine."

"You conned me into this. The more I think about it, the less I like it," I said and felt foolish about losing my temper.

"Just get your stuff out. I'll send Helga Coleman to you."

"And who is Helga Coleman?" He was working like a spider, weaving one thread to another until he had me tied.

"The nurse I picked to try out your thought-transfer device. You need somebody to assist you, don't you? Give it a trade name, that infernal machine of yours. Call it Thinkex or something. Get it patented to keep it out of people's hands."

"You seem to be scared of it," I said, picking up the amplifier, which was packed in cotton, a thing not larger than the fist of a child.

"If it is true that people are more scared of the unknown than of the known, then I'm petrified with fear," he answered. "You should be kept behind bars. But if they could do that to you, they'd have to can every scientist since that breed has no conscience."

"If we have one and refuse to cooperate, we are put on ice. It's up to the social sciences to clean up the mess which we leave behind us. We have no other responsibility except to make our imagination practical. But who is Miss Coleman?"

"One of our more intelligent young nurses. She's used to burned faces. She worked with a plastic surgeon. Be nice to her and keep her at ease."

He walked to the door. "See you at seven. Coleman will take you to the lecture room. In the meantime, order yourself a dinner. I'm warning you, it'll be lousy, of course; they do it on purpose to discourage patients from staying on.

They even give matches that say, 'Why not dine out tonight?' on the cover."

He laughed and left. His small talk covered his apprehension. Knowing O'Brian, I was aware that he was worried about my discovery. But he did not know how to stop me.

I sat down and felt myself withdrawing into my shell, a sensation that repeats itself when pressure becomes too oppressive. I am able to divorce myself from my emotions, as a wrestler slips out of his opponent's grip. I like to be an onlooker, a spectator of my own activities, the way I look at myself in my dreams.

It was clear to me that O'Brian considered me a paranoid. Paranoids are extremely clever people who can hide their thoughts from the most astute psychiatrist. I took his opinion of me as a compliment. Paranoia might be a propellant of geniuses. It might be the cause of it, the root, the soft meat in the nut.

"Just to be different is cause enough to be suspect," I said aloud to myself.

"What did you say, Dr. Cory?" a woman's voice said behind me. I turned my black-clothed face toward the door. A girl in a nurse's uniform stood there. Why hadn't she knocked? I was no patient whose room was a hall for nurses and doctors!

"You must be Miss Coleman," I said unemotionally, remembering O'Brian's concern for her. She was attractive, though the nurse's uniform would make any girl look better. She was quite tall, her hair was very blonde and framed her face softly. The waist was exaggeratedly slim. She had pulled the belt of her dress tightly, purposely I supposed, to accentuate her waistline. She had translucent skin like that of Swedish girls who do not expose their faces to the sun because there isn't any.

"I'm Helga Coleman. I only heard part of what you said, Dr. Cory. I thought you were talking to me."

She ignored that black cloth and her casualness was trained and professional. She might have talked the same way if I had horns and a tail.

"I said that to be different in this world is to be suspect. Conform and you'll fill the spot in the jigsaw puzzle. Have a different edge, and you don't fit."

She laughed and her laughter betrayed her age. "To be different has many meanings," she said. "But I don't care. People can think what they want. There is so little time in life that to bother about differences which make no difference is a waste of time."

"A philosopher! That cunning Dr. O'Brian has sent me a pensive nurse."

"Thank you." She stepped closer and peeked into the suitcase. "That was his intention. I'm mostly assigned to people who are difficult to handle or very clever like you. My halo has a soothing influence on them."

"How did you get that halo?" I asked, looking at the blonde hair piled artistically on top

51

of her narrow head. Only a hairdresser would have been able to do that. Did she sleep on a special headboard like Chinese women so as not to disturb that ornamental construction?

"I'm a natural blonde," she informed me. "'Does she or doesn't she?' I don't!" Again she laughed disarmingly.

"And why did you become a nurse?" I asked, assembling my equipment for the test.

"I was raised a Presbyterian in a Presbyterian family. But I became a Baptist," she said and her voice lost its gaiety. "I want to serve Jesus Christ. And how can you serve Him if not by bringing happiness and peace into the lives of others? All people are in need, not only of food, but also of love and kindness, patience and understanding. Even among crowds, people are very lonely. And to be lonely is the first step to unhappiness. That's why I want everybody to join the company of the Saviour."

I watched her through the slits of my face cloth. She talked with a conviction born of long deliberation—or maybe of a shock she had suffered in her life.

"And of course you are not married, because you have no time for a husband. You want to serve many people, isn't that it? What a waste of yourself! There is more to life than living other people's lives. People are leeches, don't you know? They love to sap other people's strength. They are like pebbles you kick—for a time they roll; then their inertia slows them down and stops them until the next push."

"I know you don't mean what you just said," she answered, having learned to sidetrack disagreements. She studied my face cloth as if its removal could answer all her questions. "I wish you'd take off that black mask of yours. You don't need to hide from me."

"I have no face, and I don't want you to run out of here screaming," I said, though I did not want to pity myself. O'Brian had made me aware of that shortcoming.

"I wouldn't," she said and repeated, "I wouldn't run away. You are a most interesting man; so don't worry. I'll stick around."

Her flattery and ostensive purity annoyed me. Like Joan of Arc she was inbued, probably by her mother or father, with the Holy Spirit. But her father also might have threatened to shoot through the groin the first man he caught her sleeping with, and her mother probably would have died of a broken heart if her daughter had lost her flower without the blessing of a minister. Behind parents' protectiveness hides jealousy of their children's youth. I was convinced that Helga Coleman was a virgin and that her virginity was part of that ironclad armor she displayed. I don't trust people who wave their religious convictions like a flag. But her set mind had produced in her a strength that intrigued me; I wondered how much resistance was really behind that pretty face.

"One doesn't need to go to the jungles to be a missionary; one can do it right here," she said.

"There are more heathens in Los Angeles than in Africa."

"Anyone who isn't of your faith you would consider a heathen, wouldn't you?" I said. "Isn't that the cornerstone of your religion? For you it's important if a man has been submerged in a river, not doused with holy water, sprinkled with oil, or circumcised. That makes all the difference if he is accepted in heaven or not."

"What do you believe in?" she asked.

"One day we'll have a discussion about religion," I said. "I'm quite good at that. Being an agnostic, I have converted a great many people to my way of thinking. But first let see how my equipment works."

"I'm glad you're an agnostic and not an atheist. It means that you are searching. There is an answer for everybody. Even if you think you are not looking for it, you will find out that you are and that in your heart you know you'll never give up until you have found it. And you will find it, I'm sure."

"Maybe I will. See you in church." I resented wasting time on a subject that was of no interest to me. God and man's search for Him belonged to the time of my parents, small country physicians, both of them, working in an office that had not seen fresh paint in a generation. They lived a life as regulated as their cuckoo clock, which, by calling out the hours, made human marionettes of them. They shifted to different routines as the clock's hands moved around its painted face. My parents never missed church.

The food was put on the table every day at the same minute. The weekly menus had been laid out on the day of their marriage, and the same kind of food was served on each respective day. It was always potato pancakes on Thursdays and boiled chicken on Sundays. "God has settled in my house," my father used to say, content with his lot on earth.

But God cannot be found in formulas or equations, nor in transistors or the superhigh frequencies that permeate the universe and might be the origin of creation.

Man contends that there must be a God, or how could the universe move in such harmony? He forgets to ask himself why his brain is so limited that he is constantly baffled by the working of nature. He is still using a sledgehammer to gain inside knowledge of nature's mysteries and wonders why his approaches are so clumsy. He hasn't even developed the right tools for his work and replaces with symbols whatever escapes his mind. Man's possibilities are not limited by heavenly laws, as my father fervently believed, being his own Sunday-school teacher. Man is confined only by the scope of his observations, his approaches to the seemingly unsolvable. The word frequency and its ramifications have become in my life as important as the scriptures were to my parents and still were to that frail, blonde apostle at my side.

"I hope my experiment doesn't scare you," I said, not knowing how deeply her courage was anchored in her belief.

"Why should I be afraid?" she asked. "A few things of course frighten me, Dr. Cory. Violence, for one, because I can't defend myself against brutality. And I fear pain. That's not so unusual for a woman. But what you ask of me isn't connected with pain or violence."

She looked up to me, her face pale and small. She did not look as pretty as she had when she entered the room. She looked like an undernourished child who had experienced unkindness and feared it.

"Didn't Dr. O'Brian warn you? What did he tell you?" I asked, hiding my suspicion that O'Brian had given her confidential information.

"He told me nothing," she said. "All I know is that you want to lecture tonight on your latest experiment and that you need an assistant for the demonstration. He also told me about your accident, but that he did as a matter of fact. A nurse has to know what to expect from a patient."

"Am I a patient?" I asked, aware of her slip.

"In a way you are. Of course I had heard about you before. When you taught at Berkeley I read your book on superhigh frequencies and their use in thought transfer. And you know where I came across it?" She laughed and the features of a thin child turned back into those of a pretty, young woman.

"I couldn't guess," I said. "It's a highly specialized subject and not very entertaining for laymen."

She could not be older than 22 or 23, but she talked as though she already had shed every vestige of immaturity. She might have skipped the stage of adolescence, changing from child directly to woman without the awkward transitions of growing up.

"Everything is interesting to me," she said. "All knowledge is contained in the Bible. When I studied Bible history, my favorite subject, I read your theories about thought transfer."

"What made you read my book?" I asked beginning to like her for her curiosity.

"Oh, I didn't," Helga confessed. "I read about it in *Reader's Digest.*"

"*Reader's Digest*?" As I turned, startled, she laughed.

"Yes, It explained your theory in popular terms. I guess they printed that article because of its sensationalism. I became so interested that I got your book from the Berkeley library. And you know—I didn't understand one word!"

"Some parts of that book are still obscure to me," I said jokingly. "So you're not alone."

"All those graphs and terms I don't understand. You know, we nurses here at the hospital have our own slang, which is different from the slang the nurses use at the Cedars. The doctors too have their expressions, which they make up. We hide behind words to keep patients from knowing what we're talking about. If you hear the intercom calling for Dr. Post, that means there is an interesting post-mortem, and the doctors and interns are invited to watch. If the patients knew who Dr. Post was, they wouldn't like him. A woman patient one day asked me to introduce her to him."

"What has that to do with my book?" I asked her, enchanted by her prattle. I now understood why O'Brian had picked her to assist me. She was not too smart to be in the way and not too dumb to annoy me.

"You also use slang in your book—the language of the initiated. I bet you made up many words yourself to keep away the curious."

"New words must be invented in new media to express new concepts and ideas," I lectured and sat down. I had not felt so relaxed since before the day of the explosion. I count history from that day. For me that is the year one. My life is measured in B.E. and A.E.—before and after the explosion. A world existed of which I knew precious little, a world of pleasant drift and relaxed aspirations. A world that contained happiness in its petty events. Relaxation and happiness seemed to be synonymous. Then my facelessness entered my mind, the barrier that parted me from the girl's world forever, the high fence that could never be hurdled, and I felt the pain in my cheeks, the overtight skin, the vain cries of my mutilated nerves.

"Aren't you afraid of my face?" I asked, hoping to see how far I could use this girl who did not expose one facet of her real self. She pulled in her soft antennae like a snail that meets resistance.

"I haven't seen it yet," she answered. "Take that thing off that hides it, but don't be surprised if I flinch. That would only be a natural reaction. I wouldn't be human if I didn't express any feelings, would I? You know, I often observe how much more hardened we become in this business, which is supposedly based on compassion and devotion. Sometimes I don't hear cries of pain. We let children scream for hours knowing we can't do anything for them, especially in A-12, the ward for the burned, where the pain never stops and not even morphine can help."

"I know," I said, and again I was aware of the constant grip that tore my face, those sharp invisible claws that I tried to shut out of my consciousness.

"There are three stages, Dr. Cory, we go through, nurses and doctors alike. At first we almost die with compassion for the miseries we see. We cry for hours—even in our sleep—about the unstilled pain in the world. Then we pretend to be moved and to pity the sufferers. But there is a third stage, which I hope I'll never reach. That is when we enjoy the sufferings of others. A few days ago I assisted a surgeon. I heard him marvel about the beautiful colors of decay he found when he opened the patient. Can you imagine that? Where do we stop being human beings, I wonder. But since we are dealing with human beings, everything that happens to them is part of humanity. Why should we be shocked or frightened by deformity or pain? People do not choose to be ugly or to suffer. It is only our fear that it might happen to us which makes us callous. We want to run away from responsibilities. We are selfish. And our patients resent us, forgetting that we too are made of the same stuff they are."

"How old are you?" I asked her. She offered her wisdom too readily. She might have discussions like that with O'Brian. I could hear an echo of his voice.

"I knew you'd ask that question," she laughed, "because I sometimes talk too much and act as if I had solved all the problems in life. I'll be twenty-four in a couple of months. That's not so young. I'm just trying to understand things which bother me. If you know the roots of your emotions, you can control them. If I like to do something, I want to know what makes me like it, and if I dislike something, I also look for the reason. You know, when you said, 'You are not married' I knew what you meant. No, I've never even been in love; I mean really in love. Of course, I had crushes on people. But that was puppy love, like the crush I had on that surgeon who could have been my father or that intern because he had such a cute smile. But I always found out why I was so intrigued, and I knew that it was not love at all. Unlike my love for Jesus Christ, which is not a bodily love. It is the Love of the Spirit. He has shared with us His creation of the good. I know you don't agree with my convictions. But they helped me in my search for the answer to the question: 'Why was I born?' A question, I'm sure everybody asks. I've found the answer."

"Then you are one in a million, " I said to shut her up. She sat down and I felt that she professed a strength that she did not possess.

O'Brian might know what she was afraid of and might encourage her in her religious tic. Her shield might crumble under pressure. For why should she give so much attention to herself when she professed selflessness as the objective of her existence? That perfectly groomed hair, the expertly made-up face—she must have taken at least a quarter of an hour to paint her mouth, aware that her lower lip was too thin and that a very pale lipstick accentuated her translucent complexion. Her shoes were of a soft deerskin. Every moment she was conscious of her appearance, it seemed to me. Why should she be if she was only interested in the unselfishness that her religion prescribed?

"You are very kind, listening to me," she said. "I was sent here to assist you, not to make you impatient."

I slowly lowered the mask and saw her pale, as I had anticipated.

"It is bad," she finally said. "I'm sorry for you, Dr. Cory."

"You don't need to be sorry for me," I was angry. "Hell, that's the last thing I want from a nurse."

She turned away and cleared her throat, as though she were afraid she might burst into tears. Instead, she uttered one of her basic verities, which she must have found in one of her religious tracts. "Pity is divine, self-pity is diabolical."

"You and Jimmy O'Brian talk alike." I couldn't help laughing, guessing now why he had sent that girl to me. Maybe it was he she had a crush on, and being flattered as a much older man would be, he gave her a mental hand, so to speak.

She stepped up to me and looked at me with clinical interest. "Osteomalacia," she said. "The plastic surgeon didn't have much to work with."

"I forget you were an assistant to a plastic surgeon," I said. "How much chance do I have to get a real face, doctor?"

She must have heard an urgency in my voice and rose to the clarion call. "I don't know. You might have to find other values in life."

"How does the saying go: first comes health, then beauty; the rest is cold cash?, You should know those steps, Miss Coleman. You have the first two. The third one isn't too hard for a girl to get. Get it and you'll have made it. But use your good looks as a weapon, not as a crutch." I tried to offend her, to get a reaction from her, to find out who was hiding behind that pretty face.

"You're wrong," she said and slid the cloth professionally back over my face. "You like to hide behind this mask, don't you? There is no real value in our outer shape. 'The Kingdom of God is within you. Seek therefore to know yourself, and you shall know that you are the city, and that you are in the city. Follow Me and you shall lose Me; follow yourself and you shall find both—Me and yourself!' "

"You've a good memory for all that wisdom," I said with sudden impatience, resenting that she knocked at a door that I had locked forever.

"You will find that idea in many religions, not only in mine."

"Okay," I said and terminated the excursion into the girl's white soul. I walked over to the table and picked up the electrodes. "Sit over there. Let me tape these things to your temples. It won't hurt."

I had said the same words to Kaweah, who was not curious to find out what kind of test I had in mind. But this girl was different. I might shock her and she had to be warned.

"It's good that we had that enlightening talk. Now you are not a stranger to me anymore. I need your confidence, Miss Coleman." I talked lightly and tried to seem casual as I walked over to her with the miniaturized equipment.

The word confidence alarmed her and I talked on quietly.

"My discovery has potentials which I have to explore. I'm using a live person as a receiver for electronic commands. The impulses will create physical reactions and make him say whatever is transmitted to him. The medium automatically will repeat the words which are on this cassette over here in the recorder. The cassette will direct the mechanical functions of the body. But the test has no aftereffect whatsoever. None!"

"If you say so," she answered, her face drained of its blood. "But you said that I won't have any willpower to resist, whatever I'll be doing. It isn't like hypnosis?"

"In hypnosis you still have your willpower. But this is not a suggestive thing."

"I'm not a brave person when it comes to the unknown."

"All I'm going to do is tape these electrodes to your temples. They are miniature circuits. Something mechanical."

"With tape?"

"Ordinary Scotch tape. I wish my voice would have the sound of a human voice and you'd hear that I'm quite relaxed about it. We are going to repeat this test at my lecture tonight, and I would like to find out if it works with you."

"What is on the cassette?" She tried to prolong the time, as though facing an operation.

"If I told you, you might subconsciously interfere with its monitoring. Do you speak French?"

"Just what I learned in high school."

"I used a tape on my Indian cleaning woman. She had never heard a French word spoken in her life, but she repeated the words on the cassette fluently. That is, the tape made her speak French."

"This is shocking!" She finally had found an outlet for her fear and made use of it. "Just imagine that a government gets hold of your invention. They could take away any person's willpower, or the police could make anybody confess to a crime which he had not committed! This could make people into automatons!"

"Precisely."

I fastened the electrodes to her temples. My fingers, calloused by the burns, pushed up her soft hair. The pleasurable sense of touching her skin shocked me, and I stepped back immediately, aware that the contact with her excited me. My emotions were not as completely burned-out as I had made myself believe.

"I wish you'd destroy this—discovery," Helga said, beset by the same apprehensions as her protector, Dr. James O'Brian. "What good will it do for the world?"

"It's not up to us to decide what's good and what's bad for the world," I answered and stepped back to the table, where I had laid out my equipment. "It certainly will have therapeutic values and will lead to many things which are good for the world, if that is what every progress should be in your opinion. It might cure criminals of their antisocial inclinations or store memories and languages into brains or make people less apprehensive. How can I know at the start of my work what the results will be? I can't interfere with progress. If we hadn't split the atom, somebody else would have. What does reluctance to explore new territories ever accomplish? Not even a delay. Discoveries seem to pop out of people's minds at the time when they are ripe. Looking back at history, the same inventions have been made in different countries, almost simultaneously. Could we stop the others from walking a path which we are afraid to follow?"

"You're right," she said resignedly. "Like most people I don't like to face reality, I guess." She looked up and her eyes, too large for her thin face, were out of focus. "Will I know what I'm saying during the test?"

"That's what I want you to tell me afterwards. You are the first intelligent person upon whom I will have tried out thought transfer. I'll give you credit as my collaborator," I joked, but she folded her hands in her lap, pressing them together until the knuckles showed white. I was tempted to stop the experiment and get someone else. What did I know about her? She was no scientist who deliberately submits himself to a test, accepting its outcome whatever that might be. I decided to change my approach. If she were the transmitter and I the receiver, I would get the information that had to be analyzed firsthand. It only meant switching the electrodes from her temples to mine and attaching the minute transmitters to hers.

"Let's do it differently," I said and pulled the electrodes from her temples and fastened the transmitting set to them. "Now I will know what you are thinking, and that shouldn't hurt you at all."

"What I am thinking?" she asked, startled. "You'd be able to siphon off my thoughts?"

I taped the cool electrodes to my skin. "Don't think too hard," I said, "if such a thing is possible. You might know the sad story of the man who was told he was permitted to think of everything except elephants and who from that moment on could't get elephants out of his mind. Just don't strain!"

I saw her smile. I wanted her to relax. Fear changes the metabolism and I wanted her to be unexcited.

I still had to use amplification to record the minute emanation that the electrodes on Helga's temples transmitted. The next problem I had to solve was to miniaturize the equipment even more. Since thoughts are electric brain discharges, their microamps, almost unmeasurable, have to be reinforced. The shorter the frequency, the farther it could travel. Man's thoughts might even expand into space. Theoretically, ultrahigh frequencies never stop vibrating. A sensitive instrument might be able to pick them out of the ether and, by amplifying them, bring them back into the reach of man's senses.

"All right," I said. "Here we go. You won't feel anything. Just sit quietly. I'm not using a tape. Nothing is prerecorded. You are the tape."

Since I was the receiver, I was able to watch myself with clinical concentration. Now I could experience myself what I wanted the medium to tell me. I did not have to rely on subjective information. I might be able to eliminate mistakes, avoiding personal interpretations and emotions. But I was not prepared for the onslaught of this experiment on my senses.

Sitting down, I turned on the amplifier. A sensation that I had never experienced permeated my body. I had the impression that the nerves of my body were leaving their confinement, stretching like tentacles across the room toward the girl, fusing with her, as though we were Siamese twins. The manifestation increased in strength as I tuned the amplification to its maximum. Immediately I felt the chronic pain leave me, like a cloud evaporating. My eyesight became blurred, and as I tried to penetrate that film of fog, it cleared up like the frost from a window. I saw myself sitting on the chair. Was I watching myself through the girl's retinas? My mind was clear—or was I deceiving myself like a man under the influence of LSD seeing the world with X-ray eyes, but subjectively? At once the defenses of my mind, the mind of a scientist who must doubt before he can accept, sprang into action, challenging this impression. At first I believed it to be a pathological offspring of my imagination. But the mirage persisted: I saw myself looking at the girl, whom I could not see since it was I who was sitting in the same space she was occupying. Another sensation flooded me, an almost orgiastic wave of well-being. My weariness, the constant pain that I fought like a beast trying to break out of its cage, evaporated. The muffled sounds of the hospital became sharper. Was I listening with her ears—younger ears more receptive to sound waves, the tympanic membrane still reacting to sound waves that an older man like me could not hear? I watched myself from the vantage point of an onlooker, withdrawing my personality, which I did not want to obstruct my observations. I saw myself clearly, much more sharply defined than I had ever seen myself in a mirror: that destroyed face of mine, that death head on a human body. There I sat, the electrodes taped to my temples, experiencing a communication from another body's nervous system.

I touched myself. My hands were not as callused, thickened by scar tissue, as they had been. The pressure of the incisions on my face, and the tightly pulled skin that had continuously tortured me did not hurt anymore. The awareness of my body, that of a middle-aged man, had lifted and I felt floating and vibrant. As though the inner table of my skull was lined with a different membrane, I experienced a boyancy that had died in me years ago. My sense of smell became acute, and I was conscious of the thin odor of a disinfectant that had escaped me. As I lifted my right hand to my nose—and I seemed to have command over my movements as before—I also sensed a scent different from that of my skin. A sweeter, more fragrant scent of a hand lotion or perfume.

There was no doubt in my mind that I was experiencing Helga Coleman's sensual impression through my nervous system.

"Do you see me?" I asked, looking at myself through her eyes. I did not hear my own voice, but the girl's asking that question. Words thought by me were spoken by her.

"Get up," I commanded her in my mind, and I felt a body rise from the chair, a body that was not mine. I still saw myself sitting motionless. "Walk!" I silently ordered her. "Come closer!"

There was no weight to my movements, which were really hers. The motions were quick, as I had observed in her previous to this experiment. I saw myself as she stepped closer to me.

"Go back, sit down," I ordered in my thoughts and the specter, which I could not see, but which saw me, returned to the plastic chair. I lifted my hand. At first I believed that I was touching myself, but it was the girl's body, different in resilience, her shoulders slim and pliable, her breasts firm and small, her thighs round and supple, her knees pressed together—I was in her body! Then her hands folded and I could feel the knuckles, a thin ring she wore on her right hand, even a small roughness on her index finger, where she might have cut herself and where the wound had left a tiny scar.

I sat motionless and savored the sensation of well-being, a happiness that floated through my body, a buoyancy that I had believed would never return—the elasticity of youth, which is not conscious of its existence since euphoria is its constant companion. Though I would have liked to have remained motionless, living through her body, I forced myself to switch my thoughts to the test. The amplification had to be turned off. I reached out and cut the switch. At once, as though blood was streaming back into empty veins, I felt pain resurging in my body. The tightness of my artificial face, the pressure of the electrodes on my temples became acute. My vision, blurred at first, returned to its normal focus, and I saw Helga Coleman sitting motionlessly in her chair.

"Okay." I walked up to her and removed the transmitters from her temples "You see, it didn't hurt. Now tell me what you experienced."

She stared at me, her eyes reflecting a horror I had never seen in a human face. She opened her mouth wide, but no sound left her lips. With abhorrence and terror she stared at me as if she were seeing a monster escaped from hell.

I tried to get hold of her, but she jumped up and screamed like an animal in pain. Still emitting that ghastly cry, she stumbled backwards, fell, rose hurriedly to her feet, as I tried to help her up, she threw her weight against the door, her eyes riveted on me. Blindly she groped for the handle.

"Helga!" I shouted, but my voice seemed to increase her panic. Having found the handle, she pushed open the door and ran out into the corridor, screaming without taking a breath, emitting one unending high-pitched sound.

I stopped in the doorway; it was useless to follow her as she raced down the corridor. Nurses rushed at her from all sides, popping out of rooms and from around corners. Two doctors and an intern stepped into her way, grabbing her. I heard her sobbing cry and then words that baffled me. "I'm dead! I'm dead!" she repeated over and over again.

Quickly I walked back into my room and closed the door. I had caught the horrified stares of patients.

Drained of emotions, I sat down. The pain almost blinded me in a sudden ferocious attack.

71

The magnitude of pain depends on the intensity of passion and reaction, but this pain assaulting me was not an isolated fact. It seemed to serve as a flight from reality. It distracted my attention completely, forcing me to control my agony by self-hypnosis. Pain pulled me away from this shocking incident.

Silence descended upon the room. It was as though the hospital had stopped breathing and all its life had become suspended.

I had stumbled upon a terrifying discovery. In order to understand its potential I had to analyze it clearly and unemotionally.

The disparity between reality, which the girl had experienced, and the science of abstraction, which I was on the verge of unraveling, consists in its basic essence of equations of manmade symbols. To put those symbols into their proper place, the mass of facts has to be sorted out and applied to reality. It is the ultimate task of science to convert complex formulas into workable facts. If that could not be accomplished, all that would be left of research would be some scrawls on paper, scrawls that would stand in place of laws of nature. But only by applying those laws to practical purposes can science find its results.

Helga Coleman, having experienced a secret still unknown to me, had become an important part of my research, a link to the unknown, a living portion of the formula I was trying to put together.

I had proven that emotions, like thoughts, could be transferred artificially from one person to another. They could be siphoned off, like blood from an artery. My own worn nervous system had been replaced with that of a young person.

But this was only the beginning of my experiment. How far out could its limits be pushed? Had the phenomenon been a coincidence? Could it be repeated at will? With any person or only with certain mediums? Was I going too fast in my research? Should I stop, retrace my steps, and securely pave the way to the next one?

Hastily I put on my face cloth and tied the strings. For a moment I was frightened by the dimensions of my research, because it bordered on metaphysics, a field I always avoid. For me metaphysics has the same connotation as religion, a nebulous search into the unknown based not only on beliefs that cannot be proven, but also on faith, which rejects the concept of logic. The data I find has to be solid, standing on foolproof ground. For me, there is no room for imprecise solutions that can be used as a researcher's whim. I do not concede that there are many avenues of approach to scientific regions open to man. I am searching for the most direct way that would exclude mistakes and false conclusions.

A scientist must divorce himself from emotions. I could not permit myself to be sorry for that girl. Helga Coleman, for me, had to be used like a laboratory animal for a precisely defined purpose. There is no room for sentiment in research.

The secrets of nature will be unraveled by man. The word secret in itself is man's admission to limitations.

Pondering the ramifications of the event, I was aware that I was arguing myself back into the reality of my duties.

The door opened. O'Brian stood in the doorway, squat, his shoulders hunched, his face purple, the veins of his forehead standing out sharply. He looked like a man who had been running a long way and who was not in shape for such exertion. He closed the door quickly.

"What happened to the girl?" he asked, lowering his voice as though afraid of being overheard.

"That's what I'd like to know," I said, packing my equipment into the foam-rubber bed of the cases.

O'Brian sat down, and as if I were one of his patients, he watched me, filling his pipe from a plastic pouch. Knowing him well, I could tell he was highly upset. His deliberate movements calmed him and his face regained its normal color.

"What did you do to her?" he finally asked.

I decided not to share my experience with anybody. "Nothing which I didn't try out on Kaweah," I deliberately lied. "It was supposed to be a dress rehearsal for tonight, but I guess the lecture is off. The assistant you sent pooped out on me."

There is no human being alive with the ability to accept the intricate problems related to consciousness, the shocking revelations that are bound to be exposed in the conquest of nature's enigmas. I have to treat everybody, and that includes O'Brian, like children with adolescent minds. Mankind is not ready to accept without struggle the revolutionary ideas conceived by me.

"Helga is in severe shock," he said.

I admired him for keeping his temper. Anybody else would have shouted or raved at me, but not O'Brian. "I can fly into a terrific calm" he had told me once. "I have inverted reactions," he had added. But I didn't want him or anybody else as my confidant. What could Helga tell him? She did not have any more information than O'Brian.

"Are you sure?" I said, trying to make the issue run out like a wave on the beach.

"Yes," he said. "I gave her a shot of Amytal. As soon as she wakes up she will tell me. Why did she repeat: 'I'm dead?'"

"Doesn't that prove that she is hysterical? Kaweah wasn't. But she is a borderline case, that nurse of yours, and you know it. That religious tic of hers isn't a common attitude of young girls. And she contradicts her saintliness with her careful makeup, that come-close-but-leave-me-alone attitude. I've watched her, Jimmy. She isn't very pretty, but the way she presents herself draws the emphasis to her better points, like her hair and her thin waistline. Her breasts are very small and padded."

"How do you know?" he asked surprised.

I knew—but how could I tell him? I knew her body intimately and had even to divorce myself from some excitement that crept back into my mind. Should I tell him that her thighs touched without being heavy, that her stomach was flat, and that she wore a lace slip? She carried herself straight, but with some effort, which strained her fourth vertebra and the muscles of her shoulder-blades. Her teeth were smooth inside, except for a rough filling on the lower left wisdom tooth.

"When can I talk to her?" I asked. "I'll tell her the mechanical details of that test and she won't be frightened anymore. You told me yourself that it's the unknown that terrifies people."

"I said something like that. That's true." He looked at me with his pale-blue eyes to read my thoughts—the thoughts of a mask. "But I don't want her to see you."

"That's unfair. I must find out why she screamed that she is dead!"

"I'll drive you back home as soon as you are ready," he said and got up.

"But why shouldn't I see the girl? She might know an important facet of my research."

I began to hate him and his rocklike mind that was blocked by a lack of sensitivity. How different Malcolm would have reacted in his position! I wouldn't have needed to tell him; he would have known that I had to see that girl.

"You are not being honest with me," O'Brian said. "What are you hiding?"

"The psychiatrist!" I said. "Once he has an idea in his mind, the patient has to conform. The

Inquisition has been replaced by psychiatry!"

What a mental feast it would be for him if I told him that I had lived in Helga Coleman's body! He would not have believed me, but his first question would have been: Did you like to feel like a woman? If I had affirmed his question, my case would have been solved for him, since he answers his own questions the moment he puts them to his patients.

All my life I had wished to think with somebody else's brain, to find out how other people react to their senses. Was their thinking duller or sharper than mine? How did their body feel to them? Now with Helga Coleman, I had been able to savor the five senses of another human being. I had felt young, her age. My pain had disappeared. Her sense of touch had told me about her skin by touching it. But why had she thought she was dead?

I had to find out.

"What makes you so aggressive?" O'Brian asked quietly. I must have appeared excited, and he of course used my shortcomings to put me in my place.

"You are standing in the way of research, Jimmy. I must talk to her."

He looked at me for a long time, without visible emotion. "No," he said finally. "I don't want you to use her for your experiments. But I wish you would be honest with me."

I went to my suitcases and closed them, grateful for my tin face, which could not express reactions. But he would never again catch me showing emotion.

"There's nothing to tell," I said. "Okay, drive me home."

Chapter Four

The roots of human desire are planted in man's incompletion and insecurity and in all that is crippled and marred within him. But not in my case. An attitude like mine toward my search is less a response to stimuli from without than a result of an inner dissatisfaction. This dissatisfaction, of which I'm well aware, is based on my impatience to have to deal with problems that can be solved by an empirical and mechanical approach. A few scratches on a plastic plate, a few thin wires, an infinitesimally small electric current running through an etched circuit could give me an answer to the mystery of God.

I think the Protestants made a mistake by getting rid of the Pope and keeping the image of God. They should have done it the other way around: gotten rid of God and kept the Pope. He is a secular power who would support earthly experiments like mine.

The ministers preach that it is unholy to pry into God's mysteries. They nail a no trespassing sign between science and faith. They are not aware that faith, like terror, eliminates self-respect. Terror crushes the ego, as I had seen with Helga Coleman. It caused her, a nurse used to abstract experience like death and pain, to lose her head and run away screaming. But faith is even more debasing since it asks for voluntary submission.

O'Brian drove me home from Los Angeles. On the way back we did not talk much, and I felt the tension between us. He did not talk about Helga, and I didn't ask him, but she must have been all right or he'd have told me.

He was affected by my personality, but it is also difficult to deny that we are influenced by those we impress. I knew that he hated me since we hate what we cannot be. He would have liked to have been able to think with my precision. Unable to do so, he set himself up as a judge over my actions. He reminded me that I was working too hastily by using humans and not going through the time-honored safeguards of animal tests. O'Brian took every opportunity to emphasize his supposed superiority when the chance presented itself. When he was right, he did not fail to tell me so. In many of our skirmishes he seemed to come out on top.

I'm very glad I hadn't told him more about my experiments. I might have found myself in a padded cell.

But I decided his suggestion to try out thought transfer on animals might have its value. The more I thought about it, the more my curiosity was aroused.

He dropped me at my house and drove off.

I had to wait for a few days. A flash flood poured down the day after my return; so Kaweah couldn't show up. The sky was covered with black, racing clouds. A thunderstorm and lightning created a fiery spectacle. The gulch behind my house swelled into a river, a wall of water rushing past my back door. I watched the pyrotechnics of the heavens. They seemed to be a symbol of the working of a brain—darkness prevailing constantly, illuminated by a blinding light for a fraction of a second. Our inner self is always in a state of war, and we are groping to find the enemy. Only that rare flash of clarity, like a lightning bolt, points out the way we should go.

O'Brian's idea had its exciting possibilities. What kind of animal should I choose for my experiment? A cat? A dog? A wild animal? Would I be able to think with a cat's brain, smell with a dog's nose? Experience the fear of the hunted beast or the contentment of the cow if cows are truly content? They might not be, but here I had the opportunity to find out.

The floodwater disappeared in the porous soil. Overnight the desert was in bloom: the demons' tails broke out in huge blossoms, and the yellow ground was covered with the rainbow colors of small flowers. Life, sometimes dormant for years, had suddenly exploded. Grass grew in haste and threw a green carpet to the horizon.

Kaweah's old Buick stopped in the morning as usual. She had found out that she had not been hurt by my witchcraft, and she had stuffed that experience into a back corner of her placid mind. But she brought Jose, her husband, along. I had met him before the explosion. He got busy behind the house, closing the trenches that the water had torn into the soil.

I called Kaweah from the living room in order not to frighten her again. The laboratory might have a connotation of danger. I knew she would never enter it again. I asked her if Jose would be afraid of me since he had not seen my face or the mask. She shook her head. They must discuss my affairs as a kind of entertainment. I'm sure that everything Kaweah knew about me was also known to Jose.

She called Jose in Hopi, and he seemed prepared for meeting me. He was a stocky man with a sharp, intelligent face. He was a full-blooded Indian and therefore not independent. The Secretary of Indian Affairs, his white father, was watching over him.

Race distinctions have their amusing and silly prejudices. An American will brag about being one-eighth Indian. To be a quarter Indian is still a badge of merit, though people start looking askance. A half-breed is never fully accepted and the full-blooded Indian shares the fate of the Mexicans, the Negroes, and the other-skinned people, though the Japanese and Chinese are accepted.

The Indians themselves are intolerant toward race mixtures. They insist on the 100% undiluted tribal background, if such a thing exists.

Jose was proud and dignified. He had been in the Navy, but had returned to the reservation with its poverty and high tuberculosis rate rather than mix with the whites. If he was surprised or curious about my hidden face, he did not show it.

"How good are you with a bow and arrow?" I asked him, and his leathery face broke into a smile.

"My great-grandfather gave them up, Dr. Cory," he said. "All we have now are small bows and tiny arrows for the tourists to take home."

"Can you make me a large one and put a metal tip on it?" I said. "I'd need it to shoot a tranquilizer into an animal. I don't want to hurt it, but I'll have to knock it out."

"I'd suggest a blowgun," he said, and I saw his mind working. He was thinking more clearly than I had expected. "It's more accurate and has more power if you're not too far away."

"I'd like to get a live coyote," I said.

The idea had struck me that moment, and I thought it a very good choice for my experiment.

"In that case we could bait a piece of meat, if you give me the Amytal." He saw my surprise.

"I was a pharmacist's mate," he added, not showing that he suspected me of believing him an uneducated reservation Indian. Those people have a sensitivity that I have found lacking in most people with a lighter skin.

"I also need a bull and a cow in heat," I said.

"There is no bull around here, and we have only a few cows. But I could get them in Mojave City at the cattle auction."

"All right," I said, pleased with him. "I'll give you Thorazine and Librium for the coyote. If you bring him to me alive, I'll give you fifty dollars."

"That won't be necessary," he said with dignity. "You'll have to give a few kids a dollar each for watching the bait and bringing the animal to you. I'll bring the bull in my truck. You mean a bull and not a steer?"

That's what I wanted. He struck me as being a good helper in my work. There were certain things I could do. He also would keep to himself like Kaweah, and I was sure that he would not talk about what was going on in my house to anybody.

"I'd like you to work for me, Jose," I said and I saw a wariness in his eyes, which judged me and my offer apprehensively.

"I don't know, Dr. Cory. What's my job?"

"You need only to stay as long as Kaweah. You could come and go with her."

He did not reply.

"Think it over," I said. "In the meantime let me get you the tranquilizer."

I went into the lab and picked up the drug, which would not kill the animal, but would certainly make it drowsy. It would not be able to get far before it fell asleep. Animals react much faster to soporifics than humans. The drug sometimes hits them instantly. I have seen a lion succumb in 30 seconds.

"You'll need a cage for the coyote," Jose said when I returned.

"I don't think so."

He did not question me and did not mention his work for me. His answer would be to return or to stay away. Then I would know what he had decided.

Chapter Five

O'Brian called a few days later to inquire how I was. But I knew he either wanted to check up on me or to tell me something. He must have changed his mind the last moment before I was on the telephone. I asked him about Helga Coleman, and he replied readily that she was all right. He had given her a job at Brentwood House. Since he did not offer more information, I changed the subject and told him that I was going ahead with animal experiments and that I had postponed any further tests on humans. We talked for a while like two strangers. But there was something in the back of his mind that I could not figure out. He ended the conversation abruptly and hung up.

Gabriel's Body

O'Brian is not unintelligent. He must have been impressed by my test and have weighed the possibility of letting me work on one of his inmates, one of his human vegetables, to find out if there was any response to thought transfer. His inmates often lack anxiety, or emotion. Thought transfer could be the avenue that could lead to results. He had a houseful of autistic people, children and adults, utterly withdrawn persons; their walled-up brains had no human contacts, and they could not distinguish between a live and an inanimate object. He was working on methods of breaking into these sealed minds. It must have occurred to O'Brian that my method of brain investigations might have merits.

But I was going to let him approach me. He had to come to me.

I had to face reality and leave my world of wishes and dreams. Reality is composed of forces in a constantly shifting equilibrium, and any given situation tends to produce the opposite, to restore the balance. But the observer stays in his original surrounding. He is the hub of the wheel.

O'Brian put his own slant on my objectives. I could not ask him for any assistance. As an employee of the government he could not consent to experiments that might turn out to be dangerous. If Helga's breakdown had not happened, I'd have had a chance. O'Brian is not absolute king in his kingdom whose windows are barred not only physically, but mentally as well. There were staff meetings at regular intervals, and he also had to account to his superiors, who might be spinning avidly that red tape that they always try to string around untested ideas like mine.

I'd have to wait for an opportunity, which certainly would present itself. O'Brian had already become involved in my experiments against his will. Helga Coleman was the umbilical cord that held us together. I didn't know how strong his attachment to that girl was and I didn't care, except that I might use her to make him do what I wanted.

I had to see her again; I would ask him to bring her along on his next visit. I could suggest that it would be good for her to see me in my prison-like surrounding. The Wizard of Oz was a monstrous scare only as long as the little girl had not met him.

I heard a truck stop behind the house. It was Jose bringing the bull. I glanced through the window. A black Angus was swaying on the small platform of the old pickup. I didn't know how Jose managed to drive without upsetting the truck with its heavy cargo.

The sun burned down with the force of a welding torch, and I put on my huge Mexican hat, a wheel of straw so large that it flapped around my shoulders. My skin cannot stand even one moment of direct sun without being scorched like paper over a fire. That hat and my face mask made me into a ridiculous scarecrow.

Jose led the bull by its nose ring over planks that he had brought along and on which the animal precariously balanced. It was a young animal, its fur shiny. Its square head with the widely spaced eyes had a wall-eyed look. Eyes have no expression by themselves; they are inanimate, which can be proven by covering the lower part of the face. It is the crinkles and folds around those globular structures, with their three coats and three translucent refraction media, that supposedly give eyes an expression of innocence or cunning, wisdom or lunacy.

"I'll bring the cow tonight," Jose said without giving my strange appearance a thought. I knew he considered it beneath his dignity to show curiosity or any emotion that might trespass into my sensitiveness. "I couldn't get her on the truck. But she is ready for mating."

He led the beast into the garden and fastened it to a post. The fenced-in space behind the house could not be called a garden; it was just a piece of desert like the hundreds of miles of emptiness that surrounded the house. Once I had raised cacti, enchanted by their shapes and witchlike forms. Once a year they exploded into colors more vivid than any other flower. But that was a long time ago when I could spend time on things that did not pertain to my work.

"He'll be happy there. He's got some shade," Jose said. "I'll come every day and feed him."

This was his way of telling me that he was going to work for me. I know Indians. They dislike giving a straight reply to any question and present their answer within the frame of a casual sentence.

I looked at the black beast with his quiet, listless stare, his mouth and nose dripping saliva.

"He is excited, but he'll calm down as soon as I get him some hay," Jose said. He was waiting for me to tell him why I wanted to mate a bull in my backyard.

"I'll have to knock him out for a while," I said. He nodded, having heard from Kaweah about the strange docimasies I performed in my laboratory. I don't know what he was thinking, but for him and his tribe I was a witch doctor who worked on infernal experiments. If I had told him that I wanted to operate on that bull and put wings on him, he would have helped me without displaying surprise.

His willingness to assist me proved to me that man will accept any ideas, however abstract. He resolves the contradictions that impede him in many fields. Even Jose, a man raised on a reservation, was open to extreme change in thinking and facts. Man will finally become familiar with an entirely new word characterized by occurences of vastly different magnitudes, widely separated dimensions and thoughts. The most abstract ideas, that today are only mathematical symbols without images, will become intuitive in the minds of men of future times. My experiments will be accepted as easily as television is today. But by then, there won't be any reservations for Indians. There won't be any Indians, only a great cauldron of melted races.

I went back to the house and brought a hypodermic needle, which contained a strong dose of Amytal. While Jose talked to the bull, I shot the liquid into that animal's loose skin. A minute later the large body trembled, the beast slowly kneeled down, his black eyes closed, and he rolled on his side. Jose untied the rope that held him to the post.

I slit open the thick skin at the base of his skull and inserted the sterilized transcorders, which were no larger than a lima beans. I sewed them between the epidermis and the corium, embedding them in the fat cells. He would never feel them. I then closed the tiny wound with a couple of stitches and gave him a shot of an antibiotic just in case he should be alergic to the titanium shell in which the circuits were imbedded.

The operation took no longer than ten minutes, and all the while the beast was snoring.

"Leave enough hay for him, Jose," I said. My body was bathed in sweat. The sweat glands of my face and neck had been burned away in the explosion. My cheeks therefore were like skin on a drum, that had been pulled too tightly. Pain was cutting my face to shreds. I had to go back into the house. "Leave him plenty of water. He might be thirsty after the shot."

Quickly I went back into my darkened room. The air-conditioned coolness relaxed me. How long would the Angus sleep? I didn't know anything about the impact of ten cc's of Amytal on a 1,500-pound bull.

I did not want anybody near the house when he woke up. If my calculations were right, I would experience emotions that no human being had ever recorded in medical history.

I heard Kaweah talk to Jose, and then the truck drove off. From the bedroom window I could see the garden. The bull was still asleep, his mouth open, and tongue hanging out. Flies had settled on it.

Controlling my excitement I went back to the laboratory. Our knowledge of animal's sensory reactions is almost nil, despite Pavlov and his disciples. Man only knows the reactions of animals to certain drugs or to mechanical tests. But he does not know their emotions, nor their threshold for pain. His knowledge is assumptive. He registers conditioned reflexes and interprets them subjectively.

But I would not only be able to watch the impressions. I was going to be the bull!

Again I was entering into the forbidding realms of nature. A man was a man, a bull a bull, a bird a bird. Each with its habits, its compulsory reactions, which pertained only to its species.

There is no better way of measuring man's genius than by his ability of transmuting curiosity into a creative impluse. The genius researcher is as much a dissatisfied person as the productive painter or writer. All have one basic trait in common: the desire to break through congealed conceptions to create their own world that they believe will hold the ultimate answers to their questions. Fortunately for scientists and artists, the quest is limitless. If problems could be solved and no new ones would arise, the perfect world could be created. It would be a stagnant one.

And stagnation and death are synonymous.

Like a reverent Jew putting on his phylacteries, the tefillin, I took the electrodes from their bed and fastened them to my temples. As a precaution I measured their output with the Geiger counter. They showed an emanation not stronger than a luminous watch. Taking the amplifier with me, I went to my bedroom, propped myself up, and watched the sleeping bull in the garden. Slowly I turned up amplification. My hand trembled and my heart was beating heavily. I was aware that I was stepping into a world closed to humans since creation.

The idea struck me that I might, after all, be religious. O'Brian had skirted that matter by pointing out that I had chosen a few paragraphs about martyrdom on the tape that I had prepared for Kaweah. Religion is a malady confined to man; it is not found in any other creature. Man is able to love or despise himself, for shortcomings are selfmade omissions that exist only in his mind. I knew I trembled because I had been brainwashed in my childhood by my parents, religious people who believed that religion was a matter of God, church, and holy causes. Though I had rejected their teaching, some of it must have stuck to me like tar. I saw my hands tremble, knowing that there were still roots in my subconscious fighting against this experiment, which my parents would have labeled blasphemy.

As I turned the amplification higher, my olfactory sense became pronounced, overwhelming.

I was surrounded by a smell like hay, but it was not the scent of dry grass as I knew it. It had a pungent, though spicy content, which made my salivary glands water. I felt a burning emptiness in my stomach and was drawn to that wafting fragrance, that was unlike anything I had ever sniffed in my life. It was not the hay alone; it was also a watery scent that came bodily from the trough that Jose had filled from the well. This also could not be called a smell of water since it had a sweetness to it, which water does not have.

I guess that people who devise and mix perfumes and whose noses are trained to detect minute deviations of fragrance undergo an experience as I did. There was also a dank, sweetish odor present, like offal. It was a revolting stench like that of a corpse, and it wafted in sheets toward my nose.

Only now I became aware that my eyes were tightly shut. But that admixture of scents and organic odors was overwhelming. As I opened my eyes a galaxy of blazing colors hit my iris—colors I had never seen and did not know existed.

Red grass grew in front of me. The smoke trees also were muted red, a sort of vermilion. At the right were the strong-smelling bundles of hay—hay of a violet hue. The sky was pale orange, and the house at the end of the garden that had been painted orange, was violet. The roof was blue!

In one of the windows I saw a face—my face! My skin was of a violet shade, and the scars showed up green. The bull, which I could not see, rose to his feet and was drawn to that sweet-smelling liquid, which had a strong but clean odor, an odor I could have detected for miles. For a moment I saw the bull's head reflected in the smooth surface of the transparent liquid, which did not look like water, but like metal; then the surface broke and I tasted something new and exciting. The liquid was tangy like kelp. It also had a spice to it that I could not define. It was not molasses, but something very similar, only more delicate. The water, or whatever it was, flowed into my innards in a broad stream. The water level in the trough quickly receded.

Only now I realized that I was seeing with the bull's eyes, tasting with his taste buds. I saw the world in its complementary colors. What my human eye had known as a green tree had become a red one, the blue sky a mixture of yellow and red; my own face as seen through the animal's retina, a face yellow-pale as I knew it, had, in his vision, a violet tint. I stared at the multicolored fairyland around me, still unable to comprehend.

That balmy though spicy smell that came from the violet colored hay excited my taste buds. Saliva was flowing over my lips and out my nose. Or was it the bull's? I tore off a clump of that pungent stuff, and it filled my mouth—a huge cavity—with something I had never tasted. It was an unknown delicacy that had a lingering aftertaste and exuded an ethereal fragrance. I stuffed myself hungrily then turned to the concrete basin below the old hothouse. The flash flood had filled the basin, which once had been a lily pool, with stagnant water. Scum and dead insects floated on it. I blew them away and dipped my nose into the liquid, which had a smell and taste different from the water Jose had poured into the trough. It was like drinking something cellary and musty, but brazenly strong and thirst quenching.

The sun was sinking fast. I cut off the amplification that connected me with the animal's sensory experiences. The colors were in-between colors. Odors and scents were of an unknown quality. The pictures I had seen—the house, the trees, the bundles of hay, the trough—were not three-dimensional. They had a fourth one with more depth to it. Everything I had seen was enlarged and stereoscopic, as if I could see around the objects, embracing them with my eyes. I would not say that my vision had become sharper, except for in the way that I saw things that moved. Stationary things escaped me.

Exhausted I sank back on my bed. Too many impressions had cluttered my mind. I tried to correlate them. First I had to make a distinction between myself and the originator of those sensory impressions, which in this case had been the bull. Should I register my impressions as a personal experience or as that of the animal? To avoid confusion, I was going to use from here on the word animal and not myself.

It was his impression, that stereoscopic picture. His eyes saw differently since they were placed much wider apart than mine; they were like binoculars extending over the gap between the eyes and making the frame proportionally larger. His eyes registered complementary colors. But seeing colors was a subjective phenomenon that might vary with other animals. The insects might see rainbow facets and no shapes. Though we have given colors names, the way we see them does not mean that those colors really exist.

I remembered the corpse-like stench that had bothered the beast. It had come from the direction of the fence. I traced it to a pair of gloves that I had worn that had kept my human odor. To him they smelled decayed. Is that what man smells like to animals? No wonder they detect him miles away.

I saw a wide avenue of adventures opening before me. Now the study of animal sensory reactions was possible. Guesswork could be eliminated. The observer would be able to place himself in the position of the test animal or person. The sensations I had experienced during my test with Helga Coleman had not been a coincidence. Now a doctor could put himself in the place of his patient without having to rely on subjective information, which the patient might distort. He would be able to diagnose a case precisely.

Perhaps it was a Pandora's box I had opened. But so is, potentially, all scientific discovery.

I looked at the magnificent beast that was lying in the shade of the broken-down hothouse, his mighty neck bulging with muscles, the square, hornless head weighing as much as a man. He was chewing his cud.

I turned on the amplification, and at once the picture of my bedroom dissolved in a gray haze, and the garden emerged with its red grass and blue soil. The bull moved its shoulder muscles. They were like ropes tightened by a pulley. He slanted his jaws and a ball of food regurgitated into his mouth from one of his stomachs. The cud had a tangy taste, seasoned with many unknown spices. His flat teeth and fat tongue sought hard bits and ground them down. A great peace had descended upon him. There was no rememberance of the past, nor awareness of the future. There was no fear, apprehension, or tension, only a limitless euphoria. His mind moved in one dimension—to grind the cast-up hay.

The air was a medley of scents, fragrances that I could not distinguish. They became mixed with something sweetish like blood. The beast swallowed and got to his feet. The smell, though still faint, became more pronounced. He bellowed. The sound was like air leaving a compressor, pushed past resounding cords. He had a pitiful castrate's voice, high-pitched and miserable. The thin repetitious cry emerged ludicrously from his huge mouth. Agitated, he lumbered to the fence. He could have pushed it over with ease, but he was not conscious of his strength. As he lowered his head, the incongruous cry became a falsetto.

Only then I heard Jose's truck. I cut off the amplification. At once I saw the bull standing at the fence. Jose was towing the cow behind him. I covered my face and went outside.

"She is in heat," he said. "You know that when the bulls bawl that way."

He drove the cow to the little garden.

"Keep them apart for a while," I said.

I had to go back to my room. I was trying to formulate the mysterious impression, not merely to recall them, but to sort out that portion that is scientifically important. But emotions, like my pain, sometimes attack me unawares. Emotions are basic reactions of our senses. Even if we try to control them with willpower and logic, they are like drugs, unpredictable in their effects on the mind. We are physically or psychologically governed by them. I was treading on dangerous ground. Where does our personal enjoyment begin and where does scientific curiosity end? Can a physician always divorce himself from pleasures when he touches a beautiful body? Can his sadistic or masochistic instincts be completely separated from his clinical observations? We cannot always escape the hidden desires of our body as long as our glands are working. When I realized I did not have the knowledge I needed to answer my questions, I went outside again.

"He won't play around with her for while. First he'll get acquainted," Jose said. "Cats and dogs don't care; all they want is to get at the female. But bulls are different. They're choosy. I never know if I can get a bull there or not," he said, spreading out experience like butter on bread.

I watched the cow stand in the garden staring at the bull. I wished I had my transcorders on her to find out what her feelings were. The bull stopped bellowing and turned back to the haystack. She went after him and began to lick him, first his shoulders, then as he turned, his face.

Jose grinned. "It's love at first sight. Still I don't know if he'll give in," he said. "Bulls keep away from the herd. They are arrogant. But castrate them, and they act like cows. You're a research man, doctor. That should tell you where the male pride is located."

I saw him grin. His familiarity annoyed me.

"Pick them up tomorrow," I said, and for the first time I saw him looking curiously at me. He would have liked to have known why I was interested in mating a bull and cow. If he were a psychiatrist like O'Brian, he would have a pat explanation ready. But in his mind, which I thought primitive, aberrations I smugly anticipatated and took as a matter of fact were foreign to him.

He left, after having asked me if I had further use for him that day. I didn't; I was anxious to be alone.

It is the waiting that gives weight to time. As I lay on my bed watching the two animals, time stretched endlessly. The bull was on his feet, his eyes closed, dozing. The cow was ripping at the hay. The sun was quickly sinking behind the horizon. I had the window open and the hot air wafted into the room as if it were a tangible substance.

As I lay motionless, time passed by almost audibly. I felt a contentment I never had experienced. I had no other wish except to lie and not to move.

I thought of my work, which I had carried out without deviations. But by pursuing problems passionately, we do not always mean that we really want to solve them. Bringing them to a conclusion only creates new problems, and the whole process of search starts from scratch. The same avenues of uncertainties and agonies open up, repeating former experiences. We often pursue one thing as a substitute for the object we really want and cannot have. Often it is the action that is important to us and not the object, which cannot be reached except by immense mental exertion, an exertion as painful as birth. Lying there watching the two animals, I permitted my thoughts to face away, and as I turned on the communication with the bull, I drifted off, not into sleep, but into a nebulous state unknown to me.

That sweetish smell wafted by, an aggressive smell of blood. In the body that was not mine, I felt a formidable swelling in the groin, an expansion of lungs, a movement of muscles. Ripples ran under the hide. The bull was getting up, first the hind hooves, then resting on his knees, the long tail switching. A cloud of small black flies rose. The cow came into view, walking up to the big beast. The color of the Hereford head was green with a white spot, her eyes dark violet, the nose a lighter green. She stood still as the bull, whom I could not see, walked around her and smelled her. The odor of blood was as strong as a body blow. Again his castrate voice emitted that weird non-male pitiful cry. She lowered her head and dug her feet into the ground, bracing herself for an attack that she was inviting. Her breathing became raucous, convulsive, her nose watered, and saliva dropped to the ground in a thick stream. As she moved her head, the once violet eyes showed black.

A shudder ran through her as he landed on her back, her knees almost caved in under his enormous weight, and she emitted a low painful moan.

From this moment on, I am incapable of giving a clear account of what happened. The world exploded in noises and surging waves, sensations that I would not know how to classify. But were there actually noises? Or was it a screaming silence? I don't know.

I only know that clouds of many hues rose. I felt a softness around me, penetrating a quaggy flap that sucked and pounded, contracted and vibrated. There was a sensation of elevation, but not of floating, and a sharper and sharper tightening of an almost unbearable pain, that was not a pain as I knew it. It was a pain to which I was drawn, driving into a tunnel of agonies, that were not agonies, but something to search out, to move closer to, to suffer. Whatever it was, it mounted, climbing a steep incline, crawling up vertically, spinning as if it were a torture rack, tormentingly, rising and rising to a summit that seemed to be in sight, but that at the same time retreated slowly, though the speed of the aggravation was faster than the withdrawal. Then the summit was reached. The throes of that violent convulsion and painful thing, that was something tangible and dimensional, spilled over the ridge, gushing torrentially, in spasmodic jerks. At the same time the screaming silence rose to a thunder, and just before the last impression, which was an explosion of multicolored shrieking rainbows, a deep exhaustion drowned all my senses in a pool of resilience, which closed tenderly in waves of liquid constancy.

I have to choose that word since I don't know how to name the impressions I had. I cannot compare them with any sensation known to me. One has to invent a new vocabulary, construct new words, pertaining to a newly discovered world of sensual experiences.

I must have lost consciousness. I still don't know where I could separate my clinical observations from my imaginative or sensory stimuli. Any hypersensitive awareness is very subjective and my experience might reveal itself differently to other human beings. But science will come to a median observation of orgiastic responses in living bodies, despite the subjective impressions of the testing scientist. Kinsey had to rely on interviews; the results of my method are based on direct observations.

How long I had been lying senseless I don't know. Daylight fell through the open window. I must have automatically cut off the communication with the bull. I felt drained as though the blood had run out of me.

Kaweah was working in the house. Presently she knocked at my door, afraid something might have happened to me since I was always in the laboratory when she arrived.

I closed the window and turned the air conditioning high. The bull was lying at the water trough. He did not pay attention to the cow as she walked over to him and licked him. His black eyes were locked to my window.

The emotional reactions of animals by far outstrip those of humans. Man can stay clear minded during sexual communion. But animals cannot. The graph from the moment of penetration to the moment of ejaculation in animals reaches an infinitely higher peak than that of humans since free will and therefore inhibitions are lacking. This of course is only an assumption. Statements like that cannot be based on one single observation. But one thing I know for sure. I had exposed myself to a mortal danger since man's nervous system is not conditioned to receive the impact of an animal's emotions. Certainly not those of a bull.

I did not need the cow and the bull for further research and told Jose to remove both animals. He was still hunting the coyote for me. But I was not anxious to repeat my experiment with a wild animal.

Gabriel's Body

He helped to put the bull under sedation and I retrieved my electrodes from his neck.

Should I use them on the coyote, I would never get them back.

Chapter Six

I rolled along a straight sand-dusted two-lane highway that stretched toward the horizon. Suddenly without obvious reason, the highway branched out into an eight-lane freeway that lead 20 miles to the turnoff for Brentwood House.

I had opened the windows of my car. Having been shut in my refrigerated house for weeks, I liked the dry desert air, though I could not stand that cruel, hot disk that blended with the white-yellow sky.

As I looked down the empty concrete bands of the freeway, I tried to relax. It takes a relaxed body to think out problems. People who are always tense cannot think with absolute clarity. Since the accident I have always been tense, and I long to go back to the time when my body melted into sleep—but no more. I have tried all methods, from self-hypnosis to exercise to mechanical ways like counting backwards from a number with many digits until my mind refuses to coordinate and sends my body to sleep. Once or twice a year my muscles relax and let me glide into a soft abyss of bliss. I am aware of that moment, and I try to prolong it by shutting off my mind from any consecutive thoughts. How I envy people who can relax without any effort! O'Brian told me that he hasn't a tense muscle in his body. I cannot believe that.

Antispasmodics can produce relaxation, but it is not the relaxation the body provides. Drugs create numbness, cutting off the peaks of mental awareness; they produce dullness, but not the melting well-being of an untensed body. Since the accident, it was only during the experiment with the bull that I experienced a rare feeling of euphoria that left me wishless.

After the accident O'Brian insisted that I stay at Brentwood House. It has its operation theater, sickwards, laboratories. It has the best, all paid for by taxes. Over 2,500 mentally retarded people live at Brentwood House. In spite of the fact that there are over 100 different types of mental retardation, the causes for them are little known. There are mongolism or Down's syndrome—which is the result of chromosomal abnormality—brain injuries, infection, toxins, metabolic disorders, neoplastic conditions, endocrine deficiencies and epilepsy, which causes its victims to regress deeper into idiocy with every new attack. There are also those astonishing cases of hydrocephalism: children with heads six times the size of their bodies. They look like dolls, some even smile when talked to. They are terminal cases.

O'Brian had taken me through the hospital at night, believing that misery likes company, to show me that there were worse cases than mine. After all, my mind had not been affected. That is my opinion. I wonder if it was also O'Brian's.

At first I had a room to myself among a row of little chambers, which the retarded get when they learn to look after themselves. They guard that privilege with jealousy. It gives them pride and self-respect, which is the basis of human dignity. In the wards that contain the hopeless cases, the inmates do not care about their appearance. An animal does not clean itself when it is sick.

I had no choice but to stay at Brentwood House. I did not mind. Besides, the plastic surgery was performed at the hospital, and I hoped I could go home and drive back for the skin surgery. But O'Brian insisted that I stay there.

After a couple of weeks I moved to his house on the hospital grounds. It is a very unimaginative house, among a dozen others where the resident doctors live—the psychologists, research people, and chemists who are trying to find the causes of brain aberrations by separating enzymes from urine, counting protein molecules, coloring their specimens like abstract paintings.

After a while O'Brian gave me the freedom of the hospital, letting me run around wherever I wanted. He might have thought that his problems would finally interest me. I know he would have liked me to perform research on mental retardation. But I had other problems on my mind. I was not interested in raising an idiot's IQ from 20 to 45.

Fortunately I did not need empirical research. My laboratory is in my head.

After the bull and cow were gone I suddenly dreaded being alone. I had to get out of my house. I had not taken one fact into account: the impact of the experiment on my emotions. I had experienced a tremendous physical elation, and like a drug addict I yearned to repeat it. Did that mean that I preferred the sensual existence of a bull to that of a man?

I was, of course, in control of all my faculties. The choice of action was mine. But should I continue my research, I might come across more powerful emotions of other beings, emotions that would inundate my willpower and make me their slave.

What I needed was another Malcolm, who would share with me my responsibilities. It was a pity that I had no one else to turn to but James O'Brian!

I had phoned his house as a courtesy. I knew I would need him sooner or later, and I wanted to keep our relations friendly. A girl's voice answered, and I hung up quickly. It was Helga Coleman! I did not want to talk to her over the phone. I wanted to be close to her when she saw me for the first time since the strange incident at the hospital. How close was she to O'Brian? Why was she at his house?

I could meet her by coincidence—that is, by driving up to his home. That's why I was on my way to Brentwood.

The complex hospital—with its dozens of T-shaped buildings, its lawns and well-kept roads and small private dwellings—lay in the mold of a small valley before me.

I closed the car windows and turned on the air-conditioning. I was only then aware of the searing heat that made the air vibrate in visible waves.

The hospital grounds were deserted. Nobody dared to venture outside. All life waited for the sun to sink and the heat to abate.

I stopped the car in front of O'Brian's house. Voices came from next door where Shari, the Indian psychologist, lived with his Hawaiian wife and four children. O'Brian had told me how hard it was to get American doctors to take care of the daily routine. Everybody wanted to do research and disliked working with the in-patients. Research has its glamour and its leisure. That's why O'Brian was forced to accept more and more doctors from abroad.

I tied the face mask and rang the bell. O'Brian had a part-time maid. It is not permitted to use patients for any kind of work, not even for gardening, or Brentwood House would soon be operated by slaves.

Helga Coleman opened the door. She was dressed in a nurse's uniform.

For a moment we stared silently at each other.

"Here is the devil," I said. "But this time I left my horns at home."

"I was expecting you," she said to my surprise. "Do come in, Dr. Cory."

It was cool and dark in the house. My eyes were still blinded from the sun. But I knew my way around.

"You were expecting me?" I said as she opened the door to the living room.

"You phoned an hour ago, didn't you?" she said.

"How did you know? I didn't give my name. I didn't even talk." Her intuition was disconcerting.

"I wanted to see you—and you wanted to see me, isn't that it?" With the naturalness of a girl in her own home, she closed the shades where some sunlight filtered through. Judging by her actions, I was sure that she was a frequent guest in O'Brian's house.

I only hoped she wouldn't subject me again to her thoughts about religion and goodness. It is amazing how much a religious individual is concerned with himself, in every possible and impossible way. His selflessness is concentrated not on others, but on how much holiness he derives from his devout goodness.

But she pleasantly surprised me by being matter-of-fact. She had recovered from her shock.

"You wonder what I'm doing in Jimmy's house," she said.

So it is Jimmy, I thought feeling amused about my past innocence.

"He's looking after you to keep you entertained," I said. "He told me so himself."

"Women are selfish, you know," she said, and for the first time I discovered a trace of coquettishness in her, which didn't express itself so much in her voice or eyes, but in the movements of her thin waist and the turn of her shoulders. "Jimmy is twice my age, and a girl feels secure with an older man. We have lunch here quite often—even on the maid's day off."

There was mockery in her voice; she was making fun of conventions and the gossip that was part of the conversation at Brentwood House.

"I thought you'd never talk to me again after your experience," I said, moving right to the problem that bothered me.

"I behaved foolishly, didn't I? Flying into hysterics and running down the corridor. You certainly shocked me. I wasn't prepared for that. You should have warned me."

Her beauty was charismatic and full of change. Beauty does not need to be fair all the time, and I understood what O'Brian saw in her. Her intensity might also carry from her daily chores into her emotions.

"How could I warn you? I didn't know myself," I said. "What was it that frightened you so much that you shouted you were dead? It shocked me too, you know."

She thought back and seemed to shrink in size. "It's hard to explain," she said. "Jimmy and I talked over what little I can remember. I asked him to call you to come over to clear up my memory. He went so far as to dial your number, but when he spoke to you he didn't mention it. I believe he still thinks it might shock me to see you."

"Does it?" I asked.

"No," she said candidly. "I told Jimmy it wouldn't. I've put myself in your position, Dr. Cory, and asked myself how I would have felt having a silly girl run out on me screaming. Especially on a man as handicapped as you who obviously looks at life from another point of view."

"Like a circus freak?" I asked, pinpointing her remark.

"There's no need to express it that way. But I wondered how I would feel if I had no face and your brain. How frustrating that would be! I shouldn't have acted that way, but I couldn't help myself. That's why I insisted on Jimmy calling you. But he has his own theories. He is overprotective."

"What did you tell him?"

"Not much. Only that you fastened small gadgets on my temples, then exchanged them and used them on yourself. And then I tried to describe what happened."

"That's what I want to know." I had her in a corner.

Her eyes clouded; she obviously hated to think back to that moment. "It was a sudden blackness," she said. "But I still could see. I had no control over my eyes or my body. It was as if I were locked in a glass coffin, but I couldn't move. I couldn't even think. But I saw myself! That was the most dreadful shock, seeing myself. How was that possible?"

"Is that what you told Jimmy?" I asked her, trying to find out how many pieces of the jigsaw puzzle she possessed. O'Brian might be able to put them together. "But why did you shout you were dead? Because you felt you were in a coffin? You ran, didn't you?"

"Yes, after you took those gadgets off my temples. Then I could move. I thought then: This is what it must be to be dead, to be conscious but not able to move. Silly, isn't it? People who are dead don't think anymore. They certainly are not conscious. But it was terrifying! What did you do to me?"

"Nothing. You're high-strung and easily excited. It was your imagination, I'm sure. Didn't Jimmy have an explanation?" I lied to her as I had lied to O'Brian to obscure all traces that might lead to my experiment.

"Is that what it was?" She looked at me disbelieving. "No! I'm sure that all you do has a purpose, Dr. Cory I don't think you'd do anything you had not thought out to its last consequence."

"How can anybody be that clever?" I said. Her trust amused me. It was part of her charm, which

O'Brian had discovered before me. The intensity with which she lived was not an act of will. It was a childlike ability to concentrate on a person or object with undivided strength.

"But you are that clever," she said simply. "And I know you can help Gabriel."

It was the first time that I had heard that name. Thinking back, I'm aware that moment changed my life completely. I wonder what would have happened if I had not gone that day to O'Brian's house. But fate moves its chartered way, and whatever happens to us is the crossing of two different causes that come from any direction. When they intersect, our lives take another course. We are powerless to interfere with destiny. Before we become aware of its trend, we are already too deeply enmeshed to extricate ourselves.

"Gabriel?" I asked.

"I'm Gabriel's nurse," she said and stood. "Jimmy got me that job. I didn't want to take it at first since I don't like to be a private nurse. But when I saw him I couldn't refuse. You must help Gabriel, Dr. Cory!"

She looked at me with an unshakable belief that I could work miracles, as if I were a holy figure of the Catholic church.

"Is he one of Jimmy's patients?" I asked. "If he is, then Jimmy is better equipped to take care of him than anybody."

"I'm sure you'll help him!" she said without logic, basing her wish on faith. "Look at him and you'll know why you must help him."

"Is that why you wanted me to come to Brentwood House?"

"Yes," she said with perfect candor. "You may ask me anything about that experiment of yours, and if you want to, I'll even go through another one. But I want you to help Gabriel. Your thought-transfer process might help him. It could rebuild his mind."

She and O'Brian had discussed my experiments!

"Is that all he needs? A new mind?" I tried to be sarcastic, but my broken voice did not carry the intonation.

"Yes. His has been burned-out by encephalitis."

"Then he is obviously an imbecile," I said. "Why are you so concerned about him?"

There was desperation as she said, "I am in love with Gabriel!"

She obviously meant it. O'Brian should have never let her emotions become that uncontrolled. Her job was to nurse, but she was becoming a patient!

The telephone rang. It was O'Brian calling from his office.

"Dr. Cory is here," Helga said and looked at me with an expression that I could not comprehend. Did she want to keep our discussion a secret from him?

"Yes, I'll bring him over," she said and hung up.

We walked past the parked private cars and the state vehicles to the administration building.

I wore my strawhat with the large brim and the huge green glasses that sheltered part of my face. Helga, in her white coat and her blonde hair, seemed to fuse with the achromatic sky. A few of the Brentwood House inmates walked about. A wizened woman of indefinable age ran up to me to shake my hand, babbling words that had meaning only for her. A man in a crinkled and sloppy Boy Scout uniform walked beside Helga and talked to her about recruiting more scouts. In the bright sun two women screamed at each other, one sitting on a swing, the other pushing her. In the distance a group of children were engaged in a ball game, training perhaps for competition with children of another asylum.

Life has its different levels and there is no special value or merit to any of them. Unless we can remember ourselves, we are completely mechanical like those retarded people around me who were scarcely aware that they were alive. Some couldn't even distinguish between night and day. They had no insight, which is possible only through personal memory. That is the first step in self-consciousness, which was absent in most of O'Brian's patients.

I looked down at the blonde head beside me. With all her belief in heavenly providence she had to come to me, the scientist. Science is occupied with the how and not with the why in life. Since she had not been able to figure out the why in the affliction of her patient Gabriel, she wanted to solve the question how.

117

For her, God had a purpose and it was her objective to understand that purpose. But in the case of Gabriel she had postponed that search because she had found the heavenly answers inchoate. That was where she wanted me to come in.

Belief is a luxury. Only those who have real knowledge have a right to believe. I, the scientist, see everything in mechanical relation. That is where my belief and my knowledge lie. A shot of penicillin has more effect on an inflamed appendix than a holy pilgrimage.

Helga had been on a pilgrimage to nowhere. O'Brian should have never allowed her to drift that far away from reality. Why hadn't he shocked her out of her dreamworld by telling her the truth—he, the man who believed in shock treatments?

"Why don't you take Gabriel to Lourdes? You want to help him, don't you? That would be in your line since you believe in miracles," I said.

She looked up astonished. "I'm not a Catholic," she said.

"But you believe in miracles. There are places near by, like the Madonna of Guadalupe. Ask any travel bureau. They'll fix you up."

"Why do you want to hurt me?" she asked quietly.

"I want you to look clearly at Gabriel's problem," I said, doing O'Brian's neglected job. "Being a psychiatric nurse, you must've studied the working of mental mechanisms. It is characteristic of hypersensitive people like you to feel an excessive sympathy for others. Did you ever consider that your extraordinary devotion and compassion might be a compensation mechanism for an unconscious sadism and desire to inflict cruelty?"

"You don't make sense!" Shocked, she stopped to look at me. "All I want is to help."

"Did you ever figure out why? In our mental process we are constantly aiming to satisfy our desires. You learned that in class. If we fail, we want to get satisfaction by compensation in any substitute form. Why don't you just consider nursing a job and not a heavenly appointment?"

"I don't know what you're aiming at," she said angrily. Her face looked small and pinched.

"You said you are in love with Gabriel. And you really meant it! How could that be? You've lost your footing somewhere. If nature wants the sick to be sick, and the morons to be morons, why ask for miracles to keep them alive after the medical profession has done everything in its power?"

She walked on, getting herself under control. Then she said, "When your face was blown off, they didn't let you die, though that might have been the will of fate."

"That's something mechanical. They do it to everybody as a matter of routine. But Vainhuus gave up on me the moment he knew that he had exhausted every possibility. If my brain had been crushed, I certainly wouldn't have wanted to be kept alive as a cripple or moron. Just to make the crawling crawl little faster and the morons a little more conscious doesn't make sense."

"Then you recommend extermination?" She made a sweeping gesture toward the inmates who crowded the shaded lawns.

"They are incurable, aren't they, like your Gabriel?"

"What makes you so sure? Would you like to be the man who decides their life or death? Sign the death warrants? Would you like doing that?"

"Sorry," I said, knowing she could not be reached. "I forgot that there is a perfect protection available for everybody, and that is silence."

She opened the door to the administration building. "I'll have to get back to my job. Jimmy is in his office. You know the way," she said coldly. "But if you have time, go over to Bungalow B where the autistic children are. They were hopeless cases a few months ago. Look at them now! Somebody has found a way to reach them. Couldn't that happen to the rest of the people over here?"

"You can't repair a damaged brain," I said.

"You can repair a damaged heart. Why not a brain?" she answered. "If anybody can, you can do it, Dr. Cory!"

Her eyes had a liquid, speechless eloquence as she looked at me. Then she walked off, very erect, her back straight.

The girl at the switchboard waved. The man behind the mask, as they called me at Brentwood

House, was popular with the employees, partly because my case was different and interesting to them, partly because they were sorry for me. It is amazing how much compassion can be found in the home of the mentally retarded in comparison to hospitals that cater to the sick. It seems to be that morons, since they are helpless and docile, grow on healthy people like animals grow on their owners. Patients in hospitals are transients, while most of the inmates at Brentwood House are there for life. They become part of the family.

Mullford, the chemist, shook my hand and said something cheerful. He had stepped from the university into that low-paying job, refusing double the salary somewhere else just to be able to do research in chromomatography. He worked with Hellman, the outstanding expert in katyokinesis. Passing me, Hellman mumbled a few inconsequential words, wrapped up as always in his thoughts, afraid I would stop him. In the human being the female has 48 X chromosomes, and the male 47 plus a rudimentary one, the Y, which Hellman called in his German accent, "The Vi." His life was dedicated to finding out why in mongolism female offspring have 49 X chromosomes and male offspring 48, and why their big toes are separated by a wide space from the next.

Hellman had become an anchorite like me, shut in by his monomaniacal thoughts. It seems the fate of the research man to isolate himself from the distractions of the world.

The room where the case histories were stored was open. It bulged with files, every one registering a tragedy, a story repeating itself with patterned cruelty. But it also contained in hidden details the causes of autism, schizophrenia, and mental retardation. I had suggested to O'Brian to feed all that data to a computer. The cybernetic machine would give an answer much more exact than any psychiatrist could find. With gushing enthusiasm O'Brian had at once agreed to my idea, and he had tried to assign me to that kind of work, promising me a government grant. But I had been aware of his intention to keep me busy at Brentwood House and had not fallen into his trap.

The administration building had a better air-conditioning system than the bungalows where the inmates are housed. It also did not have that permeating smell of gray, unhealthy skin and the faint stench of excretion, an odor that had never left my memory.

I passed the operating room, which I knew so well. The huge oval light had shone into my eyes for hours when Vainhuus had tried to restore my face. I knew the number of rivets that circled the chrome ring. There were 208 small ones and 36 larger ones. I had counted them and recounted them to take my mind off Vainhuus's hands, which, in my memory, had steel knives instead of fingertips.

All the doors, except those to the operating room, were open. I don't know why they never worked at the administration building behind closed doors. The Catholic chaplain, looking like a night owl from behind his desk, nodded perfunctorily to me. There was also a Protestant chaplain in residence. Both of them had avoided me since the day I had told them that the esoteric teachings of the church had to be adjusted to the progress of modern science. Only when religion and science were in equilibrium had the world seen a time of peace. But both men did not want to wake up from their comfortable sleep. They had withdrawn into the asylum like inmates. Their moronic parishoners could not argue. The psychiatrists and physicians were too busy. Only I had time on my hands.

The rabbi who came twice a month to Brentwood House had humor and earthy wisdom. There were not many Jews among the inmates, though their percentage of mental cases is the same as in other religions. The Jews take care of their own people in their hospitals.

O'Brian's door was open. The large room was filled with chairs standing in a circle around his desk. There had been a meeting. O'Brian talked to Biswell, a powerfully built young black man who worked in Bungalow eight, where the violent cases were kept. Biswell was an intern writing a thesis on Jackson's Law, which pertains to the memory functions in mentally disturbed persons.

A few months more confinement at Brentwood House, and I'd have become as familiar with as many aberrations as the professionals.

While Biswell talked to him, O'Brian beckoned me to come in. The office did not have a speck of character. Furnished in stainless steel and formica, it reflected O'Brian's neutral personality. Except for a humorous print of a vicious-looking cat, its ears back and hair sticking out in tufts, the antiseptic walls were bare. File cabinets and a couple of smaller desks heaped with pamphlets stood about.

Nothing was on O'Brian's desk but a rose in a thin-necked vase. The lone rose looked out of place. There were no photographs of family members. O'Brian, a bachelor, might not know a face he liked to look at.

"I hate to leave Oscar in solitary," Biswell said. "Would you mind if I brought in Gabriel?"

I seemed to have entered the room on cue.

"Very unorthodox," O'Brian muttered.

"It worked with the women. It might work on Oscar and the others too," Biswell said. "If you would tell Miss Coleman to bring him over. I've tried but she referred me to you."

"Okay. He might do some good. Tell her you talked to me. I'll be over in a few minutes," O'Brian said and pointed at a chair for me.

It was like a secret dance of the mind. I hadn't read the captions on the program and didn't know what they were talking about.

"I'd like to keep Gabriel in my bungalow," Biswell said. "Well, I'll tell Oscar that he's going to see Gabriel. Maybe he'll understand. I never know how much they understand and how much they want to understand. Thanks, doctor."

He left. Passing me he made a perfunctory gesture of recognition. He was going to be a psychiatrist and already measured out his reactions. With me, he had decided to be casual.

I sat down. It was cool in the office. Outside the heat trembled in waves, and from the distance the shouts and screams of playing children sounded muffled but frenetic.

O'Brian pulled the rose closer and studied it absentmindedly. "Helga finally succeeded in getting you here," he said.

"Is that rose from her?" I asked.

"My secretary puts one on my desk every day. No, it's not from Helga." He looked squarely at me.

"And I've come here on my own accord," I said. "Or maybe she's got me here by witchcraft; she said she was expecting me."

"She wanted me to call you, but I didn't see any advantage to that. Not for you, nor for her."

"Does everything have to have an advantage or a disadvantage?" I asked. I had never seen him unsure before. I couldn't figure out what he had on his mind.

"I've thought about your experiment for a long time," he said, looking at his hands. "I'm sure it's your duty to turn your research over to the government. It must be under constant surveillance. You've stumbled onto something as potent as an atom bomb."

"Is that your advice?" I felt contempt for his pusillanimity. He had been too long a government official and had lost his basic initiative.

What he needed were more files to hoard, more reports in triplicate.

"I know what you expect me to say," he said in a flat voice. "You want me to turn over to you some of my patients as guinea pigs. This I couldn't do without having the government's okay. That's what prompted my suggestion."

How I wished that Malcolm had been in his place!

"You know what's happened to you, Jimmy?" I said. "You're drying up. If I went to the government a committee would stamp top secret on everything I've done. I wouldn't even be allowed to look at my own papers without their consent. My work would end up with the FBI and the CIA."

"You must have supervision, Patrick," he said with sudden sharpness. "You don't know what you're doing."

"You mean I can't be trusted?" I said, watching him with alarm. I was prepared for his refusal to help me, but it had not entered my mind that he might put a government agency on by back.

"The subject is too big for any one man to handle." I heard a threat in his voice.

"Forget the tests I did on Kaweah and Helga Coleman," I said as calmly as I was able. "But let me warn you: should you inform on me, I'll destroy my equipment. There won't be a trace of it left. They can't take away my brains. My ideas are stored there."

"All right. If you promise . . ." He stopped and shook his head. "No, promises are kindergarten stuff. You wouldn't keep them. I'll have to go the way my conscience guides me."

"To hell with your conscience," I said and got up. "I considered you a friend."

"What did you do to Helga at the City Hospital? That wasn't the same test you did with Kaweah," he said. He must have thought of that a long time.

"I can't stop you from conjecturing. Jimmy, there's no point in telling you anything. You only believe what you want to believe. You're cross-eyed! I told you you'd lose your judgment. That snake-pit poison has got you. All you see is your routine and your government pension, which you'll get if you are a good boy for the next twenty years. Or can you retire when you have given thirty years of service? Then you have only another five thousand days to go!"

He watched me as he watched his patients through a one-way mirror. "Think about what I've said." He too stood. "I won't move before we've had another talk. I'm sure you'll see your problem my way."

I knew I had put his mind at ease for the moment. But he had become dangerous to me.

"Okay, maybe there's something in what you said. I'll think it over," I said carefully to mislead him. I had no intention of submitting to his inane demand.

We walked out of the office. O'Brian took a bunch of keys with him. As in a prison, every door leading into another department was locked. The inmates had no keys.

He sensed the tension between us. He was self-righteous, prejudiced, convinced of his infallibility. For him everybody was a patient. Only he was the doctor.

"What about Gabriel?" I said to make conversation. "What Biswell said sounded like Chinese to me."

I had even lost the curiosity to see Gabriel. Helga Coleman and her inamorato, James O'Brian, the smelly asylum that called itself a hospital, the futile care of half-wits as a life's vocation, the bottomless futility of this expensive compound—all of it bored me.

"You'll see a strange case." O'Brian suddenly came to life. He opened a door with his master key, and we found ourselves in a long corridor. Behind glass windows lay half-conscious, crippled children with harelips and bedsores. Some had to be turned every 30 minutes until they died. A few nurses passed us, smiling cheerfully. They seemed to be happy.

"Gabriel once had a good mind. He would have become an outstanding man. Then lethargic encephalitis got him and burned out his brain."

"How old is he?" I asked. He might still be a boy. That would put another slant on my conjectures.

"Thirty," O'Brian said. "He looks twenty-two. You know encephalitis cases change very little in appearance as they get older. There was a case of a girl who was standing at the window in her room, waiting for her lover. He never came to see her. She was still standing there when she was eighty, waiting for him. Supposedly she looked like an eighteen-year-old girl when she died." He smiled and the left corner of his mouth bent crookedly. That gave him a fiendish look. "That was of course the Victorian age. Today a girl doesn't wait that long."

"A female Dorian Gray," I said and hoped I had again established some rapport.

"Gabriel lost his mind about five years ago. His mother was madly, almost incestuously in love with him. She saw to it that he did not get married. Now as it turns out, this has become a blessing. He might have left behind a wife and a family. His mother kept him at her home after he got sick. But her doctor insisted that she finally turn him over to an institution. She did, under pressure. Otherwise she might have lost her mind. But she only consented after she got permission to hire a private nurse for him."

"Helga," I said.

"Yes. Mrs. Deeping looked her over herself. She found her all right."

"After she consulted with you, I guess, and you recommended Helga."

He glanced at me. "Of course. The job pays well. Though we don't have private patients, we took him for a while. He will end up in a private sanatorium. His people have money."

"Why not a sanatorium in the first place?"

"Mrs. Deeping wanted to have him observed by a competent staff. He'll never recover, but she refuses to give up hope."

A child pushing a laundry wagon collided with us. He was no taller than three feet, and his small, sallow face was peculiarly formed. The eyes, wide apart, lay flat without indentations below the temples.

"That's Jerry," O'Brian said and bent down with a tenderness that I had never noticed in him. "Doesn't he look like a Walt Disney deer?"

"He's lovely and so smart," the nurse who had run after the apparition said. She directed him back to his room, helping him push the wagon.

O'Brian unlocked another door and we walked outside the building, crossing the lawn. The heat wrapped me in a tight blanket. My skin immediately was on fire.

"Many disturbed children come from highly intelligent parents. I suspect that Gabriel had been an autistic child, but outgrew it. That cannot be traced anymore, since the encephalitis. Mrs. Deeping, of course, wouldn't know or wouldn't admit that anything ever was wrong with her son. We haven't found out either what encephalitis is. A streptococcus, perhaps a filterable virus. All we can find is a marked congestion and swelling of the meningeal vessels of the brain."

He was off on one of his lectures and I didn't listen. We now had reached Bungalow eight, O'Brian shook the bunch of keys in his hand. He looked at me like the prison warden he was.

"It needs painting," he said, looking critically at the building. "It's the oldest around here. We'll do something about it."

He unlocked the door and there it was again—the foulish air that hung in every one of the T-shaped buildings. A couple of technicians were standing about, one making entries in a book, the other polishing the glass window of the enclosure, which, like a captain's bridge, dominated the rooms.

Biswell walked up to us. "She's bringing Gabriel over," he said.

It was not very light in the large center room. Several closed doors fitted with unbreakable windows led to other rooms. Special hinges spaced the doors a few inches from their frames. Inmates used to slam the doors while others had their hands in them. It was O'Brian's idea to separate the doors from the frames after he had an epidemic of crushed fingers.

One door led to the infirmary, which every bungalow has, and another into the dining room with its cafeteria kitchen. All bungalows were entities in themselves.

"I turned the tables in parallel rows, Dr. O'Brian," Biswell said, proud of his idea. "In case of a fight we can get at them quicker. We have quarrels when Oscar is around." He flexed his bulging muscles under the white coat.

I had not been to Bungalow eight before. Through shatterproof windows faces grinned at me, some as crooked as if a hand had pushed heads of soft clay out of shape. One of the men wore a motorcycle helmet; another carried a doll with a broken face, and a third gyrated endlessly without losing his balance. One young man, his eyes closed, moved his hand to his forehead and pounded it back on his knees in a steady rhythm, which O'Brian had called a masturbation symbol. I don't know how he had figured that one out. Some men were sitting on the floor, while one was on a table covering his face with his torn shirt. One with the grinning features of an idiotic clown had the gleam of malevolent intelligence.

"That's Oscar." Biswell pointed at the mischievous face. "He's calm now and well behaved since I told him I'd bring Gabriel." Suddenly he shouted at a technician, "Take Willy out. He's ripping his face apart again."

The technician quickly opened the door with his key and pulled out a young man in Levi's whose mouth was bleeding profusely.

"We had one guy here," Biswell said, "who pulled out all his toenails. One day he got hold of a pair of pliers and started pulling his teeth. He had no protopathic pain receptors." He showed off his knowledge while keeping an eye on the technician who took the young man to the infirmary.

Breathing through my mouth to keep the sweetish smell out of my nostrils, I wondered how long I had to stay in O'Brian's private hell. His devotion, which was without hope and without future, escaped me. But was it devotion? Or was he Beelzebub, the actualized, ideally objective man? The devil's functions are stagnant like O'Brian's. Since the devil is rationalistic, he puts down his conclusions impartially. But he is incurably opinionated about his interpretations of the world. That trait too O'Brian had in common with him. O'Brian would grow no more. To grow means to ascend to a higher order of thinking. He was still encased like the meat in the nut, while I had broken my shell and was moving forward with ever-increasing speed.

My discovery that emotions can be stored is basic. Every new basic discovery is a crack in the dam of stagnant conceptions. After the first drop of water oozes out, the crack widens with increasing rapidity until the whole wall is washed away and the dam's content cascades in every direction. O'Brian wanted to be like the Dutch boy who stuck his finger in the hole to prevent the dam from breaking. How wrong he was! No new force can be contained forever in this world!

I had been a fool to confide in him. Fortunately I had told him little, but even that was too much. He could not digest it and had become panicky. Or he wouldn't have talked about government control.

But I wouldn't stay in Desert Rock. Fortunately I was not tied down by lack of money. My patents in miniaturizations gave me more income that I could use in a lifetime. I could go where O'Brian would have no chance to find me.

O'Brian suddenly smiled in the way I had seen him look at the moronic child in the ward. Then through the window in the door I saw Helga and a tall young man approaching the building. She was holding the man's hand. He walked with a dancer's grace. There is an outward sign of beauty in a human body that can be detected from afar by the balance with which the person unconsciously moves. Every limb seems to be in equilibrium with the proportions of the torso, propelling the body forward as if it were floating.

"There's Gabriel," Biswell said.

I watched with growing interest as the two people came closer. I could not see his face due to the glaring sun, but his black hair shimmered like Japanese lacquer. Some barber must have fussed with it for quite a while. He was dressed in a white jump suit closed with a large silver buckle. The material, which looked like silk, accentuated his movements, rippling as if it were a second skin. It must have been made to order by an expensive tailor.

He balanced on his feet as if he were weightless. Once, at a party in Berkeley I had watched a Russian dancer, who also had been gracefully unconscious of his body's perfect equilibrium. His too had not been an effeminate or exaggerated grace. Women clustered around him, got under his feet like cats, tried to touch him as if by coincidence. He did not seem to be aware of their desire, and never for a moment had I felt that he had been self-conscious or conceited. The man who came closer with Helga reminded me of that dancer.

Biswell opened the door and I drew a stunned breath. Gabriel's face was shocking to see for the first time because of its sudden beauty. It was not the regular beauty of the Greek or Roman statues, nor Adonis's sheepish prettiness. The bone structure was somehow Asiatic, with high cheekbones and thin skin pulled tautly over a finely chisled skull structure. Years ago when I lectured in Belgrade and Bucharest, I had seen similar faces. Gabriel was deeply tanned, which made the whiteness of his teeth stand out. His eyes were the most remarkable of his features. They too were slightly slanted. They had a violet color. Though not large, they were translucent, as if they were windows fashioned inside his skull.

His eyes met mine. There was no recognition nor life in them, no emotions or awareness. Before his illness they must have been overpowering.

His was a freakish beauty, every feature overdone in its interesting detail. I understood his satanically striking appeal. Lucifer, God's most beloved angel! I understood why that graceful young body was adored by personnel and inmates alike. He was exciting to look at and at the same time soothing.

I divined Helga's agonizing frustration—the frustration of a woman who practically owned that fabulous creature, but who could never approach him. He was a hollow shell filled with as much emotion as a figure in Madame Tussaud's waxworks.

A hush fell over the rooms. The inmates crowded the windows of their prison. Only the gyrating idiot continued his macabre dance, blind and deaf to his surroundings.

135

Helga looked at me, searching for my reaction to Gabriel. She had forgotten that I had a tin face without expression.

"How is Gabriel?" O'Brian asked perfunctorily. I was not able to comprehend his reaction to his rival—a rival who was powerful since he appealed to Helga's compassion.

"I saw him smile today," she said, still holding the creature's hand. "He wouldn't smile if he couldn't react to something. He's getting better, isn't he?"

She was pleading for hope, but O'Brian out her cruelly down, lashing out at his competitor. "No, I don't think he could ever improve."

Helga's eyes again fastened on my face with an expression of pain. She was searching for a way to reach me.

How much she must have loved that live dummy at her side! She was so close to him and still light-years away!

All I wanted was to get away from Brentwood House and its puppet show. Gabriel disturbed me.

I didn't want to be drawn into that morass of sick emotions.

Chapter Seven

The retarded stared quietly from behind their windows at Gabriel. It was like a sideshow—only the monsters were the onlookers and the exhibition a handsome human being, unmarred, except for his brain. They made signs at him, grimaced, waved at him, some only grinned. The spectacle was made obscene, not by gesture or words but by its atmosphere. Even the technicians were affected. They had banded together to watch Gabriel, who did nothing but stand and smile. There was seduction in the line of his body, the shape of his head, the deep-set violet eyes. I wondered what would happen to him if he were led inside the dayroom and left to the pawing and adoration of the morons. Would they, finally, in a frenzy, pull him apart, each one trying to salvage a piece of him?

None of them looked at the television screen flickering on a ledge high above their heads. Gabriel for them was a better entertainment. He might evoke some buried emotions in them, of beauty, sex, and, perhaps, love.

O'Brian was called from the main office. Mrs. Deeping, Gabriel's mother, had come to see her son. O'Brian told the receptionist to take her to the observation room.

The observation room was a cubicle with a huge one-way mirror—transparent on one side, reflecting from the other. Before O'Brian accepted new doctors, nurses, or technicians, he watched them working on patients through the mirror. Believing himself alone with the inmate, a doctor or a nurse might act differently from the way he had in O'Brian's presence. The patients taken alone in their rooms were given to idiosyncrasies. Facing the observing psychiatrist without seeing him, some grimaced into the mirror, some cried, and others stared with empty eyes at their own pitiful appearance.

It was in keeping with his character that O'Brian used this rather insidious spying extensively. But to him, it was a legitimate method of study.

"I want you to take a look at Phyllis Deeping," O'Brian said, opening the door of the secret room for me. "The relatives of my inmates are sometimes more disturbed then the people they bring. Their afflictions are hidden, but may be dangerous. She wants her son back."

"What's wrong with that?" I asked. "You can only accept six patients a month. Your waiting list is a mile long. You told me it takes six years to become an inmate at Brentwood. It seems that others need a bed at the hospital much more than Gabriel Deeping."

He did not answer. He had something else on his mind, and I soon found out what it was.

"It isn't a question of Gabriel, Patrick. It's that of his family. He cannot stay home without wrecking it. It doesn't help either that his mother comes twice a week to see him. She should forget him and not visit his grave."

I had never heard him talk so negatively. He had given up on Gabriel. Treatment of encephalitis is hopeless. In the chronic stage—eradication of foci of infection—change to a warm climate and many other methods have been tried. They only help the doctor's purse. One cannot even make the lives of the stricken ones more comfortable since they wouldn't know the difference.

Two women were in the room, one in her late forties, smartly dressed in white. Her hair was bluish, her nose betrayed her secret. Her face also had been lifted. It had that smooth frozen look of a statue, the death look, which my face had also. However, she was very stunning from a distance. She also had Gabriel's eyes, heavy lashes, and thick brows. The young woman with her matched her appearance: black Spanish hair and a cap-like coiffure around her delicate, finely boned face. Not one hair was out of its place.

In contrast to her dark eyes, her mouth, painted a stark red, was like a bleeding wound. The clash of color was extreme. I was sure that she never exposed her face to the sun to keep that startling contrast between black hair and very white skin.

"Mercedes Cordoba, his fiancee," O'Brian said.

I had heard the name Cordoba before, but could not place it.

"Hasn't she given up hope?" I was surprised.

"You know how it is, Patrick. Even if she met a man better looking and smarter than Gabriel had ever been, he could not match the Gabriel of her memory. His picture has not faded in her mind. Every time Mrs. Deeping shows up, Mercedes comes along."

"Macabre!" I said. It sounded funny coming from my artificial mouth. But O'Brian did not laugh.

"He is hard to forget, don't you think?" he asked.

"Maybe. Helga too is stuck on that living statue." I could not resist bringing up her name.

"Mr. Deeping called me last night. He does it often. He does not want Gabriel home."

"What a father!" I said.

"Stepfather," he corrected.

Then he walked out. I sat down to watch the performance. I had been in that room often, and each time the spectacle had stirred me. There is something exciting in being a Peeping Tom. One shares pleasures, secrets, or grief without being personally involved.

Both women had brought packages. Their voices, coming from the loudspeaker, sounded as if they were next to me.

"Why do I have to come here?" Mrs. Deeping complained. "How degrading! Can't I have my son at home? He is much better off with me."

The young woman did not reply. She opened one of the packages and took out a cashmere sweater with a marine insignia knitted onto it. Now I knew where Gabriel got his outfit—the white silk overall, the belt with the silver buckle, the Italian leather pumps.

As if performing a ritual she opened other packages. They contained a scarf in vivid colors, argyle socks, and shirts.

O'Brian entered brimming over with good will. He at once assumed his fake Southern accent. "Ah was expecting you today, Mrs. Deeping," he said and bowed at the two women, waving his unlit pipe.

"I am taking Gabriel home," Mrs. Deeping said. "I don't know why he should stay here one night longer!"

"It was you and your husband's decision," O'Brian said smoothly. "I would need his consent to release him."

"I am his mother," she said.

It was clear to me that she was unbalanced. She was in love with her son and not only in a motherly way. If I were her husband, I too would insist that idiot stayed out of the house.

141

Helga, leading Gabriel, entered, and I wondered why she had changed his clothes. He was dressed in a flaming-red blazer, a raw silk shirt open at the neck, and trousers of thick greenish wool. She led him to a chair and by pressing his arm she made him sit down. He looked at the mirror with that male-Mona-Lisa smile, which meant nothing, though it gave him an air of detachment and amusement.

"See what I brought you, Gabriel?" Mrs. Deeping dangled the sweater in front of his face. I was back in the freak show, the make-believe. "I'm taking you home. Wouldn't you like to come home?"

"Please don't imagine that he understands," O'Brian said patiently. "There is no use exciting yourself, Mrs. Deeping."

The scene sounded to me like a play's fiftieth performance. The actors were just going through their routine.

The young woman could not take her eyes from Gabriel's face. She started to cry. O'Brian turned to her, his voice brutal. On purpose, I guess.

"Really, I don't recommend bringing Miss Cordoba, Mrs. Deeping! We have had this scene many times before. There is no use upsetting her too."

I once heard a doctor shout at a young pregnant woman who ate too much. He screamed at her in the reception room in front of the patients. Shock therapy!

Now I looked at Helga. She glared at the young woman with a resentment that she was unable to suppress.

Three jealous women fighting over a man!

"Gabriel is very well taken care of here at Brentwood," Helga said. "He is used to me."

"Miss Coleman can stay with us. I have a whole floor for Gabriel and her, two bedrooms, two baths, and a den."

Mrs. Deeping talked fast, as if afraid of interruptions. "I don't know why my husband should object. Gabriel would even have his own nurse! You do want to come with us, don't you, Miss Coleman?"

"She is an employee of Brentwood House," O'Brian said quickly. "And I can't release that patient without having talked to your husband. It was at his insistence that Gabriel came here. We still are doing tests. There is a chance of improvement."

His insincerity annoyed me. That idiot would never react to anything, not even to fire. O'Brian wanted to keep Helga.

Everybody seemed to be mad—visitors, nurse, patient, and doctor. It was a wild scramble of self-interests. Gabriel was the pawn.

"I demand that you release him," Mrs. Deeping said sharply, though she had lost the battle. "If not, I'll get an injunction."

"If your husband agrees to your son's release, I will certainly comply," O'Brian said, reinforced by Mr. Deeping's secret calls.

"He will. If not I will divorce him," the desperate woman proclaimed.

"It is Gabriel's dinnertime. I'd better take him to his room." Helga helped Gabriel to his feet. She had a knack for guiding him. He stood erect, towering over the people around him.

"Yes, it is his dinnertime. We are trying to be very precise. It might create a sense of time in him." O'Brian helped her.

"His presents," Mercedes said. "His presents, please!" She held out a few shirts to Helga.

"I'll send somebody to pick them up," Helga said, in no mood for compromise, and led Gabriel out of the room.

O'Brian took the two women to his office, I presume. The presents stayed behind like props on an empty stage. The curtain fell.

Chapter Eight

When I arrived home, Kaweah and Jose had already left. I found a coyote in the garden. Jose had tied his hind feet and chained him to an iron post. He looked like a small wolf, his fur tawny gray, the hair mottled and dirt streaked. They must have dragged him. His flanks moved quickly up and down, and his lips curled, exposing stained, vicious-looking teeth. The eyes were half open. He was in a deep coma.

I tried to dismiss the unpleasant trip to Brentwood House from my mind. I depended on this world of mine that started with the front door and ended with the small driveway and the garden fence. I found the outside world diffused, confused, and disorganized. I hated it.

But hatred is based also on hope. Hate demands change.

When O'Brian tried to get me away from my house, he emphasized that a man by himself is in bad company. That might be, but for me, to be with other people is worse company. Nor do I want to own a dog, a cat, any pet. They are creatures for laboratory tests.

Life is not lonely if one has objectives. I wish I could live forever. There is so much for me to do. I am years behind in my work. Many problems have been solved in my mind. It is the mechanics of empirical realization that consume time.

Age slows down the bothersome desires of the body. I'm looking forward to the day when mine are going to stop. Then I will be able to think even more objectively.

But I could not get Gabriel out of my mind. His luminous eyes. His dancer's body. The smile on his lips that suggested aloofness and detachment from the world. For ten dollars, morticians put smiles like that on their customers. The sloth, an arboreal mammal, has such a smile of contempt on its hairy snout. How much mystery we see in the shape of a mouth!

I went to my laboratory for the electrodes, a small scalpel, and a surgical needle and thread to operate on the coyote. I had to implant the transcorders.

I was suddenly reluctant to go through with my test. Would I change into a wild animal? Could my nervous system absorb that shock?

But scientists are the banner carriers of their own research. There is no better guinea pig than the researcher himself. He is like a race driver. When the driver becomes afraid to floor the accelerator and drive around corners at top speed, he'd better give up his profession.

I analyzed my reluctance and the thought of being afraid. It was the first time in my life that I considered the consequences to myself in relation to any experiment.

Fear causes the abscission of scientific curiosity.

I cut the rope that tied the coyote's feet together and removed the chain from his neck. When he woke up he would be able to run away. To make sure he would sleep till nightfall, I gave him a shot of Nembutal. I didn't want him chased by dogs or shot in the daytime. I inserted the transcorders and went back to the house.

But again I felt reluctant to tape the receivers to my temples.

Gabriel came to my mind as I lay down on the bed, watching the coyote in the garden.

Gabriel was 40 years younger than I. He was the most handsome man I had ever seen, even better looking than Malcolm. Malcolm had the detached unconcern about his body that people who work indoors have. He did not watch his posture nor his weight. Gabriel, when he was still in possession of his mental powers, must have adored his body—like Narcissus. I am sure he had given great attention to himself, using subtle exercises that leave the muscles smooth while developing them. Despite his mental breakdown his body had not suffered. Subconsciously—if he had a subconscious, which I doubted—he still walked as if he had trained himself.

Helga wanted to submerge him in herself, but she could not since he was an imbecile. He could not be aroused. I wondered if it was not Helga's subconscious wish to see Gabriel as a man. O'Brian would have thought of such a possibility, being an analyst, a disciple of Freud who was trained to trace all emotions back to the libido. Some men who die of tuberculosis lie in the morgue with their phalluses erect. At the City Hospital they had fired a cleaning woman who had abused one of these corpses. But that man had died with his mind functioning.

To get rid of my disturbing thoughts, I pulled an idea out of the maze of problems that I had stored in my mind.

After the age of 35 it is hard to divorce one's mind from established patterns. It is no coincidence that most new discoveries are made by men below that age. In an older man's mind, theory is so well established that new ways of exploration are forever closed to him. For him they lead to a dead end. Only the young mind is able to break through the wall of artificial barriers.

I am a generation older than O'Brian. Still my mind is as flexible and curious as it was when I was in my twenties. I am unorthodox in my approach to new problems. I deliberately put hurdles in my way to create seemingly impossible challenges. Then I try to overcome them. The more unsolvable they appear, the more perfect the solution.

If I could etch circuits, using the path of electrons as they orbit in the atom, miniaturization could be reduced to a size that could only be observed through electronic microscopes.

Largeness and smallness is a man-made conception, which nature does not contain and man should not accept.

I turned on the amplification. At once the bedroom walls dissolved and I saw only gray emptiness. My body was rigid, as though stricken by lockjaw. It was fear that prevented me from moving, a phantasmal fear, chasmed and savage, the abject and bodily anticipation of dying. It was not the fear of pain or impending disaster. That fear was an admixture of awareness, defense, alertness, and instant death.

I tried to move and felt tight sinews in my body like strings of a bow.

Then I heard the cry: a faint howl, an undulating barking from the horizon. It was repeated from all sides of the desert. In its different staccato signals and long, drawn-out screams it was like a language, a barbaric message directed as a code to only one species of creature.

It was reassuring and transmitted strength. I was not alone. A haven, an end of fear called, a companionship that accepted only its own kind—me. Now I was able to move and to see.

The world swayed, but the house was there, as were the trees, the fence, and the desert beyond. But startlingly, the picture had no color, only shadings of black and white—a gray sky, black trees, a fence sketched with dark brushstrokes.

Small noises came from everywhere, half and quarter tones like the humming sounds of a gypsy's violin, a riot of insect stridulations, the zing of birds higher in frequencies than the human ear was able to hear. The atmosphere vibrated with polyphonic strains, riding on ultrashort waves. All of them were sharply defined. The medley of noises wafted through the air like an orchestra of tiny woodwinds, strings, and minute kettledrums. The moon stood full in the sky, throwing a white light over the sheet-white desert.

But that fear persisted. I was a prisoner, though that jail had no door. I could run away, but that might be a trick, a trap to lure me, to kill me. This was not a place where I had ever been before. I was inundated by odors, every one of them menacing and murderous.

Then the beast must have started running since the house disappeared and the road was racing toward me. The howling in the distance, that beckoning communication was always just ahead, as if ventriloquists were throwing their voices.

I had to go, go fast, fly to where that barking and beckoning came from. Death was surely close behind me. There was no way to hide but to move quickly farther and farther away from those menacing smells of death.

The coyote in his mad run barked, answering those calls that were searching for him. My eardrums became numb as that brazen cry rose, that blare and shriek that ran the gamut of an achromatic scale. The moon, directly overhead, dipped out of sight, as if it had hung on a thread that had suddenly broken.

The chase continued, bounding through chaparral, over brush and cacti, past desert trees, flying, sprinting, jumping, while the air, filled with a thousand scents, whistled past.

Terror rode on my back, putting its claws into me, the way Sinbad the Sailor was beset by the giant. There was the smell of game, of herbs, of animals—things to kill or to flee from. Every one of those minute smells had its sharp distinction, and though it lasted only for the smallest part of a second, it was recognizable and I could pinpoint the direction from which it came.

Mirrored sounds beamed back from the distance, leading the way like audible radar beams. From where it came there was safety, burrows in the sand, caves below the rocks, holes under Josua trees, and the safe company of the callers.

But that fear, that dread terror mounted to an unbearable pitch. I could not shake it off. What to do, where to hide, how to run faster? The enemy was around everywhere and could not be escaped.

The beast stopped, saliva dripping from its mouth. The world around blurred out of focus, shifting into two images. The Nembutal in its system, that sleeping drug, was still working, dulling its sharp senses. It sniffed the air—I knew it did since a stream of scents and odors flowed through me. Then it howled again and ran on.

The band of highway stretched to the voices that came from afar. It was easy to fly along, though pain spread through lungs pumping with exertion.

Then it came, the thing that towered. It came from behind, throwing a long light and elongated shadows on the pavement. The shadows were that of a running coyote, 100 feet long, its body fusing with the darkness. The beam was a white tunnel, the night at each side a wall that could not be scaled. The feet—jumping shadows on the road outlined without diffusing edges—moved faster and faster.

Lights, white and cold, raced closer. No escape was possible. The noise of the motor rose to a thundering snarl.

Suddenly I knew I was going to die, and the screaming terror of death rampaged through my mind, throwing my thoughts out of kilter.

I tried to rip the receivers off my temples, but my hands clawed without coordination.

There was a dull impact, a catapulting, hurtling on unfolded wings. A burning came from the lungs, a fiery stream of gray slime, an emptying of stomach, the acid juices of half-digested food.

The light slowly faded, drifting into a black void that was soft and all engulfing. All noises died. There was only darkness.

Chapter Nine

That ceiling with the thin, erratic crack in the shape of the winged snake of South American mythology was familiar to me. The snake was my companion for months after I had my facial operation.

I was back at Brentwood House in the same room.

Though I had experienced a violent death with all its impact of fear and drifting darkness, I had not died. Now I knew why Helga had run down the corridor at the City Hospital screaming.

The coyote had been hit by a car and thrown into the bushes flanking the highway to die. I too had died.

My experiments with animals had to be stopped. I should not have followed O'Brian's suggestion. The delicate filaments of the human nervous system, the fasciculi that unite the nerve trunks, are not made to absorb a shock such as I had experienced. One can shoot a 10,000-volt charge only through wires gauged for high voltage. I was lucky to have survived. The dull pain in my face reminded me that my nervous system had again taken over its functions.

To be able to experiment I had to find a nervous system akin to mine. A human body.

They had put me into a hospital wraparound, which decently covered the front of my body, but embarrassingly left the back open. My clothes hung neatly in a closet. Somebody had brought my toilet kit and the drugs I always carry with me, which I stored in every room and also in the glove compartment of my car.

The unbreakable chamberlain window was closed. The thin steel web, hinged on springs, could not be broken by a fist. Instead it would bounce back. The first thing inmates at Brentwood House did was try to break the window and run away. That the window looked like an ordinary one was the lone humanitarian feature of my prison.

I swung my legs out of the bed. At once the room circled around me and I had to lie down again. Somebody passed my open door, stopped, and quickly walked away before I could raise my head to see who it had been.

How had I gotten to Brentwood House? There was no image in my memory, not even the shadow of a recollection of what had happened.

Steps came closer, those of a man and a woman. Two faces bent over me, Helga and Mullford the chemist.

"How are you, Dr. Cory?" Helga said. I saw her in that strange angle one sometimes sees on the television screen in hospital stories—large faces bending solicitously over an invisible patient.

"I have no pain. That means that I'm all right," I said with exertion.

"Can I get you something?" Mullford asked.

"My face mask, please." Without my mask I felt naked.

"How did I get here?" I asked Helga.

Her glance at Mullford was like a message in a Morse code. The chemist left at once.

"Dr. O'Brian will be here in a minute," she said and like a good nurse arranged my pillows to make me more comfortable.

"Help me to get out of bed." I was suddenly impatient. One needs doctors to fight a virus or to set a broken bone. As surgeons, they are useful. But the body does not need the pampering of medics as long as it is fighting only its nerves. I had trained myself to overcome nervous attacks without drugs. Despite my vertigo I sat up, and she put the pillow behind my back.

"Please stay until Jimmy has seen you."

"Can you manage two private patients?" I asked, grateful for the delay that helped me to restore my strength. I wished I were able to smile. How I missed simple expressions accessible to everybody, even morons! I should preface my words with "This is said with a smile" or " this

I say in anger." How else would people know? How little words convey without the coloring of intonation and cadenzas.

"I have time. Gabriel is still asleep." She sat down, watching and waiting. "He sleeps till three, and then we go for a walk."

"Does he like to walk?" I asked. "Does he know if he is outside or inside his room?"

"He likes to take a stroll," she said. "Of course he knows."

He was a robot, but still she had not given up hope that by some miracle he might get back his brain. I knew she expected me to talk about Gabriel. The less I mentioned his name, the more eager she would be for me to help him. I acted according to my plan.

"How did I get here?" I asked, though it was not hard to guess.

"Kaweah phoned and told Jimmy you were ill. Jimmy drove to your house and found you unconscious."

"Were you with him?"

"Yes. I packed a few things you might need. But I couldn't find your pajamas. Though I took your toilet kit."

"Thanks," I said. "You should've asked Kaweah. She knows her way around the house. I wouldn't know either where she hides my pajamas."

There was that pause again, the many unspoken words she wanted to hear about Gabriel.

"You've been here for three days," she finally said. "We're glad you're all right. We were very frightened. Jimmy still does not know what was wrong with you."

She got up quickly as O'Brian entered, then left wordlessly. O'Brian sat down on the same chair. He watched me with the compassion I had seen on his face in the children's ward.

"I knew you would wake up today, Patrick," he said. "The shots I gave you were timed that way."

"You knocked me out?" I asked. He should have revived me instead of putting me into a deeper coma. Give a doctor pills and he will use them. A chiropractor will twist your spine. A masseur cures you with manipulations, a Christian-Science practioner with prayers. Different professions know only their own remedies.

"Chloropromine," he said. "The French came out with it. They put people into hibernation. That gives the body and the mind a rest. One could keep people asleep for years without after-effects. I use it on violent cases."

"Was I violent?" I asked, surprised.

"No. But your brain needed a rest. If I had my way, I'd knock you out for a few weeks. It's excellent therapy. You woke up for your meals, then went to sleep again. You even talked coherently. But I know you don't remember. Just the perfect rest cure for people like you."

"What a waste of time!" I said.

He smiled. "You couldn't have recovered that quickly. I think I did a good job. Let me check your pulse."

He took my wrist like a house physician and looked at his watch. He seemed satisfied. "At first I was afraid you were in for a coronary. You are a fool, Patrick! Why do you want to kill yourself?"

"I have no intention of doing that," I said. He had the patronizing attitude of the physician. The patient is always in a weaker position than the medic.

"You came damn close to it," O'Brian said. "You had indications which didn't fit anything I know about medicine. At first it looked like meningitis to me. When I saw those two things on your temples, those electrodes, I knew it could be a reaction to your experiment."

"What did you do with them?" I asked, alarmed.

"I left them in your lab," he reassured me. "You were doing some kind of experiment, Patrick. What was it?"

I did not trust his benevolent curiosity, and I would not have given him information even if he had put me on a torture rack.

"None of your business," I said.

He was persistent, as I expected. "I couldn't find the second pair, which you use on your medium. Who was the guinea pig this time?"

"I won't tell you anything, Jimmy. Thanks for getting me here. Now I want out of this place."

I tried to stand up and again the room gyrated around me. O'Brian watched me stoically.

"Kaweah found you unconscious in bed. She had my telephone number written down in case of an emergency. When I asked her why she had been expecting trouble, she clammed up. So did her husband. Did you tell them not to talk?"

"They had nothing to tell you," I said. Did he really think the Indians would speak about anything that happened in my house? O'Brian was the stranger, and the stranger was the enemy.

He looked at me with the curiosity and probing that he reserved for his mental patients. Usually he was able to figure them out. A small gesture, a glance that loses its directions, or a reaction betraying anxiety would give him the clue he was looking for. He had worked at the state hospital for the criminally insane at Camarillo for many years and was used to the ways of paranoics. Now he had dug out this knowledge to apply it to me.

"I took your encephalogram the first day, Patrick," he said. "The pattern was pretty irregular. I was afraid you had injured your brain. You better take it easy from now on, or you'll get yourself in serious trouble."

His words alarmed me. I don't mind losing a face or a leg. I can cope with that as long as my brain is not affected. I rely on nothing else. We are sane as long as we can look at events dispassionately. But any subjective approach, which an injured mind automatically will produce, blurs logic. If I could not trust my brain anymore, I would be finished as a scientist.

"All right, I'll stay a few days," I consented.

"Why don't you let me help you?" O'Brian asked. "I told you often enough that your experiments have an element of danger which cannot be ignored."

"Of course you can help me, and I told you so before," I said. "I need human guinea pigs. You have them here by the hundreds. Wouldn't it help your research to know how your patients react to thought transfer? I might influence their brains, put new thought patterns into their gray matter. It might even create a new thinking process. New neural pathways. Who knows? If a man has a coronary and does not die from it, his body creates a fresh system of blood vessels. The same could happen to your inmates. Tests certainly couldn't make things worse. There is nothing in them to destroy."

He was torn between his scientific curiosity and his bureaucratic thinking. "You don't tell me anything new. I've considered it since you asked me the last time. But as I told you before, I have my duties and cannot move without consent. Why not let me call in a few government psychologists? Demonstrate your method to them, and they will give you the green light. I'm sure they'll turn over every necessary facility to you."

"I know of a case where the inventor was deprived of his discovery, Jimmy. By the government! Science seems to be too serious a thing to be left to the scientists. The administration has to meddle with it. They put a top secret stamp on my friend's work and he had no more say, not in matters of development nor in its application. As it turned out it was used immorally. They gave him a medal and put him on ice."

O'Brian shrugged. "You are too suspicious, Patrick, and blind too. They won't let you keep your invention to yourself as soon as they know. It is too dangerous. Why can't you face reality?"

"I'd rather destroy my notes and my instruments than submit to any supervision," I said.

"A perfect solution. I wouldn't know of a better one." By the way he suddenly got up, I knew he was annoyed. "If that thing ever gets out of hand, I would feel responsible for not having stopped you."

"You don't need to feel responsible for me or for anything I'm doing," I said. "Why don't you stick to your problems?"

"Patrick! If a person had an atom bomb in his backyard would you recommend that it be taken away from him?"

"You're getting your analogies mixed. This isn't an atom bomb. But get it through your head: I will never work with people I don't choose myself. Never!"

He was at the door. "This is your last word, I guess," he said.

"Go to hell," I answered and turned to the wall.

He closed the door.

I was certain he would send his henchmen after me. They might put me behind bars. O'Brian only needed to write a report declaring that I was irrational, to put it mildly. I could write such an opinion of myself by putting down selected facts. You could do that about almost everybody, certainly about people who work in abstract fields of science.

For a minute I experienced a chill that made my teeth chatter.

I knew I had to act.

I had to get out of there, but I had no car.

Chapter Ten

I slept for a few days almost continuously to over-come a mental exhaustion. Every day O'Brian came to exchange a few meaningless words. We did not discuss our disagreement anymore, but the friction between us was almost physical. He continued trying to be an efficient doctor by sending me specially prepared food to induce me to eat more. My appetite was gone except for steak tartare—raw meat which I craved like a pregnant woman demands blueberries out of season.

Had my taste changed to that of a coyote's? Had I acquired his relish for raw meat? It might be that my neurons, subjected to the coyote's sensory impulses, still retained residual effects. But that sensation would disappear in time. I did not crave hay after the experiment with the bull.

Man into bull—man into coyote—woman into cat—what amusing possibilities!

Since introspection is a form of lunacy, I dismissed my thoughts, afraid an abstract idea would get hold of me and I would be off again on new research, experiments, tests. Nothing could be gained by changing the senses of man into those of an animal.

Or could there be? Developing in him an extraordinary visual power like that of an eagle, a nose like that of a dog, a sense of hearing like that of a horse? But instruments can take care of that. Man's primary objective should be to develop his brain.

I now could get up without being attacked by vertigo. I took long walks, but I disliked going through the administration building. I avoided visiting the bungalows with their sick cargo. After sunset I went out, walking the tree-lined roads that led through Brentwood House. I didn't visit anybody in their private homes, not even O'Brian.

I was looking for Helga.

Just before nightfall she walked Gabriel. She talked to him as though he could understand, and he smiled his eternal male-Mona-Lisa smile, which had no meaning, but might indicate that his bowels had worked well. For a couple of days I just nodded to her when I passed. Then we exchanged a few words, which I timed carefully, so as not to make my approach appear urgent. One evening I walked with her.

He was eerie, that tall young man between us, the quiet one whose elegant body rhythm was as pleasant to watch as a dancer's. Helga directed him like a marionette, pulling him to the right or to the left, walking him straight. He would have marched into a wall had she not turned him away.

"You love him," I said to Helga, "because he cannot be reached. I wonder how you would react if he were normal, could think and had feelings and emotions. And of course, desires."

She walked on, studying her white suede shoes, her nylon skirt clinging gracefully to her slim hips.

"I wish he were like other people," she said. "But then again, I might not have met him."

"If he were to recover, he certainly would leave you," I said.

"No, he wouldn't," she answered. "It is the fundamental truth about love that it always creates love in the other person. It never fails."

"You think you could hold him just by loving him very much?" I asked, intrigued by her single-mindedness. Conviction is energy, and energy is power.

"The truth about love," she said, taking Gabriel's hand, "is shown in the order in which religion has been introduced into the world. First came the religion of Power, then came the religion of Knowledge, and last came the religion of Love. Why in this order? Because love without the former qualities is dangerous. Power alone or knowledge alone is less dangerous than love alone. God created the less dangerous forces first and left love to the last."

She looked up at Gabriel as though for confirmation. The weird combination of characters intrigued me, characters in juxtaposition: a man without a mind loved by a girl who confessed her love for him and who had in her religious training found a basis for her emotions; and I, a man without a face who was unable to comprehend anything as nebulous as love as a foundation of existence.

"Do you think he feels better for it since you love him?" I asked.

She was immune to my sarcasm. "Of course, he knows that I love him. I can't be hurt by anybody, Dr. Cory. All true lovers are invulnerable to everybody but their beloved."

She possessed an arsenal of weapons and would never run out of them.

"It might be possible to help him" I started my attack.

She stopped and I saw her pale despite the rays of the sinking sun that painted her face golden.

"You don't really mean it!"

I pointed to a bench in the shade of a bungalow. Gently she led Gabriel to it, and like a well-trained animal that can be directed by signs—a sheep dog perhaps—he sat down.

"I've thought of a way," I said, watching her face "So far it's only theory. There are many hurdles to clear, of course. This is unknown territory."

"I know," she answered, "but even that you thought of a way . . . ."

"It isn't unselfish," I said. "It would help me in my research if I could produce some improvement in him. But have you considered that Gabriel might be quite happy the way he is? Because you are unhappy, you want to change him to suit you."

My words startled her and she thought them over. I had to know how far I could expose myself to get her cooperation and loyalty. To be able to succeed I had to get O'Brian completely out of the picture.

"I'm doing it for him." She had found the answer that suited her. "To be in love means to guess the wishes of the beloved long before they have come into his own consciousness. I know Gabriel better than he knew himself before he became ill."

"And if he were not that handsome, Helga," I asked the question that was loaded with dynamite, "do you think you'd have gone out of your way to help him?"

"Since I love him, I want him to be perfect," she said. "You wouldn't stand idly by if you could repair imperfection in your beloved, would you?"

We got up and continued walking, the robot between us.

"Helga," I said, "I don't want anybody to know about our conversation. That must be understood."

"You mean I shouldn't tell Jimmy," she said soberly. "I won't."

"Jimmy is strictly against any experiment on his patients."

"Yes. But he is not against you. He would very much like to help you. But he cannot take that responsibility."

"He is a bureaucrat and sticks to the rules," I said.

"Please, don't be bitter, Dr. Cory," she said. "I understand his position and yours too. Jimmy must do what he is doing, or he wouldn't be in this job very long. Brentwood House has two-thousand-five-hundred inmates and nine-hundred employees. He cannot gamble. And you don't want to submit to any supervision. That too I understand. You are a genius, and geniuses cannot be measured by the common yardstick we others apply to our lives. You have your own sense of values, or you wouldn't be Dr. Cory."

"Well, you see the cleavage that parts the angels from the devil," I said and laughed. I didn't want to make our discussion sound too serious.

"I will do anything you say, Dr. Cory," she said, looking at Gabriel with eyes that melted with compassion.

"Even if it means helping me secretly?"

She nodded. "I can keep secrets, and I won't run away screaming anymore. I've made my choice."

We walked to the administration building and stopped.

"Gabriel is sleepy." She put her hand on the robot's arm. "I must get him to bed."

"I can't treat Gabriel here at Brentwood House," I said, playing my trump card.

She looked searchingly at the tall, good-looking idiot, at his finely chiseled frozen face, the eternally sophisticated smile, the unruly black hair, the only part of him that still had a will of its own.

"I know," she said. "We'll get him out of here."

Chapter Eleven

After I had returned to Desert Rock, I anticipated interference from O'Brian and his cohorts and prepared a plan with the precision of scientific research.

The first step was to go to a place where I could not be found easily. A big city would be the best hiding place.

I phoned a real-estate agent in Los Angeles and told him to find me a house with three bedrooms and a small guest cottage in the Hollywood Hills. There are still remote spots off the main highways not yet suburbanized and cluttered up with homes that look like the swatches in a tailor's shop—the same pattern, only of another color.

The man at the end of the line was incredulous. First he asked for a recommendation. I told him that I had picked his name from the yellow pages. He had never heard of anybody buying a house by telephone. To prove my intentions, I mailed him a check, and he sent me a bundle of photographs of available houses. Money is the language that needs no translation.

I chose a place on top of Mulholland Drive on a small private road leading off the main highway. The house, enclosed by a wall, overlooked the valley and mountains. It was not on a lover's lane, which would have defeated my purpose.

Kaweah and Jose had not mentioned the bull or coyote to O'Brian. Of course their knowledge was scanty, but O'Brian might have been able to put the jigsaw puzzle of facts together and might have come to some kind of disturbing conclusion.

It is safer to overestimate than to doubt an enemy's intelligence. O'Brian was the enemy to watch.

How would he react when Helga and her protege had disappeared? A patient of his kidnapped? He would send the police after her, and of course me since I too would have faded away. I had to see to it that I left as few pieces of evidence of this mystery story behind as possible.

As every day, Kaweah came to work. Jose too showed up to repair fences, clean the garden, and do jobs his wife assigned to him. I called them into the living room and asked them if they would like to come with me to Hollywood for a few months.

At once I saw fear in Kaweah's eyes. She had never left the reservation. Jose was calm and shrewd. He asked me how much I would pay. Having had contact with the outside world, he knew about its values, which can be measured in hard cash.

The sum I mentioned startled him. I had made it deliberately high to shock him into accepting. I could use both of them well, Jose to drive the car and to go shopping, Kaweah to run the house. They would live in the guest bungalow and not be in my way. I told Jose about the property that I had bought and sent him to Los Angeles to open the house.

How many things had to be looked after in such a short time! Time was running out on me. I expected O'Brian's henchmen any day!

Fortunately we live in a world of ease for the affluent. A decorating firm in Los Angeles took over the job of furnishing the place. I told them what I wanted, including the room for the laboratory. They had dealt with eccentrics before and were not surprised, since the check I sent them was cleared without question.

Helga phoned me from Mojave City. She was afraid to use the telephone at Brentwood House and had driven 50 miles to talk to me without fear of being overheard.

How quickly she had switched her loyalty from O'Brian to me! She couldn't wait to go to bed with her lover—after he had been remodeled and was able to carry on a conversation.

She must have believed that she had been continent all her life because she had refrained from sexual relations. But continence is of the mind as well as of the organs. I'm sure that every night alone in her bed, she imagined herself in Gabriel's arms—a Gabriel with fire in his eyes and loins, uttering words of endearment.

The chastity of the mind is natural in very few people. Helga did not have it. All she had were walls of defense, her religious fanaticism, her self-sacrifice as a nurse. Now she was ready to lay down her arms.

Bluebeard and *La Belle Dame* were but the male and female aspects of the same psychology. They were inspired by hopelessness because of unrequited passion. Charles Perrault's famous ogre killed his wives and kept their bodies in a room. *La Belle Dame* hung the pale heads of her murdered lovers in her cave. Both were looking vainly for fulfillment of their passionate desires.

Helga was looking for the same fulfillment, not knowing that fulfillment and death are synonymous.

"Jimmy is going to visit you this afternoon," she said with the relish of an informer possessing an important secret. I wished she had felt guilt instead of excitement. Guilt would have hammered more links to the chain with which I kept her a prisoner. At the end of the chain dangled Gabriel.

"I'll have a drink ready for him," I said.

"He is bringing two people from the FBI," she continued in her conspirator's voice.

"Then I'd better put on the coffeepot. Thanks for warning me," I said. "Now this is the time to get away. Take down this address: twenty-two thousand Sumac Drive. That's the house I bought. Pick up Gabriel and drive to Hollywood. Jose will be at the house. Don't call me. I'll come as soon as I can."

There was a frightened silence on the other end of the line now that she was faced not with intention, but with action.

"Shall I pack his clothes and mine?" she asked.

"No. We will get things we need. Leave your car in the garage in the Hollywood house and close the door. If there is something you want, send Jose. He has enough money."

I suddenly yearned to get out of the desert, out of that jailing loneliness, that Hades heat that desiccates every brain.

"And if they find Gabriel and me?" she asked.

"You are not committing a crime! Gabriel is the answer. If we make him think again, we will have cured an incurable. We won't be punished for that. You couldn't wait to help him. Now you have the chance. There's a difference between praying and acting, Helga. It's easy to pray and to leave the rest to the angels."

"You're right," she said. I had slammed the door behind her. She could never go back from where she had come.

She had not called too soon. When I put down the receiver, the telephone rang again. O'Brian was on the line.

175

"I've been trying for the last ten minutes to get you," he said. "I thought you never used the telephone. I even called the operator to find out if your line was out of order."

I felt a chill. To talk over secrets on the phone is madness. There are always people listening in—linemen, operators, chance wrong connections. I shuddered at the possibility that O'Brian had been an ear-witness to our conspiracy.

"Now you've got me." I tried to put a carefree cadenza in my voice.

"How do you feel?" the doctor asked.

"Never better. It was relaxing among your inmates. You know that my business is vibrations. Those at Brentwood House are not strong enough to interfere with mine."

"But they show up on the encephalograph." O'Brian made conversation before he came to the point. I became impatient.

"What gives me the honor of your call?"

"I thought I'd drop by for a few minutes. There're a couple of people with me you ought to meet."

He might have felt uncomfortable if he had arrived unannounced.

"From the government?" I asked, making it easy for him.

"Well, yes. Would you talk to them?"

"Anything you say, Jimmy," I said to his surprise. "If that question is so dear to your heart, I will, for sure!"

"You're mellowing, old man," he laughed.

After we hung up, I looked again through my equipment. The timing was right: O'Brian's absence would give Helga time to leave with Gabriel. Nobody would watch her. I would keep O'Brian at my house until she had a good start. Before he returned to Brentwood House she might be close to the California border.

The major part of my equipment had been taken to the new house by Jose. Whatever was left was inefficacious and outdated.

Though I was sure they would never get any information from Kaweah, I did not want to have her submitted to questions that might upset her. I told her to go to her hut on the reservation.

It was not more than an hour before two cars stopped in front of my house. In order not to shock my visitors, I put on my face mask.

O'Brian brought two men along. One of them was bald, his broad face pasty; the other one was in his late twenties, thin, lanky, bony. They always work in teams, one talking, the other watching. They would watch my mask!

"Dr. Merriam, Dr. Hausdorffer, Dr. Cory," O'Brian introduced us. He must have briefed them well since they showed no surprise at a face hidden like that of a man to be hanged.

With a flourish O'Brian threw his yellowed cap on a chair, indicating that he was at home in my house. We acted out a play of the commedia dell'arte, where the twists of the story and the performance of the players are so traditional that the spectators know every move in advance.

"Dr. Merriam is working for the government," O'Brian stated ambiguously as we walked to the living room. I'm sure he felt wretched as an informer.

Merriam laughed with the restrained jovialness of the professional investigator.

"Somehow we all are working for the government," he said to appease me.

"Coffee? I could offer something stronger." I said before the inquisition started.

"Later maybe," Merriam muttered, as I expected. To accept anything might be equal to taking a bribe.

Hausdorffer settled down where he could keep me in view without being seen by me. He was the watcher, recording my reactions to Merriam's questions. But a black piece of cloth has no expression. I therefore took it off in order not to give Hausdorffer the chance to report that I deliberately and cunningly had hidden my face.

Suddenly confronted with my hideous countenance, Hausdorffer paled and gagged, his eyes riveted on my destroyed face. Stark horror has a hypnotic effect. It fixes the gaze until the brain fogs up and blots out in a faint.

"Aren't you more comfortable in the mask?" O'Brian asked, afraid Hausdorffer might pass out.

"I'm sure you must've prepared these gentlemen for my looks." I turned to the young chap. "The bathroom is across the hall if you want to freshen up." He quickly left the room; I heard him vomit and flush the toilet. He did not reappear for a while.

"Felix isn't used to this heat," Merriam said lamely. "It gets to him."

I waited for Merriam to start talking. I was not going to make it easy for him.

"Dr. O'Brian informed us of your work, Dr. Cory, and we are, of course, highly interested."

"He told you against my will," I said. "And I still don't know what department 'US' represents. Is that an abbreviation for unwanted scientists?"

Merriam laughed. As in many people who laugh forcibly, his expression was that of a villain.

"No special department! We all work together, the State Department, the FBI, the CIA, and lots of other abbreviations. But that's of no consequence. Dr. O'Brian believes that your discovery is important to the government. I wish you'd called us on your own accord, Dr. Cory."

The toilet flushed, emphasizing his reproof. Hausdorffer reappeared, but I did not put back my face cloth to make him comfortable.

"If I have broken any law, please tell me," I said.

Merriam laughed loudly, as if I had cracked a joke. "We would have to create a special law for men like you, Dr. Cory. But it isn't a question of law; it's one of public safety."

I dragged on this ridiculous blather to give Helga time to get away. She had to pass Desert Rock on her trip to California. There was no other highway. I had to prevent O'Brian from running into her.

"Are you a physicist, Dr. Merriam?" I asked.

"Yes, but not in your class, Dr. Cory," he said. "I'm a neophyte in comparison to you. Could you tell us something about your work?" He had the courtesy of an executioner who exposes his sword, proudly showing it to the condemned.

"I don't think I will," I said.

He looked at me with the proper astonishment mixed with a touch of disdain. "I can't see the reason," he said.

O'Brian squirmed in his chair. "You told me you'd cooperate, Patrick!"

It sounded like the questioning at the Committee for un-American Activities. The word cooperate had the connotation of admitting guilt.

"I'm sharing Dr. Merriam's concern, Jimmy. He may search my house, confiscate all materials which look suspicious to him; I won't stop him. I won't even ask for a warrant, which I'm sure he's got. He may cart off my things in trucks. That's all within the law, I'm sure. But he cannot force me to give him any information."

"But you will, won't you?" Merriam asked.

"No," I said.

"Then you'll permit me to go through your house?" He got up, and I heard Hausdorffer behind me rise simultaneously.

"Suit yourself," I said without rancor.

O'Brian looked unhappy. He had not anticipated that kind of development, which, as he stated, his conscience had dictated. "Why make it tough?" he asked.

"Tough?" I acted surprised. "You know that I dislike regimentation of my work." I turned to Hausdorffer, who had opened the door of my bedroom. "My lab is opposite the living room."

Without looking at me, he bowed a little. I know my face will appear in his dreams to the end of his days. Some people have an irrational horror about deformities or extreme ugliness. It is a phobia that makes them vulnerable in their work. I'd have enjoyed taking him through Brentwood House. That would have castrated him.

I followed him and Merriam. O'Brian stayed behind. He went to the liquor cabinet and poured himself a drink. I had expected him to be more cold-blooded. He needed solace.

Merriam at once found the electrodes in their small container. They were the first ones that Malcolm had built, oversized in comparison to my latest models. Merriam studied them with a fair knowledge of what he was looking at.

"I've never seen such miniaturization of circuits, Dr. Cory." There was genuine admiration in his voice. "Thought transfer! You are capable of putting thoughts into people's minds by artificial means? It's a tremendous accomplishment, and believe me, I won't let go until I know how you do it!"

People like Merriam can be trained by etching into their minds preconceived facts. Repeated often enough on tape, messages will imprint themselves permanently into the brain's neurons. People in the future won't need to think, the knowledge will pop into their memory as if jumping out of a file. Besides, no specific level of intelligence or training will be required. Any moron will do. They might even do better than those with some intelligence and will only need to be fed one certain bank of information. Merriam, I guessed, was aware of the extent of these possibilities. Any government office would be only too happy to use such a method.

"You were working with isotopes as a power source," he suddenly said. "Where do you keep them?"

The isotopes! I had sent the containers to Hollywood with Jose.

"How do you know?" I asked, while trying to think up a good explanation.

"You got them from Oakridge. You are in their records, Dr. Cory. They were shipped to you in containers which you designed. Now thanks to you, they are using that kind exclusively."

He tried to sprinkle sugar on all his questions.

"Why didn't they tell you that I returned the radioactive material to them?" I said.

Before he could find out the truth I would be 600 miles west of Desert Rock. Luckily he accepted my explanation.

"You did?" he said. Then he launched a vicious personal attack. Part of his method of investigation was to shock his opponent. "I wish you'd help us, Dr. Cory. I had hoped to find a patriot."

"Patriot?" I repeated. "I can't help you there. I don't read newspapers, don't look at television, nor get the pamphlets of the right, the middle, or the left."

"I don't understand you," he said, baffled. "The definition of a patriot is clear."

"By government decree? The Germans were our enemies, so were the Japanese, and the Russians and Chinese our friends. Then the Germans became our friends and the Japanese too. The Chinese and the Russians our enemies. Indonesians are enemies, Malaysians friends. North Congo is a friend, South is an enemy. One island is, another is not. Sorry, I'm not up to the latest tally, Dr. Merriam. I'm working in a back room, and I'm ignorant whom I should like and whom I should hate."

I saw the professional spyhunter behind his friendly mask.

"Whom do you like?" he asked.

"My friends," I said.

By now Helga should have crossed the border into California.

Merriam's conciliatory attitude flowed off him like soap suds in a shower. "Sorry, but I must ask you not to remove anything from this house," he said.

"Am I under arrest?" I asked. That would upset my timetable.

"Experts will have to look over your equipment. I'm not. But I would prefer if you stayed on." Then he again poured on the oil. "Why don't you cooperate, Dr. Cory? Why not use the immense government facilities for your work? The times are gone when a man could be a loner."

"No cooperation on my part, Dr. Merriam," I said.

"Then Dr. Hausdorffer will stay with you until the commission arrives. I hope you have no objections."

He glared at me, covering up his weak legal position.

"Of course not," I said. "I'll take good care of him."

Merriam walked out and Hausdorffer followed him.

"Patrick," O'Brian whispered at my side. "You removed some of your equipment."

"Then why don't you tell them?" I asked.

Confused, he shrugged his shoulders.

"As a Judas," I said, "you're a bust, Dr. O'Brian."

Chapter Twelve

Now that I was in my house in the Hollywood Hills, O'Brian, even with the help of the police and the abbreviated offices, had only a slight chance of finding me.

Hausdorffer, my jailer, had been polite and professionally conciliatory. To repay him in kind I had kept my face mask on. We had dinner together. For the first time I heard that Kaweah's tamales were excellent. They had been my staple food for months.

Hausdorffer had been with General Electric's research department for years; Merriam had taught at MIT. They were well trained, or the FBI wouldn't have given them this job. When Merriam called to say that the committee would be in Desert Rock in the morning, I knew that I had to get away.

Hausdorffer couldn't discuss his government job; so he talked about his old one. When he had a few drinks in him, he told me about his grievances, complaining about the red tape at G.E. and how he had to stand in line for promotion, waiting for somebody with seniority to leave or to die. The people in his department kept him in a corner. It was a conspiracy. They even claimed his ideas as their own. When Hausdorffer had a chance to leave for a more interesting job, he quit to become the investigator he was.

He was bitter like any man who has not enough stamina to stand up against adversity. A man like that never blames himself, only others and systems, which are conspiracies against the nation—black devils working insidiously in the dark. Like the Hydra, which grew three new heads for every one cut off, their sinister forces penetrate the government right to the top.

The pattern was clear. He could only live when he could hate. Hatred is a defense, a retaliation. Somebody has to act first. Hatred is retribution. Hatred also can be excused, since it wants to retrieve only what has been stolen or willfully snatched away: self-respect, pride, hope, and tangibles like women or money.

Hausdorffer hated people like me who carried out their own ideas without kowtowing to bureaucratic restrictions. It might not be true that he had been slighted in his job. His lack of drive might have interfered with his success. I didn't care about his dilemma.

Now, as a sleuth for a powerful, mysterious government agency, he had a chance to retaliate, to inhibit people like me who had not sold out as he had. In his opinion those people had to be put in chains—chains that he had willingly forged for himself.

I was still in the paradise that he had lost. Every Adam had to be driven out by him.

He had been drinking that night with the Teutonic approach to the job. He did not show any outward signs of drunkeness. Though the kidneys can absorb only one-and-a-half ounces of alcohol an hour, his seemed to be of a special capacity.

But the frontiers of his tolerance narrowed more and more as the bottle emptied. He ended with his boss, Merriam. Merriam boasted that he had destroyed Lesage, one of the foremost scientists of the decade. Not that Lesage was outstandingly inventive. But he was like the conductor of a huge orchestra who knew every instrument and directed and fused them into a symphonic masterpiece. He had advanced research into the outer atmosphere more than anyone else alive. Mentally he stood above Merriam as a skyscraper towers over a hut. Merriam had felled that giant by collecting quotes from his speeches for years, snooping in Lesage's private life, making him guilty by his association with people who were branded undesirable. He reminded me of the picture of the little man who with his long saw stands on the trunk of a giant sequoia tree. That tree had weathered the world's hazards for 4,000 years, but had been felled by a dwarf who wanted to prove that he could cut down that miracle of nature already 2,000 years old when Christ was born. That act of vandalism made the man more powerful than the tree in his own eyes.

My disgust for Hausdorffer deepened as I kept filling his glass, hoping he would collapse. But he did not. Like in an old-fashioned melodrama I finally sneaked a few drops of Nembutal into his nightcap, hoping the combination of alcohol and barbiturate wouldn't kill him. It didn't. He was snoring on the couch when Kaweah came just after midnight.

Kaweah and I drove off in my Chrysler limousine. I taught her how to use the automatic transmission, since her old Buick still had a stick shift. She learned quickly. Whenever we had to buy gasoline I hid in the backseat, supposedly asleep under a blanket. Kaweah ordered the gas and paid. Nobody ever saw my face—a face one would not forget.

At daybreak we arrived in Hollywood. Jose was waiting for us and so was Helga. Masked, I felt like the Lone Ranger.

The house on Sumac Drive had been furnished with the soulless efficiency of a decorator who is sure he knows what people like. There were the plants in Mexican urns, the highly polished teak furniture in Swedish modern, the printed curtains, the Utrillo and Picasso prints, and as an exclamation point and conversation piece, a wall-sized reproduction of a Jackson Pollock, which looked to me like the enlarged slide of an atomic fission. The bookshelves were bare.

My room, with its ivory-colored walls, chaste bed, and sparse furniture, overlooked the valley. Smog rose in the morning like ghosts. The smog drifted higher and higher with the rising sun, obscuring the mountain chain behind, but never reaching the crest of our hill.

I worked continuously in the lab, devising the new miniature transcorder that, bean-small, contained the power needed for transmitting the brain's ultrashort emanations. Based on the principle of the encephalograph, it converted the electric impulses of the brain's parietal lobes, which are the primary cortical reception level, into transmittable frequencies. But it also could receive impulses, transforming them into sensory perceptions. Following Malcolm's thoughts, I had the systems completely worked out in my mind. When he had dreamt them up, they still were abstract concepts. I now could put them into practical shape.

Jose and Kaweah lived in the small guesthouse in luxury they had never dreamed of. Kaweah could never get over the wonder of the electric dishwasher. There she stored her pots and pans. Her bathroom had a sunken tub, and she marvelled at the many gadgets, which she never put to use. Kaweah had started to blossom again. She was similar to the desert where she had been born, which she had never left before— the barren land exploding into bloom after a sudden downpour. Jose liked to sit behind the guesthouse, out of sight, watching the diminutive traffic far below in the valley. Neither wished to go to Thousand Oaks, the sprawling community at the bottom of Mulholland Drive. For them life again had found its equilibrium.

I had worked out the puzzle of staying hidden from our pursuers. Jose was not permitted to take the old truck or any of the cars. Their license numbers might have been broadcast by the police. I had Jose buy a secondhand truck to ride into town. Helga bought a small Fiat Spyder sports car for cash and registered it in a fictitious name. Whimsically she chose Gabriel Hyde. Had that car ever met with an accident, or even a traffic ticket, our adventure would have come to a sudden end.

Time, perpetually perishing, is the enemy of man. Though its flow gives him an opportunity to extract from life what he wants, only a limited amount of hours are his.

Helga was not concerned about the decay of time. She had no conscience about having kidnapped that inanimate paramour of hers, who was sitting in the garden, smiling eternally, staring at the valley he could not see, at Helga, whom he did not recognize, or at me. I don't think she would have minded if life had gone on that way forever. She knew I was working on the problem of bringing Gabriel to life, and that was all she needed as an incentive for doing nothing.

Before I left I had ordered the bank in Mojave City to send money from the account to the post office as a registered parcel. The manager of the bank phoned me in alarm. He had never heard of such a request before. I insisted and Kaweah picked up the package.

Having access to abundant money—my money—Helga used it lavishly. Since I left the bills in a drawer to which she had a key, she took whatever she wanted. I did not mind. Money, the symbol of exchange, has no meaning for me. Besides, new funds come in every month. Industries all over the world use my patents. A lawyer in New York takes care of the collections. I do not want to be bothered.

Almost every day Helga drove to Thousand Oaks to go shopping for herself and Gabriel. She had not brought any clothes when she absconded with that robot. In new outfits, she was pleasant to look at. The nurse's dress had stamped its own attitude on her daily life. Now she had shed that sterile white costume and with it that peculiar frame of mind, that devotion to a cause. She did not even flaunt her religious asseverations anymore. She was preoccupied with Gabriel.

Knowing Gabriel's size by the measure of her hands—as one measures a horse—she bought suits, shoes, ties, and shirts for him, spending untold hours dressing her dummy, brushing his thick black hair, shaving him in the morning with the electric razor. When I heard its hum in my laboratory, I knew she was fussing with her life-sized puppet.

Nobody ever had a doll such as hers, beautiful and patient, as if it were artificial. A doll that, though it did not talk, could perform all the other actions children expect from their toys. How much pleasure she must have extracted from that giant marionette, dressing and undressing him, wrapping his smooth body into silken sheets at night.

What could be more perfect for her? She could play at love. There was no mind to oppose her, no quarrel, no disagreement, no friction. She could play with the devil without the danger of ending up in hell.

She had her lover and still kept her virginity. If anybody ever had his cake and could eat it at the same time, it was Helga. She did not care for the house or for anything alive. Like an autistic child who cannot distinguish between a living and an inanimate object, she was wrapped up exclusively in Gabriel.

We were a cartoon strip of monsters: an anchorite Indian woman, her silent, withdrawn husband, a male robot, a religiously fanatic girl in love with the robot, and I, a man without a face. All of us wanted urgently by the police and by an asylum for the mentally retarded!

Jose, returning from Thousand Oaks, brought groceries and newspapers. They never contained anything about Gabriel's abduction, nor did the police ever mention that crazy scientist who had absconded with his fearful invention. But I was sure that Merriam and his departments were feverishly looking for us.

People hide to escape from themselves. Hermits are the acme of selfishness. They do not want to share. None of us wanted to share any of our pleasures. Each one of us lived in his small circle, stagnated, kept conscious solely on the thought that something might happen, an impending thunderstorm, an earthquake, a disaster. But that was far away, like the clouds on the horizon that might drift away.

Helga's room was next to Gabriel's. At night she left her door ajar. It was like the engagement of two virginal people who one day might get married. Helga must have dwelled in this pure abstract irreality. I don't know if she ever thought about what would happen if he had back his mind, and therefore power to act, to think, to resolve, to impose. Her dreams were the substitute for her desires. They were, in a way, similar to my nightmares that the explosion had not occurred, that Malcolm was alive, that I had my original face.

In her case she might dream of being Gabriel's wife with all the wild ectasies only a virgin can conceive. Like me, she might not want to wake up. In my case I was faced with facts that the dream was just a reeling off of that shattering incident. She was faced with the opposite: though her lover was there in the flesh, her emotions could only find fulfillment in her dreams.

The night had cooled off and the smog had sunk back into the ground when I finished working. The first daylight framed the top of the Simi Valley mountains opposite.

I went into Gabriel's bedroom, carrying two of my third-generation transducers with me. They were bean-small and flat. The early sun's reflection painted his sleeping face white. He looked at peace. There was no thought to disturb him. His brain might have started to atrophy.

I sat next to him on a chair. The sheet that covered him had slipped down; the ocher silk pajamas he was wearing were half open and exposed a tanned skin and a hairy chest. As he breathed the muscles of his stomach rippled and contracted like that of an athlete. A bluish hue indicated the growth of a heavy beard. The cheeks fell in below the eyes. Thin, delicate skin creating a cavity filled with shadows. Very long eyelashes lay on his face, deep black as though painted. He snored a little. That eternal smile hovered on his lips, the corners drawn out thinly and turned up slightly. The mouth gave the face its curious attractiveness. His hands were long and strong like a tennis player's, the fingers tapered, the round nails manicured and highly polished with a touch of pink. Helga had sissified her doll. The toenails of his exposed foot also were shined. The toes were of a peculiar shape, like elongated fingers.

I fastened the transducers behind his ears, gliding them into his shiny hair, which was soft and smelled of thin perfume. Helga must have shampooed him the night before. What else did she do, alone with him for days? She had turned him into the image she wanted a man to be: well-groomed, artificial, sweet smelling, precious—the way a man likes an exquisite whore in bed.

Gabriel's Body

I peeked into Helga's room. She was asleep, her face hidden below the bedsheet, her legs drawn up like that of a fetus. She wanted to be back in her mother's womb with its dutyless security.

I returned to the lab and spoke a few words on tape. I now was ready with my first experiment on Gabriel.

Chapter Thirteen

Days shaped into routine. Kaweah got up at five every morning, as she was accustomed. Jose slept till a quarter to six, then started his gardening. The hill sloping down precipitously behind the house was ablaze with flowers. At eight, after one hour of primping, Helga was ready for the day. She always dressed as if for a fashion show. I never saw her with hair curlers or without carefully applied makeup. At eight o'clock she started Gabriel's day behind closed doors.

Gabriel was displayed in different disguises: as a mandarin in a flowery Chinese gown, as a gentleman in a finely striped suit of cashmere, in a silk overall with broad belt and buckle, in shorts, bare knees, and canvas shoes as though ready for tennis. One day she had put a riding outfit replete with boots and spurs on him.

She did not care how much of my money she spent on him or herself. Every day she bought him a present: a tie, a Panama strawhat, silk shorts with his initials. One day he showed up with a Patek Phillipe wristwatch.

I let her have her diversion, not wanting her to become restless, pensive, or remorseful. She had violated all her former taboos. She had run away with Gabriel, who had been entrusted to her; she was hiding out from the police and had broken her trust with O'Brian. She could only be vindicated should Gabriel regain his mind.

She was like a gambler who had put all his money on one number at roulette. The ball had been tossed and was circling the wheel. There was no doubt in her mind that the ball would fall into the pocket with her number on it.

I rarely left my laboratory. It is amazing how quickly a room takes on the character of its owner. Electronic equipment has a soulless abstraction. This was the world in which I felt at ease—a world of wires, plastic, stainless steel. In a way, the lab was a symbol of myself.

As I passed the breakfast nook I saw Helga feeding Gabriel. The peripheral nervous system acts as an external mirror for the physical world. These impressions are passed on to the central nervous system to provide for the necessary immediate adjustments or reflex activities. Gabriel's lower brain functions had not been completely destroyed. The activities connected with circulation, respiration, digestion, and phonation were still working, or he would not be alive. The mechanical action of eating and sleeping, of being toilet trained fortunately had never been affected by his illness.

But he had no memory. Memory also disappears partially in old people whose voluntary nervous systems become calcified. I once saw two old men meet in the corridor of a hospital, trying to figure out if they were going to the dining room to have lunch or just coming back from it. Although they might have remembered every episode, however trivial, they had lived through 50 years ago, they had lost the ability to learn new behavior.

I was ready with my first experiment with Gabriel. I was not able to watch it, but I certainly would hear about its success.

Inserting the prerecorded tape into the transcorder, I turned on the current. It was the same test that I had tried out on Kaweah. A moment later I heard Helga's scream. She came out of the breakfast room and, in headlong flight, crashed into a chair in the living room.

"Dr. Cory," she cried "Dr. Cory!"

A moment later she stood in the doorway of the laboratory. A strand of hair had fallen into her face, her eyes were wild with shock, and she had smeared her carefully applied lipstick.

"He talked," she shouted at me, as though I were a mile away. "Gabriel talked!"

"Good, that's what I expected."

She did not listen.

"He said: "Helga, more coffee please. . . ." He said it quite clearly! And he went on talking. Maybe he still is!"

Only now I diagnosed the expression in her eyes as terror. "Aren't you pleased?" I asked.

"Yes," she shouted, then controlled herself and pushed back that willful strand of hair. "It—it was such a shock . . . . I was sitting there and he suddenly talked!"

"That's what you wanted, wasn't it?" I said, reeling the tape and starting it again. I had added half a minute of blank tape to give me time to walk into the breakfast room.

Gabriel was sitting erect and smiling behind his cup of coffee. He was dressed in a sports shirt, which showed a tuft of black hair creeping from its open collar. There was no expression in his large violet eyes. But now he opened his mouth and his white teeth flashed.

"Helga," he said, "more coffee please, and some of that oatmeal, no . . . no sugar, no cream, just oatmeal and coffee."

There was no oatmeal on the table.

His voice was resonant, well modulated, and had the sensuous throaty inflection that men dislike to hear in other men's voices. The voice fitted his looks and must have been part of his invincible charm.

Kaweah appeared in the doorway, startled, a pan in her hand. When she caught my eye, she disappeared quickly. I was sure she was running to Jose to tell him that the silent idiot had found his voice.

"Helga, more coffee please, and some of that oatmeal, no . . . no sugar, no cream, just oatmeal and coffee," he said again. The tape ran out. He was silent.

Helga was leaning against the wall, visibly shaken. She had become so pale that her makeup was sharply defined against the pallor of her skin. "He talked, you heard him," she muttered, unable to comprehend that miracle.

"I made him speak, Helga," I said.

Now regaining her composure, she turned her large eyes toward me. "You did make him talk," she said, waking from the dream that had started the day she had run away with Gabriel. "How did you do it?"

"It's a mechanical reaction produced by a stimulation of the lower brain functions. I can make him say anything, as long as he is wearing these."

I stepped over to Gabriel and removed the tiny transducer that I had hidden behind his ears.

She stared at the bean-like elements in my palm. Her voice was hoarse with fear. She must have remembered her shock at the hospital when I had experimented with her.

"Terrifying," she said. She walked quickly over to Gabriel and touched his face with the compassion I had often seen at Brentwood House.

"You didn't hurt him?" she asked.

"Of course not. There is no pain connected with my experiment. You should know that, Helga."

"No pain," she shuddered, "just shock and fear."

"But Gabriel does not react like a thinking person," I said. "Not yet. I will make him walk, teach him to dress, read. Though I cannot make him understand right away, I could make him do many things."

She looked at him and her eyes clouded. I could guess what she was thinking about: her innocent honeymoon was nearing its end.

"But he would need you to do all that?" she asked.

"No," I said. "But we will have to train his responses by stimulating his reflexes, the associative and voluntary activities. My theory is that his illness has shocked them into chronic cramps. If this tension could be released, he would have a chance to recover. His brain matter might not necessarily be destroyed. Diagnosis depends on the theories taught. Encephalitis has been the private domain of the epidemiologists. They might be wrong all together. His cure might belong to the research of engineers like me."

Her mouth opened with astonishment. I had heard that expression, but here was proof that people do act that way when they are startled.

"You mean you could strengthen his nervous responses by artificial stimulation?" she asked. "Like training the polio patients? That also is a disease of the nerves."

She began to believe me. My cure descended from the level of miracle to that of therapy, where she was at home.

"You have just heard that I can make him talk." I opened my hand with the transducers.

"If I insert those under his skin close to his brain stem and the tracks which convey rostrally the several streams of sensory impressions, he might regain his senses. Not necessarily his memory, but he would be aware of the world around him, and he would be able to act on his own will."

She nodded. I had made sense to her. "Yes. We were getting responses from autistic children by commands and small electric shocks. We even got cures."

"Mild jolts of current through their bare feet," I said. "O'Brian showed me a few cases, and I witnessed a session. That gave me the idea, Helga. Mild jolts of current through the thalamus would stimulate paralyzed nerves."

She reverted back to the nurse. "How would you go about it?"

"For the last few weeks I have worked on tiny circuits to be placed under his skin. They generate their own power. Will you assist me in operating on him?"

"You need me as a nurse," she said, smiling at me while she touched Gabriel's hair for a fleeting moment.

I was glad that my voice had no color, or she might have become aware that I had deliberately fooled her.

I was not giving my secrets away. It was true that I could bring him back to life, make him talk coherently, intelligently. I could give him emotions, make him into a man.

I could, by lending him my personality.

Chapter Fourteen

That night I was attacked by pain more severe than I had ever experienced.

Suffering passes, but the fact of having suffered stays in the mind forever. The fluid medium of languages retains some of the connection between physical pain and human existence. The word pain derives from the Latin *poena*, punishment. Pain is evil. It is death's shadow. Death is an end without meaning. It cannot be brought into harmony with life, however much religions try. Pain is the destruction of self in the body of agony.

But it could not reach me anymore. I had discovered a way to escape pain, wipe it out without a trace. Though it might still ravage my body, it could not find a fiber to crawl into my consciousness.

We had led Gabriel to the laboratory. I shaved his hair at the neck, which I anesthetized just below the axis. From the sterilizer I took my latest transducers; I had reduced them to the size of a rice grain.

Helga assisted me. Acting with the precision of a surgical nurse, she sterilized the operating room—a part of my laboratory—painstakingly. The small scalpel she had boiled for an hour. She insisted that I use surgical gloves, though all those precautions were hardly necessary. I complied to alleviate her concern about my skill as a surgeon. It was less complicated an operation than removing a splinter, but she behaved as if it were major surgery.

Only a few drops of blood were oozing from the two tiny cuts I had made. I did not bother to sew up the skin, but I used an antibiotic. In a couple of days the wound would heal and the hair would overgrow it. Nobody would ever suspect that Gabriel Deeping's actions were triggered by two tiny gadgets.

As an added precaution she bandaged his neck, then left with him to put him to bed so he could rest after that ordeal.

I expected her to return. But she did not. Wasn't she interested in what would happen from now on to Gabriel? Or was she afraid to know? I had the answers to her questions ready.

That night pain struck.

I have seen people receive injections into the eye itself to arrest glaucoma. Though the eye is anesthetized, the pain is excrutiating. Numbed by the stab of torture, no one cries. They have no time to convulse since that torment evaporates as quickly as it strikes. Some who have experienced it before laugh. It is, in its enormity and quick disappearance, funny to them in a morbid way.

But the suffering that beset me stayed on. The lancinations in my skin burned like red-hot needles, algospasms choked me, and a paroxysm of fear increased my agony.

I fell to the floor, clawing it, not knowing how to detach myself from that frenzied onslaught.

As I stumbled to my feet to find the prepared hypodermic that would give me relief, my blurred vision misled me. I could not remember where to look for it. I even wanted to call Helga, but only a croak escaped my throat.

As I groped, I found the two transducers. They would connect me with Gabriel. I pressed them against my temples.

All algogenic sensations suddenly disappeared, a black void rose soothingly, all enwrapping. I seemed to fall into a soft whirlpool of silence. For the first time in many weeks—perhaps since the day I experimented with Helga— I felt at rest. My mind blotted out. I was asleep.

When I woke up I saw a rosy shine behind my eyelids. Floating euphorically, I did not move. I heard a door quietly open, and light steps came closer.

Helga stood in front of me in a diaphanous negligee. The lacy, thin material outlined her body nebulously. The gown was revealing without giving the eye anything definite to see. I did not know where she had gotten it. It certainly could not have been found in Thousand Oaks, that suburban appendix of Los Angeles. It came from a very expensive store.

The gown was the acme of coy enticement and virginal provocation, a shield of gossamer chiffon. To get close to her body, it had to be destroyed. She was dressed like a bride for her wedding night.

Soft meat in a soft shell!

The Picasso prints from his blue period on the wall, the blue clowns, the blue absinthe drinker with his cadaverous face and long bony hands, blue flowers on the dressing table, blue curtains—I was in Gabriel's room.

I was Gabriel!

He did not move, nor did he give an indication that he saw her.

"Gabriel," she whispered, "you are awake!"

Scant light fell through the thin drapes. It was just daybreak, an hour before sunrise.

She sat on the bed beside Gabriel. "Are you going to leave me?" She hardly breathed those words. Her hand caressed his cheek, slid behind his neck, touched the bandage that she had wrapped around it a few hours before, and came to rest on his chest. She sighed from fear and the uncertainty of parting, the apprehension of the future. She felt troubles ahead, but her mind could not penetrate the darkness.

She must have come every day to his room while everybody was still asleep and she knew she would not be surprised. Moving like a shadow, the fine fabric floating around her thin body, she locked the door as an added precaution.

Then she returned to the bed and, slowly turning back the covers, lay down beside him. She took his hand and laid it on her eyes, which were hot as though filled with tears that could not find release. Then she slid his palm over her mouth, breathing into it, and her tongue traced the lines of his hand.

"What is going to happen to us?" she asked, her voice scarcely a whisper.

It was quiet except for the river noise of the faraway traffic. She turned her face to Gabriel and guided his hand to her breast. The small nipple became hard, and her flesh quivered with passionate recognition. She rolled over close to him and pressed her body to his, her hand sliding into his pajama top, unbuttoning it.

"Gabriel!" she breathed close to his chest. "Why? Why?"

It was a riddle she could not solve since she was unable to lift the cause of her fear into her consciousness. Any psychoanalyst could have given her the answer at the first session. Her thin hand moved over his body, his taut stomach, the hard solar plexus, and she pressed herself closer and closer to him, kissing him in a sudden frenzy.

Gabriel did not move. His eyes, wide open, stared into hers. She pulled up that chiffon gown and threw her leg over his, to be still closer; and with a moan she pressed her head and mouth to his hairy chest, as if she wanted to become one with him. Moving in tense tortured repetition, pressing her laboring lap against his, she suddenly exploded into a long series of contractions and threw her head back, her teeth gripping her small lower lip.

Suddenly she drew back, crying out in shock. She rolled off the bed, fell to the floor, but quickly got to her feet. In terror she stared at his groin. She had felt the distention, the life that had unexpectedly sprung into him, which she had been sure could not be awakened.

With both of her hands she suppressed a scream. The abject fear that had possessed her at the hospital engulfed her again, and she ran blindly out of the room. The door slammed, and the key turned in the lock, as if she were afraid he would follow her.

I again was in my laboratory, the transducers in my hand. Dull pain, the aftermath of the hurricane that had swept over me, ebbed in my face. The main assault of torment was gone.

Slowly getting up, afraid a sudden jolt would revive the revolt of my tortured nerves, I went to my room and fell on the bed without undressing. But I could not sleep. Had I reached the plane where nothing mattered except that elation of life and youth? I had slipped out of my broken body, as I had intruded into the bull's and the coyote's nervous systems, taking with me my senses, my brain, my emotions, transferring them into another shell as the hermit crab

208

searches and finds another house for its soft, vulnerable body.

The soft body in the hard shell!

My experiment was completed. I should end here. I had achieved what Malcolm and I had started. I had pushed the empirical proof to its limit. Emotions could be transferred. So could sensual impressions. The receiver, with the help of auxiliary powers, could turn them on and off at will. Man was in control. It was possible for him to live in any body he chose. The body was helpless to resist.

That was the fermata in my research. Now I should move into the next phase, that of dissemination, expansion of my ideas, of useful application. My discovery could teach brains to accept sensations they themselves were incapable of spawning. It could be applied by O'Brian for example, to retarded children and possibly cure them; he could also use it on the mentally disturbed and force them to experience buried emotions. I could also cure frigid men and women. Its application was limitless and beneficial.

But how could I voluntarily retreat into my half-broken shell, masochistically submitting myself to suffer to the end of my days? There was a body I could live in, wholesome, strong, powerful, 40 years younger than mine.

It was mine if I so desired.

My decision had to be weighed carefully. Once having alerted my fellow scientists, there would be no road back. They would police me from that moment on. I would be in the limelight, a light as dark as solitary confinement.

Didn't I too have a right to live a few years more, at least?

I, Gabriel!

Chapter Fifteen

Kaweah knocked at my bedroom door. She was disturbed. The day had not started with the usual routine. When she saw me dressed, she was relieved. Contrary to my habit, I too had overslept.

She told me that Helga had left very early in the little sports car, but had not taken care of Gabriel, who was still in bed, unwashed and unfed.

I went to Gabriel's bedroom. He was awake and stared unblinkingly at the window, his long-lashed violet eyes without expression.

Helga had fled the house to recover from her shock. The devil—whom she knew existed, but had never confronted—had suddenly popped up, brandishing his hellish lance. She was very good at theorizing how people ought to comply with her way of life. But reality terrified her.

She had left her protege behind, abandoned and helpless.

I too was helpless. How would I get that hulk out of bed? Would he get up if I pulled him by the arm? And what then? Should I lead him to the toilet?

I was no nursemaid, but I had an idea how to handle him. Besides, it would be part of the experiment. I went back to the laboratory, locked the door, and put on the transcorders.

The picture of the lab dissolved and I saw Gabriel's bedroom. I gave him commands, as I would myself. I had to think of every moment, since none came to him automatically—stretching out the hands, pulling back the cover, moving the feet, standing up, breathing deeply, and yawning, as a man would after a good night's sleep. I wanted him to be completely natural.

I enjoyed the well-being of his muscular body, the surging energy of his young flesh. He went to the bathroom, threw off his pajamas, opened the shower door, turned the faucets, and tested the temperature. When he found it right, he stepped inside and soaped himself. He hummed a tune. Men and birds often start singing when they hear the sound of water. The muscles of his well-proportioned body moved smoothly like ropes under the supple skin. His long hair fell into his face and he whipped it back with a spray of droplets. Then he stepped out, turning off the faucets, which he had at first forgotten to do, and he wrapped himself in his terry-cloth robe. He dried his hair vigorously and then plugged in the electric razor. His face was reflected in the mirror as he moved the cutter over his bluish growth of beard. He grinned into the glass, examining his tongue and teeth.

Throwing off the robe, he walked naked into his bedroom, opening the large closet to choose a suit and matching shirt and socks.

It was time to stop Helga's masquerade party. He laid out a flannel suit, the only one he possessed, and I thought of getting clothes for him that were not as gaudy as the vividly printed Hawaiian shirts or as conspicuous as the English riding outfit with boots and silver spurs.

He did not know how to part his hair—that was I did not—and finally brushed it straight back. Helga liked it long. He needed a haircut.

Still standing naked, he admired himself, that broad-chested torso covered profusely with hair, the dancer's long muscular thighs and legs. He saw Helga in the mirror. She was watching him fixedly with the incredulity of a person confronted with magic tricks. They seem to be mysterious, though are obviously based on slight of hand; tricks are incomprehensible to the uninitiated until they are explained.

I didn't know where she had been, maybe in the hills trying to get her thoughts untangled.

Once a sculptor friend of mine made himself a life-sized doll of rubber with all the intricacies of a human body. But he found his creation unsatisfactory. She had no vaginal warmth, he told me with a laughter that hid his disappointment. He wanted a beautiful mistress, pliable, without a will of her own—Olympia of *Tales of Hoffman*. But it was not enough to have the perfect shape; there must also be the touch of live skin with blood pulsing underneath.

Helga had made love to a zombie, but that walking death had come to life and had shown emotion! She had panicked—the natural reaction of a virgo intacta. Before that incident it had been her choice of approach and rhythm without regard for her inactive partner. But how did she know if that doll might not now suddenly crush her in his arms by a force that had sprung up in his inanimate brain?

Gabriel did not give any indication that he saw her. As though he needed purification, he doused his face and armpits with shaving lotion, generously rubbing it over his skin. He ignored the powder puff in its embossed box—one of Helga's presents.

He stood like a Roman gladiator, his skin tanned and hairy. Slipping on rose-colored shorts, which he looked at with disgust—Helga had bought them—he picked up his trousers and slid his long legs into them. He hummed playfully.

As Helga stepped closer, he passed her to pick up his shirt. His eyes met hers without recognition, and still humming, he turned away to choose a tie from the rack.

"Gabriel," she said hoarsely. "Look at me, please!"

He did not hear her either, and as she stretched out her hand, he walked past her to the closet, where his shoes were stacked. She had gotten hold of his shirtsleeve. He just moved on, pulling away from her slight grip.

A sudden sob, like the sound of pain, escaped her. She threw her hands over her face, as a child would, and cried uncontrollably. Gabriel moved about the room as though she were transparent, whistling, putting on his shoes, in the routine of recurrent days. Tears streaming down her cheeks, she suddenly ran out of his room.

I was prepared for her when she knocked at my door. Leaving the transcorders behind, I stepped into the living room. She looked at me with tearstained eyes. Helga had come for sympathy. I was not sorry for her. She was a hysterical girl who broke down if the world did not respond properly to her selfishness.

I like to work with guinea pigs since their souls do not concern me. But here I had to cope with human elements.

"What's the matter?" I asked. She felt that I was annoyed, though I could not display emotions.

"Gabriel dressed himself today without me," she said, still shocked and disbelieving.

"You didn't dress him? Why not?" I asked.

She did not reply.

"I thought it's your duty to look after him," I said. "You wanted him to have back his mind. Now that he has started to do so, you ran away. I thought you had more discipline."

"He doesn't know that I exist," she cried. "He looked at me and didn't see me! Looked straight at me, but didn't see me!"

"What did you expect?" I asked. "A complete cure?"

I had no use for her anymore. She had forced me to return to my own body, to give up that beautiful healthy shell. She had no more function in my game than a chess piece that had been taken off the board.

"Why didn't he recognize me?" she asked, upset that she had lost her toy. It had been handy as long as it could be packed away or used as a plaything. Now its mechanical innards had developed a flaw. The spring had moved by itself.

"I don't know. It might be that he acts like one of the autistic children who only recognize what they want to see and only use what is useful to them. Give me time."

"Give you time?" She looked at me warily and with suspicion.

"Yes, me. So far I have only been able to stimulate his motor nerves and only part of his memory. His mind now recalls part of the automatic movements which are connected with getting up and dressing. He remembered how to eat and how to defecate when he was with you, didn't he? He still has emotions. Or has he?"

She blinked and let the lids slide over her eyes, recalling the shock when the doll in bed had reacted physically. I wondered if she had the courage to talk about it. She surprised me.

"Yes, he has," she said, having decided that there must be no subterfuge; we both were concerned about Gabriel. "I touched him and he responded—like a man."

"That's some progress," I said. "It's what you wanted, isn't it? The next step might be that he recognizes you and falls in love with you."

She was not aware of my sarcasm. In her pilgrimage to the hills that morning, she had analyzed the problem that faced her. Drawing up the bridges, she had returned to her fortress. Her foray into enemy territory had ended.

"I've thought it over, Dr. Cory. Your experiment is against the will of God." She was back in her religious shell. I now regretted that Gabriel had not raped her. That might have made her human.

"You amaze me," I said. "As long as Gabriel was a puppet, you were happy. Now that he has become a man again, you cannot take it. Why?"

"I went up into the hills to pray," she said, slamming the door in my face. "I formulated my thoughts and feelings. I have sinned. I had unclean desires and lost my humility."

"Okay," I said. "Humility is necessary. That I understand. But it must be followed by tolerance. And what you tolerate is only yourself."

"No!" she said, and her face—wan and rather bruised looking—had that glow of detachment that I had noticed when I first met her. "That is not true!"

217

"Isn't it? The will of God! What an easy way to avoid responsibility! 'Follow Me and you shall lose Me; follow yourself and you shall find both— Me and yourself!' End of quote by Miss Coleman! You told me that you love him and that love begets love. You were convinced of it. What's happened? He's returning into the world from his mental vacuum. But you are running away. Why?"

"I don't know," she said desperately. "I don't know!"

"Of course you do. Now that he might take what you thought you were ready to give to him only a few days ago, you are terrified. Why don't you sleep with him? That might be the right therapy for him. But for you, virginity, the physical one, is like a badge. For a few dollars to pay for a marriage license, you would lose all your scruples, wouldn't you?"

"You are cruel," she whimpered like an exhausted, fretful child. "How cruel you can be!"

I had to make her hate me. Then she would go away, even without Gabriel. "I'll tell you what you can do to save your lily-white soul," I said. "Go back to Jimmy. He adores you. You would make a fine couple, a kind of humanitarian communion. You could do good without endangering your conscience. Go to him. In the meantime I'll give Gabriel back his mind."

She stared out of the window. "I couldn't do that," she said with the single-mindedness of a woman who does not know how to compromise.

"They won't throw you in prison," I tried again. "Tell them that Gabriel is getting better, that he might be cured. I need a few more months to make him whole again. Completely. You could help by leaving him to me."

She walked to the door. "The day you told me that I should run away with Gabriel I prayed. In my prayer I thought I heard the right answer. Now I'm lost."

"Then go up into the hills again and formulate your thoughts and your feelings. I can't help you, Miss Coleman!"

She walked out and determinedly closed the door. I was curious what she would do—give me away and have Gabriel sent back, restore the status quo: the love play in the morning, the ownership of the Kewpie doll, the drifting, happy life that helped her imagine that she was the Joan of Arc of Brentwood House? Maybe marry O'Brian as I had suggested, having that lover on the side, a Madame Bovary without the stain of an illicit affair?

I was sure she'd never give up Gabriel.

"Dr. Cory! Dr. Cory!" she screamed from Gabriel's room. I knew why she was shocked. Gabriel had returned to his impassive state, reverted to the puppet since I had removed the transcorders from my temples.

Chapter Sixteen

Gabriel drove the sports car toward Beverly Hills. He did not know the house of his parents, only the address.

He had to cope with a past that was a blank to him. His mother's face was known to him and that of his fiancee, Mercedes. He had heard about a stepfather. Here the knowledge of his past ended. Who were his friends? What college had he gone to? Was he a member of clubs, a golf player, a tennis champion? Could he swim, dance?

I had to cope with a formidable task. A man's past is like a complicated machine, consisting of millions of parts. It is, for an outsider, impossible to unravel the intricacies of another person's life. How can the investigator know about a smile, a secret yearning, the drop of a voice that forms or breaks human relationships, a fleeting impression that can change the flow of life? It is not only facts that decide, but also relations to others, the minute delineations of likes and dislikes, of dependence and obligation—a huge mosaic of related causes that form a character.

I knew nothing about Gabriel except his case history, half a page of clinical facts. He came from a rich family, had a good education, had never had an accident, and had been healthy until he contracted the brain fever. That was all I knew.

At daybreak Helga had entered his room as she had always done. Gabriel woke up as she stood in front of his bed, clad in a robe, her hair falling loosely over her shoulders. The hair, long and straight, framed her pale anxious face, fraught with determination. She might have stayed up all night thinking over her problems. They only concerned her—her relation to Gabriel, her attitude toward him, her power over him. She thought she had found the answer. For her, it was a desperate decision.

"Gabriel?" she said in a hesitating, soft voice.

Lying prone on his bed, he turned his head and looked at her without recognition. But she was encouraged that he had reacted to her voice.

She opened her robe and let it slide to the floor. She was naked. Keeping her eyes on his, she lifted her arms and pushed back her hair. Her adolescent, high breasts lifted and the skin over her hips tightened, marking the solar plexus with sharp definition. Her skin was very fair, unblemished; her light pubic hair glittered on its plump hillock. She stood motionless, staring into his eyes, trying to detect an answering sign.

Fearing she was going to lose him, she had thrown all her fortune into one desperate gamble. What would be her hold on him should he recover completely? She must have figured that since he had responded to her caresses his memory might also be awakened by them. Giving herself to him would complete her hold on him. They would have something in common, something more than her one-sided love.

Orgasm is a shock to the nervous system; no other of that magnitude and impact exists. She thought she could buy him with her sacrifice.

As she bent over him, her hair covered his face and head, and with a sigh she let out her long-held breath. With her mouth slightly open, she kissed him. Her kiss had a curious flutter and probe, which she might have been taught by a lesbian. Then she leaned her forehead against his.

"You know why I'm here?" she asked in a desperate voice. His eyes were locked with hers; Gabriel did not move. She threw back the covers and unbuttoned his pajamas, fast, with knowing fingers, then slid beside him, leading his hand to her curved back, as she had done many times before. Slowly moving his hand over her ivory-smooth stomach, she guided it with a slight hesitation into the hollow of her groin. She quivered and her teeth chattered. Overcoming a sudden shyness, she touched his breast, moving her hand lower over his concave stomach until she felt his organ. His reaction gave her a sense of power and victory.

But she was not experienced. She might have read many books, *Patterns of Sex Teaching, The Sexlife of the Unmarried Adult, the Ideal Marriage and its Psychology and Technique*. She might have gone through library files, delving in medical books. But she was still unprepared. All she knew was how to obtain her own satisfaction. Wild, rapturous, without a trace of modesty, she kneeled above him trying to make love to him and herself, with a wild brutality and undulating movements, the hot thunder of her voice in his ear, pleading, cajoling. Her excitement reached its climax, and she buried her mouth in his, throbbing in a long ecstasy.

Exhausted, her head rested on his chest, the damp of her body mixing with his. Finally she rolled away from him, defeated in her purpose. With an infantile gesture she touched him again searchingly.

Putting her head in the hollow of his shoulder, she cried, not because of a lost virginity, but because she had not been able to lose it. She had gambled desperately and failed.

Sitting up, she cupped her small breasts, her tears falling on her hands.

Gabriel seemed to be asleep, his face turned sideways so that she could not see his face.

With a tiny moan she got up and sat on the bed beside him, her hands in the hollow of her thighs. Her determination had led to nothing.

The decision to give herself to Gabriel, the fears and qualms, even her prayers, the death march to his bed dressed only in her robe, the preparation of stripping naked, and the anticipation of the next day's repentance—all that agony had been in vain.

She kneeled beside him, stroking his averted face, then got up with a heavy sigh, picking up her robe and slipping into it. She stood for a minute, watching him, listening to his faint breathing, which had the rhythm of sleep. Then she returned to her own room.

Only then it dawned on me that I had made an irreparable mistake. I had not foreseen her cold-blooded determination to give herself to Gabriel, a decision that had been the outcome of unemotional planning. Now, since she had been unsuccessful in a complete union with him, she would not stop at anything from fulfilling her desire. Women have no comprehension for certain conceptions of ethics. I had seen mothers pervert their own children, making them into drug addicts to keep up their domination. In therapy, they only were sorry for themselves, not what they had done to their offspring. In certain aspects they lack a common decency that is inbred in the male. They are propelled by fixed ideas, stamping out ruthlessly any obstacle in their way. They topple kings from their thrones, destroy tightly knit families to reach their goal without any compunction, never being able to grasp the size of their immorality.

Helga had her mind set on Gabriel. Now that she had failed in her attempt of seduction, nothing short of death could deter her from trying to wipe out her defeat.

She had to be shocked out of her love for him, which was conscious love, not instinctive or purely emotional. Conscious love depends on effort and intelligence and has no chemistry as its base. She loved Gabriel unemotionally.

I might have to send Gabriel abroad, putting an ocean between them, to remove her from his life.

I made Gabriel get up very quietly. He dressed, but did not shave, lest the electric razor wake her up. Not taking any of his possessions along, he was ready to leave the house.

The car keys! She had the keys in her room!

Gabriel pushed the door quietly open. Helga was asleep, her unruly hair spread over the pillow, her narrow body pulling in its limbs, the arms across her face, the legs forming a z. Gabriel looked for her handbag, which contained the keys. The alligator bag stood on the dresser. He picked it up and slipped out of the room, turning over its contents on his bed. A wallet, a compact, and lipstick fell out, then a key ring. It was a very orderly bag, not the mess most women carry.

As Gabriel walked out of his room into the garden through the French windows, Jose, carrying a shovel, was just leaving the guesthouse. Startled, he stopped as Gabriel walked past him, then drove the sports car out of the garage, expertly turning into Mulholland Drive.

A moment later Jose knocked at my bedroom door, but I could not open it. If I switched off the transcorders, Gabriel surely would crash into the next car or house wall or topple over the precipice into the valley below.

Here the intricate interplay between myself and Gabriel began. If he was active, I had to lock myself up, shutting out the world. Whenever I returned to my own existence, Gabriel was void of any thinking process.

Jose finally gave up trying to wake me and walked away. I made Gabriel drive up onto a small dirt road. There hidden behind trees, I had to stop the car. Nobody would see him or disturb him, I was sure. He leaned back and closed his eyes to sleep. That was what I wanted him to do. I had to keep him inactive as long as I lived my own life, thought my own thoughts.

Then I went out of my room. Jose and Kaweah were in the kitchen, agitated and perplexed.

"Gabriel left in the little car," Jose related the news, "and Miss Coleman is still asleep. I didn't want to wake her up." He sensed an urgency that concerned me, and his loyalty to me had prompted him to make the right decision.

"Yes, please let her sleep," I said. "Gabriel is okay."

I was not interested in giving him any explanation or appeasing his concern. Both had seen Gabriel walk out of the house and drive rationally like a man in full control of his mental powers. Jose would be a very good witness in case Merriam or O'Brian caught up with me.

Jose and Kaweah did not play any part in my scheme. I wanted them to stick to their duties. People working for me are cogs in the machine, assigned to certain tasks. That's all I permit them to be. I cannot tolerate any trespassing into my own domain.

I went back to the lab, but before I could lock the door, I heard Helga enter the living room. I had to put her in her place. Besides, the pain in my face started to rise, that tic douloureux, which if not checked would drive me out of my mind. I wanted to return to the body that protected me.

Helga looked worn, her skin gray, her hair without luster. Having lost her Shangri-la, she had left the glow of youth behind.

"Gabriel is gone," she said. Again she had come running to me, as if I had the keys to all locked doors.

"I know," I said. "I heard him take out the car. Don't worry."

That was no explanation for her. Her mind was blank, paralyzed with too many unsolved problems.

"Worry?" she repeated. "Why aren't you concerned? What do the transcorders which you inserted do to him?"

"Reactivate his brain," I said vaguely.

"Where did he go?" she asked. Everything had to go her way. She did not know how to accept adversity.

"To his mother. I'm sure of it. There he will be safe. She won't let anybody get close to him—

a hyena defending her young! That's where he should be, don't you think so?"

She must have thought back to the previous night, because she said, "What about me? He can't just disappear from my life. What am I going to do?"

"Go back to Jimmy. I promise Gabriel will knock at your door," I said." I'm sure his memory will return and he will remember you and how close you were to him. There is no need to tell Jimmy or anybody else. Gabriel should be left alone, or he might suffer a relapse."

She looked searchingly at me, but there was an expression in her eyes I did not like. What if she was smarter than I thought and had with a woman's deadly perception guessed my scheme, seeing it clearer than I could conceive it? Females at the age of 12 already know more about sensuality in their little finger than men learn at any age. What if she was playing a game of chess in which she knew beforehand every one of my moves, while I, foolishly convinced of my smartness, had become her patsy? What she wanted was Gabriel's body. She was not interested in his mental capacities. She was ruthless in her desire for him. What made me believe that her inside matched her outside, that of a pristine blonde flaunting her purity like a flag?

The fog in my mind suddenly parted and I saw my own situation in this journey for Gabriel's body. I had ceased being a pure scientist. I too had acted with desires and selfishness. I thought I knew what I was doing, but had not the foresight to judge properly my own actions.

"I won't go back to Jimmy." She had made the decision I wanted her to make.

"What are you going to do?" I asked.

"Go to Gabriel. He needs me, Dr. Cory."

I liked that idea. As long as she was with Gabriel I could control her.

Chapter Seventeen

I locked myself in my lab to return to Gabriel. He was still in the car on a side road off Mulholland Drive.

How far would thought transmission carry? Would it become fainter, finally slipping out of reach like the beams of a radio station? Or was it like light waves in space, the distance unlimited?

I had taken a grave chance with Gabriel's life. Only seconds of interruption and, like a man falling asleep at the wheel, Gabriel would crash. My next test would be to let him drive on and to call him back as soon as the signals diminished.

I suddenly became unsure of my experiment. Was I on the right track or running into a dead end, as I had so many times during my work?

Suddenly I doubted myself. Belief in ourselves, like any belief, needs acclaim. And I still was working alone. Again my thoughts involuntarily went back to Malcolm. He judged clearly when I became unsure. But when he groped for new approaches to our problems, he accused himself of being stupid. But stupidity is not always a lack of intelligence. It is often a fear to walk unchartered roads.

I suddenly had lost the path that only dimly had been outlined by my research. Here was I, Patrick Cory, transmitting myself into another body at will. I might, one day, be unable to leave that body, incapable of removing the connections, as when the coyote was run over by the automobile.

Every time I submitted myself to that experiment, my life was at stake.

But I had reached the point of no return. I could only go forward. Like a cat whose pleasure center is artificially stimulated comes back for more of the electric shocks, though its brain is slowly burning out, I could not stop picking up the transcorders to become Gabriel.

A few seconds later I watched through his eyes.

A policeman stood at the sports car, a lost expression on his officious face. He was a rookie, guided still by the police manual, not trusting his own judgment. His companion was talking to headquarters on the prowl car's radio. They must have spotted the parked car, investigated, and found a dazed man with whom they could not communicate.

The young cop waved a flashlight close to Gabriel's eyes. If the pupils remained dilated, he had found an addict. They did contract. No heroin!

Gabriel suddenly came to life. His dead eyes became animated and, sitting up, he started to talk.

"Sorry," he said, "I must have fallen asleep, officer. I felt tired and stopped for a moment."

The fluency of his speech, the sudden change from an obvious coma to completely rational behavior startled the policeman.

"You were not asleep. You were unconscious," the officer said. "I shook you, but you just looked at me dazed. What did you take that knocked you out?"

"Take? Nothing," Gabriel said. "I'm hard to wake." He grinned amicably at the policeman. "Say, it isn't against the law to sleep off the road in a parked car, or is it?"

The second policeman joined his younger colleague. He was older and knew how to project his authority. "Your license," he said.

Gabriel went through the motions of looking through his pockets. He had no identification. I had forgotten.

"I must've forgotten my wallet. Sorry. I had a late night. She wouldn't let me go home," he said with a slight innuendo to include the two men in his supposed adventure.

There is rarely a moment of ease between a citizen and the police. Americans don't like uniforms. Even generals look funny to them if no bullets fly around them. Germans adore uniforms. For them a man with epaulets is a superior human being. Even their postmen gird themselves with sabers and go to parades. In England, where the police are not armed, they are on equal standing with the citizens. But the American police with their billy clubs and ready six-shooters are hopelessly entangled in wrong relations with the citizenry. They are trained to be exceedingly polite, and that politeness carries a superiority that the citizen resents.

"Your name and address, please?" the older officer said, producing a pad and pencil.

"Gabriel Deeping, twelve-twenty Bel Air Lane," Gabriel said. I knew that address.

Since the affluent lived in Bel Air the policeman became even more conciliatory. "Is this your car?" the older one asked.

The law is a spider's web, enmeshing its prey. The automobile was registered in a fictitious name. My address was on the registration. The shell of my anonymity had been cracked. Suspecting a criminal action behind any unusual fact, the law machine would move. Was there a law against registering an automobile in the name of a nonexistent person? I didn't know.

The patrolman pulled out the registration, which had been fastened to the sun visor. "Twenty-two thousand Sumac Drive," he read and made a note of it. "Gabriel Hyde. Same first name as yours?" His pencil continued scraping.

"That's what it says," Gabriel acknowledged.

The policeman looked at well-groomed Gabriel. His clothes were expensive, but he had not shaved. Blue-black fuzz covered his cheeks and chin.

"You must have some identification on you," he said. "A credit card, anything."

Gabriel had none. "I told you I left my wallet behind," he said, but that did not satisfy the cop.

The policemen exchanged glances. Here was a suspect. He had no papers. Man is only an appendix of official paperwork.

"We better run him in," the older cop decided. Taking Gabriel to the station would relieve him of any responsibility.

"What's the charge?" Gabriel asked indignantly. "Has sleeping become an offense?"

"Don't be a wise guy," the policeman said. "We found you doped in a car that doesn't belong to you. It might be stolen. You have no papers, no license, nothing; that's quite a package, Bud!"

"I wasn't doped and I'm not now," Gabriel said.

"You can argue that at the station." The older one carried on the conversation. The younger one listened to learn. "And don't worry about that car. We will have it towed away. It will cost the owner a few bucks to get it back." He opened the car door and waved Gabriel out.

He walked with his dancer's grace, and the smile on his handsome face deepened, as if he enjoyed the situation. His compliance and the mystery of his smile made them even more wary, as if he had a weapon the police did not know about. They shook him down, then covered him, one at his side, one walking behind him, ready for any emergency. They led him to the prowl car. Half-a-dozen automobiles had stopped to watch the free spectacle.

I removed the transcorders from my temples as soon as Gabriel had settled in the car, letting him slide back into idiocy. Suddenly having an incommunicative imbecile in their car would certainly confuse the law officers.

I was confronted with almost unsurmountable difficulties. I would never be able to merge myself completely with Gabriel. Whenever I had to think or act in my behalf, I was always forced to return to myself. What was Gabriel going to do during that time? If he lived in his mother's house and fell back into his state of idiocy, she would surely call the doctors. She would get in touch with O'Brian. To live through Gabriel I had to take him to another city, another country perhaps, build a new life around him and me.

When I connected myself with Gabriel again, he was sitting motionlessly in a small, bare room at the police station. They had stripped him to the waist. A police doctor was with him, an old man, very matter-of-fact, who had seen every human frailty and sicknesses, had stared into every abyss of human existence. Nothing could ever surprise him. But he had never encountered a case like Gabriel's.

"This man is an idiot," he said to the police lieutenant, a heavyset man who looked like a wrestler. "There is no doubt about that. He has an IQ of five, if that. How could they arrest him?"

The lieutenant turned on the two policemen who stood behind him, dumbfounded by the doctor's diagnosis.

"But he talked to us," the older policeman said, "and quite rationally. He drove that car too. He told me so himself. He also gave me his address and mentioned a girl he had been with the night before. You must be mistaken, Doc!"

"That man couldn't drive a car to save his life. He wouldn't know what to do with a girl if he lived with her on an island for ten years. I can't make it out. It just doesn't make sense," the doctor said to the lieutenant, who did know whom to believe.

"He's faking, that guy," the older cop said and stepped up to Gabriel. He jerked him to his feet. "Now come clean, Bud. It's no use horsing around with us. We got your fingerprints. There's a computer downtown that's going to tell us your life story, if you don't."

Gabriel did not react and the cop turned helplessly to the physician. "But he did talk. Isn't there a case, Doc, where an idiot could suddenly talk? I've heard about that, haven't you?"

The doctor shrugged. "There is," he said. "There's the idiot savant, the idiot who can perform mental feats which you and I wouldn't be able to do. I know of one with an IQ of thirty who couldn't remember his name, but when you let him look at a freight train shooting by, he could remember all the numbers of the carriages and repeat them for twenty-four hours. Fifty numbers or more, all in the right order. Then he lost them again. And there was that whiz in Elizabethan history who could read fluently and remember all the dates and even memorized letters she had written. But he couldn't be toilet trained. But that doesn't fit this man here."

The lieutenant studied Gabriel with the suspicion that was part of his job. "I called that address he gave," the lieutenant said. "It's true, a family called Deeping lives there. A man answered. He said it's impossible that his son is in town. He couldn't drive a car. Gabriel Deeping is an inmate at the Brentwood House for the mentally retarded. He suffered an illness which left him with no IQ. It can't be the same man."

"Of course he isn't! This guy here knows Gabriel Deeping. Maybe he works at the hospital. Now he's playing the idiot." The older policeman had a sound of triumph in his voice, having solved the problem his way. "Come on, Bud, come clean!"

He stabbed Gabriel just under the floating rib with three fingers, cruel, sharp.

Suddenly something happened for which I was not prepared. It was not my doing. Gabriel's hand shot out with lightning speed, the edge of the palm hit the policeman's throat. The man collapsed. The lieutenant lifted his arms as Gabriel turned fast as a ferret, smashing his knee into the man's groin. The heavyset man sagged against the wall, his head hitting the back of a chair.

The third policeman was still trying to get his gun clear of the holster when Gabriel grabbed his wrist, twisted it, and threw him over his shoulder.

Shaken and terrified, I quickly took off the transducer. Without thought transfer Gabriel might stop. I sat dumb for a few moments, trying to organize my thoughts. But I could not desert my alternate body.

At once a pain unknown to me shot through my system, my solar plexus cramped up as if it had received a hard blow, and my shoulders and forehead burned. The room was filled with police, two were holding Gabriel's limp body, another hit him with a rubber hose. They all shouted at the same time, trying to get in a kick. Gabriel was mercilessly beaten and I was powerless to help him.

The picture blurred. He must have lost consciousness. I was unable to get through to him.

I took off the transducers. My hands trembled, and the instruments slipped from my grip.

Gabriel had acted on his own! He had reacted to an exterior stimulus, the stabbing of his abdomen. Pain had awakened a response in him, the echo of his body in danger. It might have been that a sudden outpour of adrenaline had triggered this violent reaction. But his defense had been coordinated, vicious, and expert. He had used karate. I once had been proficient in that kind of defense. So had he. It might be that his dancer's balance came from extensive training in self-defense. It might have started as a hobby.

Karate is a fashion among young people who can afford the training.

Were there still human emotions in him, buried in his stunned nervous system? Was it possible that the transcorders and electrodes embedded in his skull had affected his atrophied brain?

Every experiment into the unknown opens up new avenues of metempirics. I had believed that my thought transfer process was a mechanical device that did not affect the brain itself. Could it reactivate deadened tissues as I had frivolously proclaimed to Helga and O'Brian? Restore damaged thought processes? Or change imbeciles into raving monsters? If that was the case I could never be sure of Gabriel's reactions.

But whatever the answer, I, Patrick Cory, was responsible for Gabriel's torture. I had disassociated myself from him. I should have at least siphoned off the pains he was suffering from the cruel beating. Used to pain as a constant companion, I should have suffered for him. Since he had fainted under the blows, he must have reacted, though his dull brain was not able to realize what was going on around him. Behind the frosted glass of his consciousness there was no comprehension.

Pain—my own—tightened my features, driving through the fiber of my spine like a thick awl. For the first time in years I took a heavy dose of codeine to deaden the revolt of my nerves, to protect myself from suffering.

The police had thrown Gabriel into solitary confinement. In the dark he sat on a bench, his face bloody, his eyes vacant. That sloth smile that meant nothing was on his lips. Light from outside fell through clerestories into the cell. His elegant jump suit was ripped, his legs caked with blood. Pain still pulsed behind a sheath of dulled sensitivity. Maybe deadened by the codeine I had swallowed.

The door opened and bright lights were turned on. Phyllis Deeping stood in the doorway, a man at her side. With them were the lieutenant, his face pasty, and the doctor. Behind them were two officers with nightsticks.

"Do you know this man?" the lieutenant asked.

Phyllis stared at Gabriel in horror and disbelief. "Gabriel," she whispered, "what did they do to you?"

The lieutenant hid his disappointment. He would have liked to hear that Gabriel was an impostor. Further troubles would have been avoided and the case would have disappeared in the files.

"It's our son," the man at Phyllis's side said. "What in heaven has happened to him?"

Phyllis kneeled on the gray concrete floor and took Gabriel's head into her hands. She whispered to him as she might have when he was a child waking from a dream.

"He got into a fight," the policeman said, skirting the issue. His fat cheeks trembled as if words had reached his lips, colliding with his teeth to disappear again in his throat.

"Impossible!" Mr. Deeping exclaimed.

"He became violent, hitting me and a couple of officers. It took six men to subdue him," the lieutenant said sternly, as if reprimanding Deeping.

The police doctor still stared disbelievingly at Gabriel.

"You hit him!" The deep fury in Phyllis's voice had the tinge of hysteria. "You! You hit Gabriel!"

"We had no choice, Mrs. Deeping," the lieutenant said in a voice trained not to show anger. "He'd have smashed up the whole station. He wrecked the room he was in."

"Liar!" Phyllis said in a dead voice that carried more threat than if she had screamed. "You hit my child! He didn't attack anyone. He couldn't, ever!" But suddenly it dawned on her that should the police officer have told the truth, something miraculous had happened: Gabriel had come to life! She wanted to have the miracle confirmed.

"Who saw you being hit by Gabriel? Who?" she said, and her immovable face paled, revealing the fine scars that the knife of the plastic surgeon had left behind.

"I was there, ma'am," the doctor said. "But having watched your son I'm not sure if he isn't faking."

It was I who was playing the idiot. I could not fool an expert for long. Gabriel's pupils might have reacted; a flicker of comprehension might have changed his features. I don't know what

241

made the doctor suspicious. I should have withdrawn at once, but I stayed on to see the drama unfold.

The lieutenant reacted as expected. If he had arrested a helpless man, he would be involved in a scandal. Now since the doctor's suspicion confirmed his report, he had found an ally.

"I'm going to file a complaint for assault and battery against this man," he announced, dramatically raising a finger.

"He is going home with me!" Phyllis took Gabriel's hand. Her palms were thin and dry, her fingers extraordinarily long and surprisingly strong.

"You won't," the lieutenant raised his voice. "This man has committed a felony."

"There is such a thing as a bond," Mr. Deeping said. "As it happens, I'm a lawyer. And this case won't do you any good, Lieutenant. Gabriel is an inmate of the Brentwood House for the retarded. His brain has been affected by sleeping sickness. He is not able to talk, nor does he understand what's going on around him. How could he ever have hit you?"

"You tell that to the judge," the lieutenant sneered. "Your son talked sensibly, not only to one but to two of my officers."

"Did you hear him talk?" Deeping started his cross-examination. "Did you, Lieutenant."

"No, but my men did. It's in the report," the officer said. "My men are witnesses. They wrote down what he said."

"Did you hear that, Vernon?" Phyllis exclaimed. "He did talk!" Her shock was a disguise for her hope. "He talked rationally!"

"Don't let these people raise false hopes in you, Phyllis. A medical examination will tell, not their report."

"This guy is a faker. He drove a car. How could he drive a car if he is not supposed to know what's going on?" the lieutenant said.

"An automobile!" Phyllis clasped her hands. "Gabriel drove a car! Gabriel—tell me—did you drive a car, did you?"

Her voice broke as she moved her face close to his; her large violet eyes flickered, unable to focus. The scent of her perfume was overpowering.

"Please," Deeping said, "please, Phyllis! Don't get so upset. There can't be any truth in that police report."

"He talked—he drove a car," she repeated, not listening to her husband. She might not even have heard her own voice. "Talk to me, Gabriel. Talk, my Gabriel!"

"I don't know how he could have left Brentwood House, if he is an idiot. Somebody must have taken him! Or he got electric-compulsive therapy, which woke him up for a time. It's possible!" the doctor said. "No, it can't be. This man here is a faker, I saw it in his eyes. But an hour ago he wasn't. Astonishing!"

"I'll get in touch with O'Brian." Deeping laid the case out like a defense lawyer.

Everybody talked without communicating with anyone else in the room. It was like the Tower of Babel, where everyone spoke the language only he himself understood.

"If that is the case then Mrs. Deeping should take her son home." The lieutenant referred to something somebody must have said sometime before. He wanted to get out of that confusion.

"Let me take him to the infirmary," the older policeman voiced a positive idea. "We will clean him up and you can have another close look at him."

"I'm sure he's faking," the doctor said. "I bet my bottom dollar. Nobody can fake imbecility for any length of time."

"I heard him talk," the policeman said and took Gabriel's arm. Gabriel got up docilely.

"Tonight, my Gabriel, you'll be home," Phyllis said. "Whatever they say, you'll be home, home, your home!"

She followed the policemen, but the lieutenant held her back.

At once I disconnected myself from Gabriel. Again he became Gabriel the idiot. The doctor would make a report about him. Gabriel Deeping had acted rationally only to be submerged again in the quicksand of imbecility—a case that would sound unbelievable to any psychiatrist. There wasn't such a thing in medicine as a sudden flash of intelligence followed by the darkness of a burned-out mind.

Chapter Eighteen

Jose entered the living room, his bony face taut with anxiety. He told me he was leaving with Kaweah. That of course, I had anticipated. Too many incidents had disturbed his tranquility. Helga had left without telling Kaweah where she could be reached. Gabriel, unexplained, had taken out the sports car and disappeared. Then there had been that incident with the police.

In the morning a prowl car had driven up to the house; one of the patrolmen had questioned Jose. The officer wanted to see Jose's driver's license. But they did not asked to see me.

The reason for their curiosity was easy to deduce: Helga's sports car had carried my address. The license was registered in the name of Gabriel Hyde. Helga's silly joke had backfired.

Jose said he did not know a Mr. Hyde, nor did he know about a sports car.

The best defense is knowing nothing. I once had been to the reservation to see Kaweah. That was a long time before the accident. The owner of the general store in Desert Rock had recommended her as being quiet and dependable. Driving to the reservation to talk to her, I met a woman in an old car and asked for the direction to Kaweah's house. The woman driver did not know her. It had been Kaweah herself who had denied knowing anything about Kaweah the Indian woman. The stranger is the enemy. A couple of days later she showed up and took the job. We never mentioned that we had met before.

Now they wanted to return to the reservation. It was no use holding them. Jose politely might agree to stay since it is impolite to give a direct "no". But I was sure that he and his wife would pack up and leave secretly.

"Sorry to see you leave," I said to Jose. "I hope I can manage without you, though it won't be convenient."

It was no use to appeal to their sympathy. They lived in a world different from mine and the word "sympathy" had another connotation. Jose did not want to get further involved with the police. He also had lied for me and that he did not savor.

I paid him and without delay he and Kaweah left in the truck. I wondered what I was going to do. But Jose had already thought of that. A market in Thousand Oaks called asking for my orders. They would send up anything I needed. The man on the phone expressed his regrets that "Dr. Cory was ill." He would leave the merchandise in the garage or the kitchen refrigerator if I left the door open. Nobody would disturb me; they would send the bill by mail. Jose and Kaweah had arranged that I could shift without them.

I could. I preferred to be by myself. For years I had lived at Desert Rock alone. Now the time again had come to detach myself completely from the world.

But I was not alone if I so chose. I could always switch over to Gabriel's life. If it was my wish, I could make him talk, let him live an active life with all the diversions and pleasures of a rich young man. Nobody would suspect that I, Patrick Cory, talked through his mouth and lived through his body. But so far I decided to keep him silent and not to show any activity that would complicate our lives—mine, his, and the people around us. I had to wait a few months, let him recover gradually until the shock of his coming to life had worn off.

Gabriel was lying in bed in a well-furnished room. I made him get up. It was early in the morning, Gabriel looked into the garden, which was covered with flowerbeds deliberately left wild among old trees. It was quiet except for the rumbling of a garbage truck in the distance and the first cries of wakening birds.

It was an old house, as California houses

go, sprawling, well cared for, furnished with antiques that had been handed down for generations. Gabriel stopped to look at himself in the man-high mirror of an Early American armoire. A grandfather clock chimed five times and the weight came to a growling halt.

Gabriel showed no signs of the beating he had received from the police. He breathed deeply, flexing his muscles. The top of his pajamas was open and exposed the hard cords of his abdomen. His hand moved over the hairs of his chest, followed the tapered line that led to the waist's indentation. He pushed back his mane of thick black hair and examined his strong teeth. He then went through the karate exercises that were familiar to me, but that I had never been able to perform as expertly as Gabriel: the quick thrust of the leg, the lunge of the suddenly outstretched arms, the shadow dancing as if he were surrounded by aggressors. Next he stood on his head in a yoga position, bending his flexible spine like a contortionist. He was in absolute control of every muscle in his body. And with that agility came the elation of radiant health.

He tiptoed into the corridor and peered down into the foyer. A staircase swung up to the floor where he stood. Pictures of the eighteenth and nineteenth century hung on the high walls. There was a Juan Gris clown, the original of prints I had seen in art magazines, and some dark Ruisdael paintings. On the stairs hung a huge abstract in vivid colors, looking like a cliff above an ocean or like a painting by one mentally disturbed.

Gabriel's Body

Soundlessly, Gabriel walked down the corridor. The door next to his room was ajar, and he pushed it open.

It was another bedroom. In a huge four-poster bed sat Helga, wide awake, staring at him. Her hair fell over her shoulders, and her thin nightgown—the same she had worn before—outlined her slim contours. She must have been waiting for this moment. She had lived through experiences like this: when he had talked to her at breakfast, when his body had moved under her hands. She also knew the police report about his arrest. He had left with her car. He also carried those transcorders in his neck—a secret she had not given away. She had been sleeping so lightly the touch of a feather would have wakened her.

Gabriel walked to her and smiled. As he stopped at her bed, her mouth trembled but she did not speak.

I was sure she had shown up at Phyllis's house the day after Gabriel disappeared and had asked for the job as his nurse. She had been accepted. Anything connected with Gabriel's past, anything that would keep him at ease, was welcome to Phyllis. Anything concerning his future she was going to decide. Having Helga around, a nurse who knew how to take care of Gabriel, pleased Phyllis. She believed that Helga would help her son. The Germans have a saying: *'den Bock zum Gaertner machen'*—to give the billy goat the job to guard the garden.

He sat on her bed and took her hand, which

249

trembled in his, but did not close. As she moved, he made an almost imperceptible gesture that he did not want to be touched and she at once stopped. The understanding between them needed no words, a union of thoughts as though they formed an esoteric society against the tribulations around them. Their unity was deeper than any single emotion could ever produce. It was a moral relationship. Whatever involves mental, emotional, or physical waste is called immoral. But that moment when he sat wishless beside her, still refusing to touch her, was the answer to all her desires. Their relation again had become chaste. Forgotten and forgiven were her wild, selfish desires, the secret mornings that had led nowhere except to remorse and desperation. There is no fall where there is no temptation.

He got up to return to his room, leaving that secret with her, that mute, complete understanding. She would not impart it to anyone. By giving away that secret she would bring down on herself an hysterical mother and a possessive fiancee who waited to get hold of Gabriel. The secret of his silent appearance was a weapon Helga alone possessed.

I had an ally who would not desert me even in death!

I knew how she explained Gabriel's activities to herself. She assumed that my method of thought transfer had stimulated his brain. She was not aware that Gabriel Deeping was I, Patrick Cory. What would she have done if she had known?

Making love to someone who had Gabriel's body? She was after his body not his mind, though, of course, who believed in that heavenly union that dispenses with carnal pleasures? But would she have resisted if he had put his arms around her? Wouldn't she have complied, cooperated, let him lose himself in her? Fear had made her complex. I could not be bothered to figure out her real desires. Once having believed that heaven and hell existed, she would never be able to divorce herself from that crushing despair of guilt—pleasures only permitted in the hereafter.

Gabriel went to his room and sat in a chair, looking out into the garden, enjoying being alive. He was relaxed. If happiness exists, it is in that stillness of a new day.

I took off the transcorders and went to sleep for the first time without pain. Gabriel's quiet nerves had finally penetrated mine, eradicating my torture.

But I didn't have a long respite. O'Brian arrived at my house early in the morning.

Chapter Nineteen

Without bothering to greet me O'Brian walked into the house. He was wearing a dark suit and a new strawhat, which made him look less bucolic than his old driver's cap. That jauntiness he usually affected was gone. He must have been baffled by the contradictory reports about Gabriel and did not know how to approach that partly realistic, partly mystical problem that confronted him. O'Brian, lacking immagination, did not know how to deal with mysticism. He also was smarting under Helga's betrayal and, I'm certain, blamed me for it.

"Come in," I said after he was already inside. Like a cat that has been taken to a new house, he peered into the kitchen, and even for a moment in my untidy bedroom, the door of which was wide open.

"I was expecting you," I said to make things even more mysterious for him, proving that I could outthink him. "See—there's the coffee waiting for you. You never drink in the morning as I remember. Isn't it strange that in our Puritan society the word drink applies only to hard liquor. If you want water you have to ask for it. But when you say, 'I want a drink,' you mean hard liquor. To mention that word is taboo. The word drinking has the connotation of excess and sin. Or one has to call it social drinking, which is limited in its number of cc. More is a weapon of the devil to corrupt mankind."

He did not react to my civil observation. He might not have listened.

"How did you find me?" I asked, and he turned his washed-out pale eyes on me. They were lined from lack of sleep.

"It's hard to hide for any length of time, Patrick," he sparred, not yet wanting to come to the point.

"I didn't hide," I said.

He poured himself some coffee. Obviously he was trying to avoid any increased tension between us. "You ran away, didn't you?" he said reproachfully.

"Do I have to tell anybody where I want to go?" I asked. "You, the police, the CIA, the FBI, or anyone?"

He sipped his coffee, looking around the room for clues to the secrets that confused him. "You had Gabriel kidnapped," he said. "You know what that means to me, having one of my patients disappear from Brentwood House? It's a federal offense crossing state lines with a kidnapped person."

"I know the Lindbergh law. They send you to the electric chair," I said.

"Helga took him," he continued. "But I'm holding you responsible. You put that idea into her head. She would never have done it without you."

He put his angelic conception of the girl back into its jeweler's box. In his mind she could never do wrong on her own. The guy with the horns and the tail always seduces the innocents, leading them from the straight though very narrow path of honesty. He obviously did not believe in free will. I wished he had seen that girl in bed with that idiot, trying to seduce him. To sexually abuse the feeble-minded is a criminal offense also.

"Of course she wouldn't have done it without my asking her. She stayed here in my house with him. That should be enough proof," I said to purge her.

I had been Gabriel when O'Brian arrived at Mrs. Deeping's house. The police, having called the computer in Sacramento, had received the answer: Gabriel Deeping, encephalitic, missing from Brentwood House. Contact James O'Brian.

Knowing where to find Gabriel he had mounted his steed and ridden straight to Bel Air to confront the dragon that guarded the treasure.

He knew, of course, he would never be able to pry Gabriel loose from his mother now that she had him securely at home. That was precisely what I wanted to happen. Gabriel could not have been safer behind bars.

O'Brian had his showdown with Phyllis. Her voice had reverberated through the large house.

"Phyllis, please, no use shouting," Mr. Deeping had said. O'Brian had insisted on seeing Gabriel without Phyllis, and she had finally consented after she had been assured that her son would not have to go back to Brentwood House.

In Gabriel's room O'Brian confronted Helga. I marveled at her calm, which betrayed her lack of ethics. She might not have been aware how deeply she had hurt the man who loved her. Her life revolved around Gabriel; all other things were appendixes, trimmings, to be cut off and discarded as the situation demanded. O'Brian too was startled by her obvious lack of remorse.

"You ran away with him, Helga," he said, not daring to mention the word kidnap as he would callously use with me. She did not respond to the hurt tone of his voice.

"He's much improved, Jimmy," she said, giving the nurse's report. "He'd never have gotten better in Brentwood House."

It is remarkable how our personal behavior adjusts itself to the character of other people. To some we appear as towering giants; to others we portray deep-set inferiority. To others we feel that we are ugly or handsome, smart, dumb, old, or young. As chameleons blend with their surroundings, our unconscious attitudes alter with every person we know. Helga behaved toward me like an intelligent nurse, though biased in her personal beliefs. With me she lacked the childlike coquettishness and soft dependence that she emanated like ectoplasm in O'Brian's presence. Alone with Gabriel she became the moonstruck little girl, dream walking, ready for any sacrifice, losing her sense of ethics or even shame. Toward O'Brian she was the helpless kitten, carefully keeping in her claws. He might not even know that she had claws. The half tones of her voice and movements were that of budding sex asking to be released, well aware that O'Brian could not know how to wake it. Nor would she have responded except perhaps via the legal way of marriage. But still, an affinity between them made them understand each other. Even by having betrayed his trust she knew that relation had not changed.

"The police told me that he could talk," O'Brian said in the low voice he used when speaking to her—a spy who had come back from a mission. "Did you hear him speak?"

She nodded.

"Here, at this house?" O'Brian asked, startled.

"In Cory's," she said.

I had been very cautious not to let Gabriel speak after the incident at the breakfast table, except, of course, by necessity when the police apprehended him. Helga could not tell O'Brian that Gabriel had acted on his own initiative, that he had been to her room. Nor could she talk about her visits at daybreak.

"What did he say to you?"

"Not to me—it was thought transfer," Helga said. "It was not he himself. It was Cory."

O'Brian sighed with relief. One of the mysteries had been cleared up. He walked over to Gabriel, who did not look changed to him. There was that same docile deadness about him, that mindless expression.

"What did Cory do to him?" he asked.

She shook her head. If she had told O'Brian about the transcorders in Gabriel's neck, the walls of my fortress would have crumbled.

O'Brian produced a small case with the stethoscope and the inevitable sphygmomanometer. "Please remove the top of his pajamas."

I had to leave Gabriel; then O'Brian would examine an idiot, a task for which he was eminently well suited.

"What did you find out about him?" I asked O'Brian.

He looked curiously at me. Sometimes he startled me with his looks, having thoughts that I could not easily interpret. There was no continuity in my question.

"Find out what?" he asked.

"You must've examined Gabriel. The first thing you doctors do is to listen to the heartbeat and take the blood pressure."

He closed his eyes a little and poured himself another cup of coffee. His calm was remarkable.

To me, accustomed to his juxtapositional reactions, it proved that he was excited.

"I'll have to take a few encephalograms. You, of course, worked on him," he said matter-of-factly. I knew he had come all the way from Arizona to hear my answer.

"I made him talk like I did Kaweah. He spoke to Helga."

"That was all?" he said, not believing me.

"Ask her, she was around all the time."

"The police found him asleep in a car. According to their report he talked rationally. He also drove—by tape?"

I laughed. "We went through all that before, Dr. O'Brian, didn't we? I told you once, and what happened? You brought the government down on my neck. Now you ask me again. Whatever I say wouldn't be good enough for you."

"What did you do to him?" His voice was flat and impersonal

"I'm taking the Fifth Amendment," I said. "I don't want to incriminate myself."

"You know what you're forcing me to do."

There was genuine unhappiness in his voice. It was like dreaming the same dream all over. We had been through the same scene once before. Sometimes we can't distinguish between present and past. The deja vu . . . but this time I remembered.

"I haven't broken any law."

"You know if the government wants to get somebody they work out a case and always win. Always. They will force you to answer questions or sentence you for contempt of the committee. Committees they have, and if they don't, they create one specially for you, Patrick. What is it that you want?"

He had lost the varnish that had protected his emotions. Having seen so much emotion in his profession—people bringing their relatives, their mongoloid children, their hydrocephalics, epileptics, encephalitic cases—he had become the immovable object. Should he too sway, the unhappy world around him would collapse. For the first time since I had known him he had lost that carefully guarded stability.

"Whatever it is," he continued, "I'm going to figure it out. If there is a reawakening of Gabriel's brain, it is criminal that you don't share that knowledge with me. You can't use it yourself."

As if the darkness in which he was groping suddenly had been illuminated by a shaft of light, he stared at me, startled. "Or could you?" he asked.

"You want me to sell out. You're not helping me, though I asked you to. You never stick your neck out for anything."

He listened gravely. "You lied to those two government men," he said. "You told them you had sent the isotopes back to Oakridge, which isn't true. That's all they need to put the hooks into you. Then you drugged Hausdorffer; he slept for ten hours. That's number two. You ran away though they asked you to stay. That's three. You obviously have an invention or discovery which is a menace to public safety. Number four. Now, you could get out of that mess by making a few concessions, which are not real concessions, but common sense."

"Let them put me behind bars," I said.

"They will." He got up, slowly, hunched. "And don't believe that your condition will stop them. Now won't you tell me what you did to Gabriel to make him talk rationally and to drive a car?"

"No. That's final, Dr. O'Brian," I said. I knew I had to leave town with Gabriel as quickly as possible. But how difficult it was to hide even in a country the size of a continent.

"What made him so violent, Patrick?" O'Brian continued probing. "You know that violence is a spontaneous outburst. If you were able to control him, why did he become violent, and of all things with the police?"

"I haven't heard about that," I said and got up.

"You've lit a fuse. The bomb will blow up in your face."

"One did before," I said. "I took it the first time; I can take it the second."

He looked at me with a pitiful expression, a wish to help, to protect me from mortal folly. But I knew, though he seemed to be honest at that moment, that his bureaucratic mind would again betray me when it had simmered down to the daily chores.

"You don't need to walk me to my car," he said.

Gabriel's Body

A minute later he drove away.

The pains in my face penetrated my consciousness. I longed to delve deeply into Gabriel's body. A body at peace.

Chapter Twenty

I knew why I rested so well: I was enjoying
Gabriel's sleep. When I woke up, I heard the
hushed voices of two women locked in battle.
Mercedes, Gabriel's fiancee, stared snakelike at
Helga; even her voice had a hissing sound.

"You wormed your way in here," she said, "and,
of course, Phyllis fell for your line. She doesn't
know what you're up to, but I do. I watched you
at the hospital. You certainly didn't behave like
a nurse!"

Helga's blonde hair was unruffled, her features calm. She controlled her voice, injecting
that soothing lilt nurses have when they talk to
someone very ill.

"Mrs. Deeping engaged me," she said. "I'm
sure, Miss Cordoba, that there isn't any point
to our discussion."

"This has nothing to do with Phyllis," the lady snake answered. "This is between us."

"And I have nothing to do with you." Helga's claws showed. "Do you mind if I go on with my job?"

At once Mercedes sat on Gabriel's bed, blocking Helga's way. She was a statuesque girl with a sports-trained body. Her expensive, though very simple, black dress was low cut, displaying a shimmering area of white skin in sharp contrast to her shiny black hair and large dark eyes. She was alluring, sensual, at the peak of her beauty—a cymbidium that unfolds stunningly for a short time.

Suddenly Mercedes stated in a matter-of-fact voice, which carried a greater impact than if she had screamed, "You're making love to Gabriel."

"Ridiculous!" Helga laughed without mirth. She did not show surprise at Mercedes's shocking accusation. The two girls were almost of the same age, Mercedes perhaps a year or two older, and their minds worked in similar progressions. Their empathy was mutual; Mercedes understood Helga's reaction to be a confirmation.

"I've watched you. The way you took possession of him wasn't like a nurse. It's like a girl having an affair. You can't fool me, my dear. Your relation to him is anything but professional."

Where the love for a man is concerned, women can spot rivals behind closed doors.

"You're upset, or you wouldn't insinuate such a breach of ethics, Miss Cordoba," Helga said. Not a flicker in her voice betrayed emotion.

When women were tortured in the Middle Ages, they rarely confessed. They lied until they died. Men haven't got that ruthless stamina. Woman's determination leaves no loopholes for guilt to weaken her.

"I don't want you to sleep next door to him," Mercedes said harshly. "You are going to resign this job—if it is a job and not a honeymoon."

"I'm sorry. I won't listen to you, Miss Cordoba. Besides it isn't up to you to dismiss me," Helga said. Her calm expressed superiority—a nurse forced to argue with an unbalanced patient.

"Phyllis will when I tell her," Mercedes said.

"I have Mrs. Deeping's full confidence, and your improper insinuations might do you a great deal of harm."

"Really?" Mercedes scoffed, putting her cool hand on Gabriel's forehead. "Let me go into detail. You are in love with him. I don't blame you. Everybody is. But I'm his fiancee. I won't give him up ever! So he is ill! But what he has been to me cannot be replaced by any other man. I'd have married him—or stayed unmarried. It isn't necessary today to buy a license for love. I live my life as I want. Gabriel is part of it."

"Nobody wants you to give him up, Miss Cordoba," Helga said patiently. "Now since he is waking up would you mind leaving? I'll have to get him dressed."

Mercedes moved closer to Gabriel. "How did he leave Brentwood House? How did he get into the car where the police found him? Since you were paid to look after him where were you?

Did you drive him to Los Angeles and why? Did you hide him during the week he was missing? You showed up promptly after Phyllis took him home. How did you know he was here? Just answer these questions."

"I again must ask you to leave," Helga said, "or I shall call Mrs. Deeping."

"I'll give you a chance," Mercedes said. "You can get out of this mess. Just quit!"

Helga sat down, biting her lip, her eyes half closed. She was forced to make a pact with her enemy in order to get rid of her and to escape accusations that she could not answer. Her voice dropped conspiratorily.

"I'm telling you something I shouldn't," she said, "but Gabriel has a chance to recover. He is receiving therapy which he could not get at Brentwood House."

"He's getting it here, from you?" Mercedes scoffed. But Helga's revelation had made her unsure.

"Dr. O'Brian is testing a new approach. I know almost nothing about it. But he could tell you."

She used O'Brian as a shield. She could not mention my name, not because she was loyal, but because she was selfish. Mentioning O'Brian was a delay. If she told Mercedes about me, she would lose Gabriel. Should Gabriel recover, then the real fight for him would start. I didn't know what made her so sure she would win. Mercedes certainly was better looking, had known Gabriel before he became ill, and must have shared intimacies with him.

Coming from another class of society, Helga had nothing in common with Gabriel Deeping. She would never be able to convert him to her religious beliefs. Mercedes came from his social strata. She was knowledgeable and not frustrated like Helga, who could never match the affinity that had existed between Gabriel and Mercedes.

But she certainly had mixed the right poison to stun Mercedes.

"Why should it be a secret?" Mercedes asked. "If there is a therapy, why make it a mystery?"

"Dr. O'Brian would need the consent of the state health department, and he is afraid of delays and refusals," Helga said.

Mercedes got up reluctantly. Gabriel's eyes were wide open, but did not seem to recognize her. "If you're lying I'll see that your pretty nurse's pin is taken away from you." She could not help lashing out, knowing she had to leave Gabriel in Helga's grip.

"If you really love him," Helga said, reverting back to the sober-minded, unselfish nurse, "then please be patient. Of course I'll forget your accusations. You were upset. I wonder what I would do if I were in love with him. Gabriel has a big chance. You don't want to destroy it!"

"But what kind of treatment is it," Mercedes insisted. "Tell me something about it!"

"Dr. O'Brian believes he can reactivate Gabriel's brain. He might give it a sensation of presence; that's how he expressed it to me."

"Of presence? Will he remember the past?" Mercedes asked. "If he doesn't, then he won't remember me."

"I can't answer that," Helga said. "We will have to wait and see."

The two snakes stared at each other, one bitten, the other hiding her triumph behind a calm, compassionate face.

Mercedes left and Helga locked the door. Once alone, she looked gaunt and confused.

I had to detach Gabriel from his past or my objective to exchange my body with his would never succeed. I had to get him completely away from those predatory women. Phyllis had him in the prison of her house and did not care much about Mercedes's possessiveness. She had dealt with it for years and knew how to cope with it. But Mercedes was watching for her chance. For Helga there was only one avenue open: to run away with Gabriel and hide. But she could not do that without my help. I held the key to his recovery. She depended on me, mentally and financially. I had to take Gabriel away from all of them.

Exhausted by the ordeal with Mercedes, Helga sat down. She did not know which way to turn. I was going to show her.

Gabriel sat up slowly. At once Helga came to life, watching him. His movements were different from any she knew. His eyes slowly turned and stared at her as motionlessly as she was sitting.

It was not the Gabriel whom she had led by the hand and who docilely had obeyed her signals like a sheep dog, nor the Gabriel who had talked like a parrot at the breakfast table. The perpetual idiot's smile had vanished and he looked at her intelligently. Petrified, she did not move. She was aware that his brain was functioning. When he had sat on her bed the night before, she knew that he was able to think. But he had not talked. Now he did.

"We must leave here," he said almost inaudibly.

She still did not move. The transition had been too sudden, though she had prepared herself for it. She did not inquire how that miracle had happened and simply accepted the fact that he was able to speak.

"I'll get dressed," he continued. "You take me to the garden for a walk. Should we meet Phyllis, you tell her I need exercise. You know what to say. We will get out through the little garden door and take a taxi. If we take a car, they'll trace us."

She tried to react, but only a small sigh came from her lips. Since she had become his nurse, she wanted him to be able to think and to talk. Now that it had happened, she was terrified.

"I know Mercedes just left." He slowly got to his feet. "She won't let go of me, nor will Phyllis. I don't want to go back to my old life."

He walked over to a chest of drawers and pulled out a shirt. "Where are the cuff links?" he asked.

"In the same drawer," Helga said. She could not have replied to any question except a casual one. Walking soundlessly, she brought his gray suit from the closet and took it off its hanger, then picked out a tie. Almost in a trance she repeated familiar movements that did not need much thought.

"I've been watching you and Mercedes and Phyllis for days," he said, throwing the pajama top on the floor. "My head is clear for hours. But then suddenly I'm asleep. It's like a light turned off. I don't see anything, or maybe I just don't remember. I certainly have no recognition of where I was and what I was doing. But other times I'm wide awake. I could have talked just now, but I didn't. I had to find out for myself what was going on in me. And around me. Last night I was in your room— that I remember. When my mind clears, I recognize you."

"You do," she exclaimed. "You do! Always?"

He put on his shorts, with the routine movements of a man who has slipped them on thousands of times, and took a long step toward her, looking down at her blonde head.

"Of course I do," he said. "There was a moment when you held me in your arms. But it wasn't here. Or was it?"

"No—it wasn't," she managed to say.

As he walked still closer, she took a small step back. Now that she was confronted with a Gabriel who could act on his own and whom a signal of her hand, a short command or two, could not control, the walls of her anxiety were quickly up again.

"It was in a bed," he said with the charm of a man who is aware of his looks and who believes that he has only to stretch out his arms to make a girl fall into them. "There was a bed—whose was it, yours or mine? We started something we should've finished!"

Helga was shocked, though the shock did not penetrate completely her consciousness as something she had hated and despised all her life—that shallow sexual banter and playful approach to emotions as deep and awe inspiring as the intimate meeting of two bodies. Sin incarnate was confronting her. Her reaction was automatic and true to type.

"I don't remember, no . . . I don't." She stepped back farther. She had been in situations before where she had been physically threatened. That was as a nurse, and her emotions had played no part in it. But here a man had come to life whom she desired and for whom she had been prepared to sacrifice herself. Now that that situation had become real, she was not ready. She might never be.

To attack her was to lose her forever.

Gabriel laughed softly. His upper body was still naked. Black hair covered it like a fine fur. That silky hair indicated an animalism and a brutal sensuality she most hated.

Where was that perfumed, docile lover for whom she had herself so thoughtfully and diligently prepared? Here was a powerful hairy beast, a forceful ape. He could squash her in his muscular arms, take her without kindness, bent only on his own base gratification. That was not the man for whom she had shed her convictions and carefully groomed morals.

"Don't!" She stepped back farther, but his arms quickly closed around her. "Not here." Her voice gave out.

"You've locked the door." She felt his breath short and hot, close to her lips. Forcing her mouth open, he kissed her. She clenched her teeth and tried to free her arms, which he had pinned to her side. Her wide open eyes were filled with terror. She did not want to be forced. Whatever she desired had to be on her terms, at her time.

"Not now," she gasped. "Tonight."

"There is no tonight," he said and bent her down on the bed, grabbing her breasts, pressing them with both hands. He tried to hurt her deliberately. Afraid of calling in Phyllis, she did not dare to scream. She tried one of her judo tricks, but he only laughed, pinning her knees down with his. His large mouth, with its long, drawn-out lips, grinned as he searched her mouth. She moaned in panic as he wantonly forced her legs apart with a strong hand. Her narrow white skirt ripped, that thin nylon of her nurse's uniform, that badge of aloofness.

The blood had drained from her face. Forcing her arms behind her body, he had her completely in his power. Every move hurt her. She felt him between her open thighs, and with clenched teeth she stared at him, gathering all her remaining strength in her eyes to keep him away.

As he looked at her that mocking gleam in his eyes reappeared, and still standing above her, between her forced legs, he slowly let go of her.

His hand that clutched her thigh opened, and she was free, but did not dare to move.

Now he laughed audibly and stepped back. Picking up his trousers he slid into them. She pulled down her torn skirt and sat up.

She had escaped, but there was no road back to him. Though she thought she had won, Gabriel had freed himself from the web that she had spun around him.

"Okay, if that's your feeling for me," he said, putting on his shirt. Now that his hairy torso was hidden, the immediate menace disappeared. Helga got up and looked at her torn skirt.

"I'll have to change," she said. When the hurricane has blown past, a woman's first concern is about her looks.

"Yes, get rid of that hospital shroud," he answered. "I'm not the patient anymore. You are from now on. And let's get out of here."

"Where shall we go?" She quickly stepped over to the door and unlocked it.

"To Cory."

"Cory?" she reacted, startled. "What do you know about him?"

He laughed his soft, endearing laughter. "Everything. Now change and pick me up. I'll be waiting for you here. We'll never come back to this place."

"Will we be staying in Cory's house?"

"You'll be with me, isn't that enough information?" he said. She seemed to resent his unaccustomed domination. Besides, she was frightened of him.

"I don't know you, Gabriel," she finally said.

"You will," he laughed and walked toward her. At once she opened the door and looked out like a girl who had visited her lover in his hotel room. Noiselessly she closed the door behind her.

I made Gabriel sit down.

To evaluate my situation, which had become more and more complex, I needed a few minutes to myself. I had to use that antidote of brutal sex to scare off Helga. Never again would she expose herself to Gabriel's aggressiveness. From now on he would be safe in his own bed. There was no pleasure for her in a relationship that almost every girl encounters in her lifetime: that love game of the young, attacking, impatient male and the defending female, who does not want to be rushed, but wooed. It usually ends up in unison. But for Helga brutality in lovemaking was agony. Love, as she visualized it, was the touching of angels in midair, the faint breath of moving white ethereal bodies, the brushing of butterfly wings—or the secret use of Gabriel's unconscious body to satiate her own desires. Her ecstasy was not made to have witnesses or memories other than her own.

I could leave Gabriel safely with her. She would show up at my house—with an idiot! I wondered how long she would be able to stand that constant change in him. She might, like a

Pavlov dog reacting to signals, become neurotic and unbalanced—those signals did not produce the expected result.

My mathematically trained mind is able to forecast incidents, and therefore the future. But women posses an X factor, variable and unpredictable. I had not taken in account that Helga would double-cross Gabriel.

Chapter Twenty-One

I had the limousine parked on a dead-end road in Hidden Valley. Some of my clothes were in the trunk, and some of Gabriel's—the necessary ones for a long trip.

In a sudden attack of decency, O'Brian had not disclosed my hideout to the government. They still were looking for me. All the police had was the phony address of a Gabriel Hyde who did not exist. Jose had led them astray. But I was on their wanted list, maybe a mug shot in post offices all over the country among the murderers and forgers and con men. They might even, via satellite, broadcast my features and Gabriel's around the world. Phyllis would do that, I was sure, to get back her beloved son. My face was easy to remember, even a description would do. A faceless man traveling with an extremely good-looking one in a Chrysler limousine. That was ample description.

To make sure they wouldn't find me I had to get rid of the car as soon as possible. I had taken with me the Blue Sheet, a Valley advertising paper that listed private cars for sale. It would be wise to buy one of them, pay in cash, and drive away without changing the registration. Then the police would have no record. The limousine could be stored in a garage or left in a parking lot. Traveling at night and staying in a motel in the daytime would also make it difficult for the police to trace us.

I had worked out our escape to the most minute detail.

I had enough cash.

My scientific curiosity, the devotion to my profession, had been an important part of my life. But more important still was to go on living without pain. To trade scientific curiosity and the physical suffering that was inseparably attached to my body for health and well-being—as Gabriel experienced—was the decision I had made.

All I wanted was to live through Gabriel.

How many people wished to be young again, to start life all over! *Si la jeunesse savait et si l'âge pouvait*—if the young knew and old ones could do . . . . I was in the fortunate position to add my knowledge of life and my experience in life to the body of youth—Gabriel's!

Nobody was around when I stopped the car at a lover's lane. The circular tire tracks revealed the nightly traffic. One of the virgin canyons of

Beverly Hills—that surprising part of the city that mixes absolute wilderness with the most sophisticated and expensive homes—lay before me, still inhabited by snakes and foxes, racoons and deer. Here the dirt road ended, strewn with pint bottles and telltale signs of illicit love affairs.

I left a few dollars on the driver's seat, withdrew into the back of the car, and put on the transducers to become Gabriel.

He was still in his room, sitting on the chair where I had left him. The door was open and the house in an uproar.

"I didn't see her leave!" Phyllis shouted. "Did you?"

"I'm sure she'll be back in a few minutes," Mr. Deeping consoled her.

"But she's getting paid to look after Gabriel," Phyllis cried. "How can she leave without telling me!"

"She will be back shortly." Deeping varied the same sentence.

Then Phyllis burst into Gabriel's room. She lived for excitement, waiting for catastrophes to enhance her life.

"She's dressed him to take him out," Phyllis shouted through the open door. "It's time for his daily walk. I'm going to fire her!"

"Take him to the garden," Deeping suggested, entering the room. He had walled himself in with philosophy to keep up with Phyllis's constant agitation. He had the affinity, carefully groomed in him, never to get involved, a wisdom that he had acquired in order to exist.

"Take him," Phyllis said. "I'll call the employment office and get another nurse! The cheek of that girl! Mercedes warned me. I should never have given a young girl a job like this. They all neglect their duty!"

"Yes, dear," Deeping said. Her voice passed through him without an echo. He was like a deaf man who could cut off his hearing aid to detach himself from his surroundings.

Reluctantly he took Gabriel's arm. He had never touched him before and was uncertain about his approach. Gabriel at once got up. They walked hand in hand down the stairs while Phyllis shouted into the telephone.

Leading Gabriel to a garden bench, Deeping made him sit down as he had seen Helga do. Too quickly Gabriel followed the pressure of his stepfather's hand. It surprised Deeping. He stood for a few moments watching Gabriel. Then, shaking his head in bewilderment, he left.

At the far end of the garden, a small gate led to an unpaved road behind the house. As soon as he was alone, Gabriel got up and quickly walked in the shadow of the trees toward that gate. It was not locked. He left the yard and walked down Stone Canyon Road toward the Bel Air Hotel.

A car stopped and a young man offered Gabriel a lift. A well-dressed pedestrian is assured of transportation in that busless part of the city. Gabriel took a taxi at the hotel and a few minutes later was on his way to meet me. Behind him he left the mystery of his disappearance. Phyllis might throw one of her fits looking for him, and

Deeping would have a bad time, having neglected his duty.

The taxi drove up Coldwater Canyon, and turned into Hidden Valley Road. The driver stopped. "There's no house down here," he said, having passed the last building.

Gabriel made him drive on. He found the limousine, picked up the money I had left on the seat, and dismissed the taxi. I put him behind the driver's seat and we drove up the canyon and down into the valley.

Now every trace of us had been erased. The only witness was the taxi driver, but his evidence was too vague—a man answering Gabriel's description boarded his taxi at the hotel and left it on a dirt road a few miles away.

I hid inside the car as we drove along Ventura Boulevard. Gabriel took a suite at a modern motel and registered under a fictitious name. The woman at the desk lifted her head as I walked past the office a few minutes later. She had expected a girl to follow Gabriel. But since it was a man hiding his face, she shrugged. All she was interested in was that the suite had been paid in advance.

Behind Gabriel a beehive had been stirred up at the Deeping house. First Helga had disappeared—I didn't know where she had gone and was not at all concerned. Then Gabriel had vanished. I imagined Phyllis alarming the Los Angeles Police Department, sending detectives after her beloved son. She might have called

O'Brian too. But all that was conjecture and of little interest to me.

My second pair of eyes and ears was with me, my alter ego, that doppelganger who did not look like me, but like the archangel Lucifer before his fall. I had accustomed myself to living through Gabriel—without pain, elated, vigorous. Every moment I had to return to myself was agony. I hated to eat or to drink since that demanded that I disconnect the transcorders. It is a fact that man very quickly gets used to luxury. My luxury was experiencing Gabriel's perfect body. I had fallen in love with it, the way perhaps he had loved his body before his illness. O'Brian, of course, would have called my emotions proof of my bipolarity. But I was sure it was not—it was a flight from purgatory into the spheres of heaven.

The motel was built in the style of a fake Polynesian village with huge images of gods carved from hairy trunks of palm trees. Colored lights sprayed on streams of water, which converged in a pool shaped like a giant green kidney. Cabanas opened toward the large patio, and music was constantly playing. Other strains of TV and radio came from rooms, and the cacophonic music blended not unpleasantly since all beat the identical rhythm.

We had a lanai with a queen-sized bed and a living room. A balcony overlooked the patio. Gabriel was lying on the bed. He had taken off his shirt and his broad, hairy chest moved up and down in the rhythm of a sleeping beast.

Gabriel's Body

Among the clothes that I had taken along for him were vividly colored swimming trunks and fancy Tibetan sandals—samples of Helga's taste.

I ordered food from the restaurant. When the waiter knocked, I told him to leave the food.

After the waiter left, I walked back into the sitting room and ate quickly. Pain accompanied my food. Pain and food became synonymous for me. I gulped down a few morsels and turned to Gabriel. I told him to eat, watching him, directing him.

Was that the way I was going to spend the remainder of my life, nursemaid to my other half like a Siamese twin? How long could such a relationship last? Supposing I got sick? Supposing Gabriel did? An accident, anything disturbing the flow of our matched lives would create insurmountable obstacles. It was a kind of relationship that never had existed since the evolution of Homo sapiens

The sun was sinking. The heat of the day still hung over the valley like a canvas cloth. The colored lights hitting the fountains and the pool became sharper, and the noise of the bathers and the mixture of tunes increased as darkness deepened. I watched the pool from my bastion and wondered what it would be like to move among those young people. I don't think I had joined a crowd for the last 40 years, since I received my Ph.D. and left for the seclusion of the research laboratory. My love affairs too had been scanty, clandestine, and unimportant. I had never wooed a woman, despising that mating game men and animals perform. In animals those rituals have a reason. It mates the same species. The male duck dances around the female, beats his wings, lifts his head, dives under water at a certain instant of the mating dance. If he is of another breed, she expects him to rise up instead of going under—and from that moment on she cannot be approached by the male. He is not her kind. Nature opposes miscegenetion.

Humans conduct similar rites. The girls provoke the male with their tight shorts, the nakedness of their thighs, the war paint, the perfume, the wiggle of their walk, the exposed bodies in scanty bikinis, which leave no part of their anatomy to imagination—and the boys with groomed hair, jeans glued to their hips and legs, outlining every elevation and depression, the muscles of their bodies exercised to sharp definitions, their shiny cars—like plumes of the male bird—to attract the opposite sex, the loud voices forcing attention, the cooing and shrieking—they are preludes to one thing only: the embrace in the dark. The juke box moaning about sex: the moon, the heart, the kiss, only you, the heartache of the waiting, the pain of the deserted. A climax resolving all that effort: propagation. Songwriters possess a vocabulary of 200 words, no more.

Propagation and survival are the only objectives of nature. Once an animal cannot propagate anymore, its usefulness is over and it soon dies. Once having reared children, man's duties on earth are fulfilled. The rest of his life he spends amusing himself in his own peculiar way. If he is rich, he may become hedonistic, buy himself the best food and human bodies. Or he developes a social conscience, spending his days in doing good for others, proud of his assumed usefulness or humble about it, the greater part of conceit. Or he becomes a scientist like me, trying to break the code of nature's mystery. To what end? Self-gratification and vanity, which is entertainment of the ego. Man lives on, without the purpose that nature demands.

I had never cared for the pleasure of the senses. For me, food was only a necessity. I had never shared with any female the pleasures troubadours sang about. Sharing is exchanging emotions. I have always walked alone, except perhaps for my work with Malcolm. Malcolm and I used to talk about his exploits in sex, and he told me about certain peculiarities in women and their reaction to his advances. It sounded to me like the description of special breeds of dogs and horses. The dog is a guardian; a horse can pull a carriage or transport a rider. These creatures are bred for usefulness.

But now I had a body to find out about those pleasures man treasures so highly.

I woke up Gabriel. He dressed for the pool. His body was magnificent—humans are conditioned to admire the shape of another human body. Animals don't see beauty in anything, but man's eye possesses that aberration. Beauty itself has no usefulness, except to excite sexual desires in humans. For an animal, any female of the same species is only desirable when she is in heat. Man, constantly in heat, needs the stimulus of certain shapes that he calls beautiful.

Gabriel threw a large towel over his shoulders. The larger the towel, the better the quality of the hotel. Then he walked out onto the patio. The colorful G-string he wore scarcely inhibited the picture of his gladiator nakedness. Wide shouldered, hipless, with his dancer's walk, he stepped out toward the pool. A sudden hush fell over the crowd that had been screaming and laughing, pushing each other into the water, holding on in tight embrace to feel each other's bodies.

Dropping the towel, Gabriel gracefully dived into the pool, sank to the bottom to come up spouting like Triton. Throwing back his black hair with a fountain of droplets, he reached the rim of the pool with a couple of powerful strokes and jumped out with the leap of a huge cat, his tanned body gleaming. He landed close to the group of young people. There he sat with that aloof smile on his wide-cut mouth. He could feel the titter and excitement of the girls. They went through their mating rites, like birds that coo, chirp, and squeal to attract attention. As he again dove into the chlorinated water, some girls jumped after him, leaving the boys behind.

A head bobbed up close to Gabriel, a mass of dark hair floating like shiny silk, eyes sparkling, the starkly painted mouth exposing white teeth like a toothpaste ad.

"Haven't I seen you before?" the naiad shouted. Somebody pulled her screaming body under water. A head bumped his shoulder and a smooth face was close to his.

Soon after they marry those faces and trim figures fall apart, their fine bones seem to grow heavier, the flat stomachs cover with fat. The powder of butterfly wings that attracts the male blows away. It is impossible to realize that gross matrons ever have been slender sirens. They fight for a time against the drudgery of everyday routine, then find consolation in food that bloats their bodies.

"I bet he's a TV star." The pretty face smiled at Gabriel. "What's your name?"

Suddenly a young man's disgruntled, morose face shot up between Gabriel and the naiad and he jealously pulled her away. Among the shouts of protest Gabriel jumped to the flagstones, picked up his towel, and walked back to me, leaving the disappointed pool nymphs behind.

Thinking back to that evening, I'm aware that those were the only moments of contentment I can recall. I had plunged into the lives of the nondescript multitude that had no face of its own, and I had liked it.

In a suburb 10,000 boys could interchangeably get married to 10,000 girls. The same product would come of that merger, the same amount of happiness and trouble. Their children would somehow look alike, their houses would be furnished in approximately the same style. The women would wear stretch pants when they were in fashion, sailor slacks if they were in demand, shorts if they were the vogue. The marital difficulties also would be practically identical. Soon the slender young men would become heavyset, drifting more and more toward their own sex for company. At parties men and women would separate like water and oil; on one side the men would congregate, on the other the women. With marriage the pursuit of sex would be abandoned. Any man mixing with married women was suspect.

But that night at the motel the noisy love prelude had created in me an excitement instigated, I was sure, by my glands so long neglected. Through Gabriel I had been aroused. I even began to daydream, which I had not done since I was a teenaged boy.

Gabriel returned to our room and soon fell asleep. I watched that tanned, strong body beside me—my alternate abode. If I were not forced to hide with him, I could start a new life.

I could study at a foreign university where nobody would know Gabriel. I could go to the Sorbonne, where O'Brian had experienced the best years of his life, or stay in Oxford or Vienna, visit the University of Ravenna or Bonn—be among young people, sharing their hopes and desires, their joys and petty despairs.

The deterioration of the mind accompanies the aging of the body. Since Gabriel was 40 years younger than I, I would add 20 years of youth to my span of life. I also could try to live a commonplace existence, get married, have a home, friends with whom I could make idle conversation, dull my mind and drift through life without mental anguish.

But where would my body hide? In a room at Gabriel's house? In a hotel? I, a living cybernetic machine that had to be fed and that was complicated by body functions?

I would never be content with such a life— my dream did not fit my personality. It was impractical. I knew that my relation to Gabriel had to come to an end. The maze of probabilities that could happen to both of us was too intricate even to be analyzed.

One day extraordinary brains might be allowed to borrow healthy bodies that were useless otherwise. There has been much talk of preserving the sperm of important people. Why not assign young bodies to them? My experiment was ahead of its time.

Chapter Twenty-Two

In the morning I picked up the newspaper that gratuitously was put on every door of the motel as a reminder that the Nirvana atmosphere of music and colored lights was only for escapists.

On the front page Gabriel's face and also mine, as I had looked before the accident, appeared. The newspaper had no other photograph of me, nor did the police.

At once I threw our belongings into the two suitcases and sneaked with Gabriel into the underground garage. A few minutes later we were on our way.

"Mystery Disappearance of Famous Scientist," the headline screamed. All the wars that were going on in different parts of the world, the government crises, the hurricanes, and disasters took second place.

"Noted scientist Patrick Cory and Gabriel Deeping, his helpless tool." They didn't mention Brentwood House. I appeared as the ogre who had the power to destroy civilization with his sinister top secret invention. They also did not say what kind of invention. But my burned face was described. That gave a better picture than any photograph could ever convey.

I was Jean Valjean, the Miserable, traveling with Cosette—Gabriel in this case—pursued by Javert the detective. Javert this time was the combined police, sheriff, and highway patrol.

A $100,000 reward had been promised for my arrest and the return of Gabriel Deeping. Now every clerk in every motel, every person along every highway and in every restaurant would watch for us. I wondered if it were government money or Phyllis's. She would spend any amount to get back her beloved son. I was surrounded by millions of informers! Our pictures would be shown on television.

I stopped the Chrysler in a side street in Canoga Park, close to a house where a late-model Ford had been advertised. Gabriel bought it from the owner and, to the man's pleasant surprise, paid cash for it. I left the Chrysler behind in the street. They might find it in a few days.

I had put sunglasses on Gabriel and he was unshaved. He drove the speed limit. The highway patrol would have no reason to stop us.

The question was where to go. To cross into Mexico was too dangerous. Though no passport was necessary, the Mexican police would keep track of every foreigner.

We could cross into Canada. I could buy a house near a lake, 100 miles north of Toronto. We could live there quietly for a long time without being found.

I stopped daydreaming. My ideas were not practical. The first flurry of the search had to die down. I had to stay in hiding. But where?

We drove along Highway 99 and stopped at a filling station with a restaurant as an appendix. I stayed in the car while Gabriel went to eat. He had half of the food wrapped for Bowser, his dog. I was Bowser! The waitress, flirting with the unshaved Gabriel, had packed scraps from other plates to please him.

We went on. A highway patrol car passed us, but did not stop. Finally it turned off the road.

Suddenly I was dead tired. The strain of watching the road from the backseat and directing Gabriel had worn my resistance thin. We drove along a frontage road and stopped. Taking off the transducers, I closed my eyes. Pain stabbed at my temples. I did not dare fall asleep, recalling Gabriel's previous adventure with the police. It was better to take a rest at a small motel. I was also hungry and thirsty. The heat was beating down from a sulfurous sky. The parched San Joaquin Valley stretched endlessly, the straight band of a road fusing with the horizon. Was it different from the road from Desert Rock to

Gabriel's Body

Brentwood House? What had I gained except a few hours of respite from pain?

I took the wheel and let Gabriel sit numbly in the back. The pain kept me alert, sharpening my mind, shutting off dangerous and impractical dreams. If I ever approached a scientific problem that way, it certainly would end in failure.

"$25.00 for two," a shabby motel on a dusty side road proclaimed. "Air-cooled."

There is a difference between air-cooled and refrigerated. Air-cooling is done with water, and the humidity in the rooms is unpleasant. I had no choice, so I drove the car up to the row of tiny bungalows no larger than donkey stables.

Gabriel went to the office and registered. The young woman, her dyed red hair showing black roots, smiled at Gabriel. She echoed a beauty she might have possessed only a few years ago before the loneliness and heat of this rickety halfway house had killed her spirit. She led Gabriel to one of the cottages. Seeing a man in his car she peered at me. She would have expected a good-looking man like Gabriel to travel with a woman.

I waited until she had disappeared, then quickly crossed to the cottage. It had two narrow beds and a stall shower. The air-cooler was turning deafeningly.

As I pulled down the fly-specked blinds, I saw the woman outside staring toward me. I was not sure if she could see me through the screen. But I was developing a persecution complex, suspecting a spy in everybody.

We stretched out on the beds and I took off the transducers to think. It was a mistake to hide in small motels. Only a large city could give us protection. Why not take a suite in a San Francisco hotel? It was easier to hide among a million people than in a place guarded by a bored, curious woman.

Someone knocked as soon as I had fallen asleep. The police?

"Who is it?" I shouted.

"I got ice water for you," the woman's voice said.

"We don't need any, thank you." I walked back to the bed and sat on it heavily to make it creak. Then I sneaked to the window and watched her standing undecidedly with the water pitcher in her hand. She had fixed her hair and changed her skirt and blouse. She also had smeared new makeup over the old. She must have wanted to lure Gabriel out of the cottage. But I did not like the way she looked over the car.

I hated myself for being so jittery. Valjean running away from Javert, who had used the mask of a red-haired slut to spy on me!

Could the morning papers have already reached this forlorn spot off the highway? I looked around. There was a television antenna, and she certainly would have a radio!

I woke up Gabriel and left with him. Had she taken my license number? I did not know.

While I was driving I kept an eye on the rearview mirror. For a time a car followed us. A man was in it. I stopped outside Bakersfield and he overtook us, staring at my green glasses and the floppy hat that shielded my face.

Javert again!

On the way to Paso Robles a sheriff's car trailed us. In Cholame it stopped. Another took over on Route 101. Were we followed and watched? Did they radio ahead of us? Why didn't they stop us?

Become aware of a new word from the dictionary and at once it will crop up in your reading matter and in conversation. Become aware of the police and they will appear at every crossroad.

I tried to dodge them by cutting over to Route 1, the highway that runs along the coast. From Big Sur to Santa Cruz they supplied us with an honor guard. I finally shook them off in the dense traffic to San Jose.

There I had Gabriel take over the wheel. My huge green glasses and floppy hat were too conspicuous. Sitting close behind him, my face near his neck, I directed him—a real backseat driver!

I wondered if he would go on driving forever. Would he finally collapse or would energy added to him by thought transfer propel him indefinitely like a perpetuum mobile? Drained by fatigue, would he make mistakes?

I had observed that after meals and sleep he was more responsive and slower in reactions as the day drew to an end. Helga knew when he was tired, knew his bed time. I had paid no attention to that, just to his sensory reactions. My taste buds experienced the sensations of his eating, but the food went into his stomach, not mine. I could have starved to death enjoying the food he masticated. What a pleasant way for people to lose weight! It might open up an industry for the obese!

In San Francisco I chose the Atlantis Hotel on Lafayette Square, where I had once stayed. It had automatic elevators that went to the underground garage. One went directly to the penthouse. I could go there without being seen. Gabriel drove the car into a stall. No attendant was around. Then he went to the lobby and rented the penthouse apartment—two rooms, living room, bar, roof garden. The clerk solicitously speeded up the registration when Gabriel showed impatience. Guests paying $3,500 a day for their accommodations are rare. He rang the bell for the porter.

"Thank you, I've only light baggage," Gabriel said. "I'll take it up myself."

The clerk glanced at the registration. "Malcolm Unwin," he read.

Malcolm was dead; his name could only be found on a small plaque at the Mojave Cemetery. Nobody would remember him.

"You traveling alone?" the clerk asked. There might be a woman whom Gabriel wanted to hide.

"My father is with me. He isn't feeling well. We don't want to be disturbed. Just give me the key. I know the hotel."

"Of course, sir." The clerk handed him the key. "The express will take you up directly from the garage."

"I know," Gabriel walked off. I had thought it best to pretend being related to him. That would eliminate any curiosity.

Gabriel returned to the garage. I picked up the two suitcases and we took the express to the top floor.

A strong wind blew across the penthouse. Doors of unfinished rooms were open. It smelled of paint. A few ladders stood about and men in overalls walked around.

The suite overlooked the bay, Telegraph Hill, and the remains of nineteenth-century wooden houses. As though fertilized by their decay, skyscrapers shot up between them, incongruously mixing with them and patches of parched grass, paved streets, and sandy foot paths, where only a couple of years ago century-old trees had spread. San Francisco is the only city in the United States I know that has the flavor of a European town. Despite its constant growth, its Barbary Coast character is still attached to it.

Only a couple of years ago old man Herbert, the gold miner, had died in Desert Rock. He was the first white child born in that part of the country. Before him were only Indians and some white immigrants. He was 89.

Four men of Herbert's age, each born the day the other had died, would cover the whole history of this city, the oldest on the Pacific coast. Twenty-five Herberts would span the time from the year one A.D. to this moment when I stood on the roof garden of the Atlantis Hotel. Fifty Herberts would reach back to the time of the Pharaohs. Three hundred to the Stone Age!

If the time since the forming of this planet were measured by the height of the hotel, the appearance of man would take no more room than the thickness of a sheet of paper. I measured the shortness of man's time against my impatience.

I, who had been planning all my life, who had never taken a step without considering it like a mathematical problem, looked down from a roof garden where I did not want to be, at a city that I had no wish to visit, into a future that had no horizon, no landmark.

Helga had searched for her objective in life and believed she had found it; so had O'Brian, Jose, and Kaweah. To have only one objective limits one's own existence. So far I had thought that my brainpower would produce the answer to all questions, unsolved and beckoning.

The Greeks of the sixth century B.C. believed that man could solve all the riddles of nature. The Ent, or the existent, is; the Non-Ent is not. Man's search is to distinguish between the two. But man lost his courage and turned more and more to God to do for him what he no longer felt able to do for himself. He walled in his curiosity with cowardness. Now after 2,500 years of this darkness of the mind a new breed had come into its own—a breed that mankind for centuries had incarcerated, tortured, and burned at the stake: the scientist. He does not believe in the stability 2,500 years of cowardice had created. His mastery of technique will be modified by his wisdom and will not enslave the world in stagnant conceptions. But should he ever lose his courage, the world again will be enchained by taboos and dogmas, by wars and hatred— the way it has tortured itself since it forsook the ideas of the enlightened Greeks. A new belief will be created by science, a belief based on logic, not on the mysterious or the nebulous, not the Non-Ent, but the Ent.

There is no use forecasting the shape of things to come. The judgment has to be made from day to day. All prophets died with the Old Testament.

For a moment, I had doubted to use my life to the best of my ability, unharrassed by the conventions, laws, and obstructions that the O'Brians and Merriams had tried to put in my way. I had to make the best of my powers.

I suddenly knew how to cope with the destructive forces, which a world that cherished the stable and therefore was destined to die had been trying to thrust upon me.

The devil would take Dr. Faustus to hell as soon as Faustus was content with his fate.

I was going to call Mercedes Cordoba!

Chapter Twenty-Three

Broken strains of music drifted into the penthouse. It was late afternoon. We had had a good dinner and had settled in our luxurious abode. I decided to stay for some time.

Like most modern hotels the bar was on the roof, the dining room on the second floor, the shopping center in the basement. The architects laid out their plans in conformity to make it easy for the guests to find their way around in every hotel. People staying in hotels of the same chain in different cities or countries should have the impression that they never left one for the other.

From the bedroom I watched Gabriel walking about, healthy, handsome. Through remote control I soon would also enjoy all the amenities a man could desire. And as an added jewel to my crown I possessed my own seasoned mind.

Gabriel watched the waiters stack the refrigerator with champagne and white wines, the rack with *premiers crus*. As he had ordered, they put fresh flowers in the vases.

If I kept up this high living I soon would run out of cash. In a few days, when my life was set as I had planned, I could send for more money.

I had located Mercedes. She lived in Newport near Los Angeles. Information had given me her telephone number. Now I could call her long-distance myself and not go through the hotel switchboard. My call could not be traced.

I sent Gabriel to the shopping center. He bought a white tuxedo, a silk dress shirt, shoes, and socks. Having traveled without Helga, who had been his butler and barber, he needed a haircut and a manicure badly.

The way the manicurist held his hand—a strong hand with black hairs growing on its back—and the way she looked at him proved again his attractiveness. She made small talk and moved erratically, as young girls do when they want to draw attention to themselves. Gabriel, his face hidden under hot towels, did not talk to her. She would gladly work in his hotel room, she said, anytime, even in the evening if he needed her. Her advances were blunt. She was a girl with cleverly dyed bluish hair, her mouth big and starkly painted with too many gleaming teeth, and as she moved his hand, she brought it close to her breast as though by coincidence to let him know she wore no bra.

The barber took off the towels and smiled at Gabriel in the mirror. "You must be her type," he said. "Marianne flirts with nobody, not even with me."

The girl giggled and pressed Gabriel's hand.

After he returned to the penthouse I made him lie down and phoned Mercedes.

It was about seven in the evening. She answered. She must have sat there all day waiting for the call.

"Miss Cordoba?" I asked. My broken voice sounded as if I were talking through a cloth. It was my voice, but she must have thought that I was disguising it.

"This is Miss Cordoba." I heard her breathe heavily in anticipation and fear of bad news.

"I'm calling about Gabriel," I said.

The pause was tense with anticipation.

"Where is he?" she finally asked.

"He doesn't want you to inform the police," I said, surprised that I enjoyed that game. A kidnapper must feel this excitement talking about ransom.

"Is he all right?" she asked.

I looked at that idiot who sat motionlessly as I had ordered him, at his lacquer-black hair, the heavy hands with highly polished nails.

"He couldn't be better. But he does not want his mother nor O'Brian or anybody else. He wants to see you."

"To see me!" she exclaimed. "Did he say so?"

"Yes, he did," I said. That made it clear to her that Gabriel could think. The slow poison that I had injected worked and made her obedient.

"Are you Doctor Cory?" she asked.

I didn't answer her question. Instead I said, "He wants you to come to the roof garden of the Atlantis Hotel in San Francisco. But if you tell anybody, he won't be there. Is that understood?"

"Yes," she said in a small voice.

"At six tomorrow evening."

I hung up. Since she was afraid Phyllis would confiscate Gabriel I was sure she would not tell anyone. Should she phone the Atlantis to ask for Gabriel Deeping or me, they wouldn't know what she was talking about. Nor could she check my long-distance call.

I liked her throaty voice, the deep purr that she might have acquired going to a voice coach or that might be natural to a sensuous girl like Mercedes Cordoba.

I knew I was moving in the right direction, had got myself back into the right frequency, the wavelength of success.

For many years I had studied the rites of the Catholic Church as they are practiced in Italy and Spain, where the priests exorcise the devil with Latin chants and censer scents. Surprisingly often it worked. The devil is the personification of bad luck and can be driven away. What is the background of fortune-telling, of astrology, which are as old as history and therefore must contain a grain of truth?

Good luck might be related to emotions. Since I was able to trace emotions by instrument, I might be able also to detect the frequencies on which fortuitous incidents travel. I could then amplify those vibrations, imprison them on tape, and release them at will, directing man's mind to that elusive band he calls luck. Since chemical companies send their biologists into the jungles to find new remedies from the natives, and to study the medicines and rites of the witch doctors, I am certain that in people's superstitions are hidden ways for exact sciences to determine the timing of fortuitous events. People say, "It isn't my day. The stars are against me." The priests with their mumbo jumbo lead the minds of the believing back to the wavelength of success, that elusive vibration, intuition.

My idea to trace emanation, which will exclude mistakes in timing and will add fortuitous frequencies to important decision, has unlimited possibilities. The world, working out its difficulties electronically, would find the exact remedies, plan its conferences for the time when success is certain. The world would become lucky.

If I had come across this idea when Malcolm was still alive, we could have discovered that mysterious wave band, tamed it, and created artificial luck.

The explosion that destroyed him—and part of me—would never have happened!

Chapter Twenty-Four

The roof garden bar was crowded, and guests danced to a small orchestra on a diminutive floor. The city, deep below, was shrouded in bluish haze—the heat sinking to the ground unveiled the sky.

Gabriel was sitting at a small table half hidden by a huge philodendron plant. He wore the white tuxedo, which made his tanned face even darker. The skin, tightly drawn over his cheeks, glistened as though it had been polished with a horse bone, and the violet eyes had the iridescence of an animal caught in a beam of light.

He had a martini in front of him, which he did not touch. I did not know how he would react to alcohol.

The women in the square, crowded room behaved like the young manicurist; their voices became shriller, their movements exaggerated. Though they talked to their escorts they seemed to be addressing Gabriel. Wherever he looked he met a pair of eyes fixed on him. It is the minute lingering that betrays interest in another person.

A waiter presented Gabriel with a folded note. "Dance? Third table to the right. Come for a drink in Room 226 any time," it read. It was the third offer Gabriel had received during the half hour he was waiting for Mercedes.

I marveled at the callousness of those bored women. Discovering a handsome man who appealed to they fancy, they sent him an invitation skipping the preliminaries, starting with the last act of the love play. A man would confine himself to the law of mating, send the girl a drink if he were boorish, dance with her to mellow her for the conquest, sense if she was willing. But those female drones—if this contradiction could be used—took it for granted that any man could be bought like a drink at the bar. They would not have tried such an uncouth approach if most men didn't jump to their tunes.

Gabriel crumpled the note and threw it into the ashtray. He was watching the door.

My mind was blank about his past, his philosophy—if he had any—his temperament, his attitude toward women. Had he been aggressive with them? Or did he like to be treated like a pretty boy by appealing to their motherly instincts?

Phyllis's relation to him would bear that out. Was he talkative? Withdrawn? Intelligent? Dull? Vain? Did he trade only on his looks?

I knew nothing about him. How would Mercedes expect him to act?

To be on the safe side, I would let him be mysterious. That she would accept without becoming suspicious. He had been ill and that illness would excuse such behavior.

Mercedes entered the bar. She moved like a high-priced mannequin, knowing how to attract attention. The simplicity of her dress enhanced the fine lines of her body. She wore black—which she seemed to prefer—and the satin made her white skin glow. Discovering Gabriel she stopped, overcome by her shock, a shock for which she had prepared herself. But seeing him sitting there without a nurse still stunned her. Then she made her way past the tables.

Slowly he turned his deep-set eyes on her, studying her as if searching his memory. He did not greet her as she sat down.

"Champagne," Gabriel said to the waiter who stood behind her. "And take this drink away."

The waiter offered a wine list.

"Any kind," Gabriel said, still holding Mercedes with his unemotional, curious gaze.

Mercedes's light face had even become whiter; her dark eyes behind the thick veil of lashes also seemed to have deepened their color. He smiled that Mona Lisa smile, which she knew well and which had stayed with him through his illness.

305

"You are Mercedes," he said softly. "I know you are!"

"You recognize me?" The shock of hearing him talk was reflected in her voice.

"I remember you and a few other faces. Very few—most of them are blurred. But yours is not. Can you help me remember? My memory isn't what it should be."

Since she was asked to do something for him she was getting back her self-assurance. "I'll be your memory," she said.

The waiter brought the bottle and showed the label to Gabriel. "All right, sir?"

"Yes, yes," Mercedes answered. There was no room in these minutes for a third person.

The waiter discretely worked the cork from the bottle, filled two glasses, and left.

"Who treated you? Cory?" she asked.

It was too early to talk about me. Gabriel ignored her question and got up. "Shall we dance?"

"You remember how to dance?" she asked and rose.

"Not this kind," he made a vague gesture toward the crowded floor. "I've been watching. It doesn't seem difficult."

He put his arm around her. She was soft and pliable as if she wore no clothes.

"I'll have to learn all over again," he said as the dancers drifted by.

"I'll teach you." Her face was almost at the same level as his. "Gabriel!" Now that she felt him close to her, her tension lessened.

"I remember my mother's face," he said, "and my father's. A blonde young girl . . . ." He looked questioningly at her.

"Your nurse, I suppose," Mercedes said. "But she's left you."

She stuck a voodoo pin into her competition.

"She did?" he asked. "I have the vague memory that she was around for quite some time."

"You don't need her anymore," she said. "I'm with you."

I did not know how long I could continue this dangerous game without making a wrong move. But she had to be conditioned to a new Gabriel.

"Are you still under therapy?" she asked, trying to lead the conversation to me.

"Not the way you think," he answered mysteriously. She stiffened in his arms. Maybe her intuition, sharpened by love, deepened by their past relationship, sensed that foreign core in him.

When the music stopped they quickly went back to the table.

"Did I used to dance?" Gabriel asked.

"We even won a few prizes." She forced herself to be gay, to shake off that gray veil that seemed to hang between her and her lover. "One in New Orleans for our tango. And one at the Waldorf in New York. Don't you remember the thunderstorm?"

"No."

She put her hand on his, but his hand did not reply. "It was in the terrace room. A thunderstorm mixed with the music. All the doors were open, and the drapes were flying. Lightning flashed around us as we danced. You asked me to marry you. It was very romantic. Don't you remember?"

"No," he said. "That night is in between."

She picked up her glass. The champagne had become flat. Suddenly she emptied it, trying to drown the insecurity that had gripped her which she could not explain to herself. Gabriel, too, drank.

"A long, long night," she said. "I would have looked after you, but your mother wouldn't let me."

"My mother," he repeated.

"She kept you with her until your stepfather finally persuaded her to send you to Brentwood House."

"What is that?" he asked.

She laughed hard. Hidden in that laughter was her real nature—that of a determined woman with a streak of masculinity. I gussed that she had dominated Gabriel too. More and more of his character appeared, mirrored in the attitudes of the people around him. His pronounced physical manliness was perhaps an overcompensation for an inherent softness.

"It's no use talking about it," she said quickly. "Let's cut out that time completely. You've said that it was a dream; let's let it stay that way. Let's pretend we fell asleep and woke up just now. Isn't that best?" Since he did not answer she added, "Would you like to dance again?"

"No."

The waiter filled the glasses. Gabriel drank. He felt light-headed and the problems that faced him seemed less unsolvable.

"I didn't look quite the way I do now," Mercedes continued. "I was slimmer, much slimmer. I did modeling then. You called me your sea gull. I was like a sea gull—always hungry. You wanted me to put on some weight, remember?"

"I don't."

Desperately searching for that contact that once had existed between them she said, "But one doesn't need a memory when there is a future."

If he did not remember anything about her, he also would not be able to recall their closeness.

"The week we wanted to elope, to run away from Phyllis, you became ill. They say it was a mosquito bite. We had been to Palm Springs, and you came down with the fever. Thirty-eight people got encephalitis. When you became worse, Phyllis had you taken to Los Angeles. That's when I lost you."

"When was that?"

"Five years ago—almost . . . ." Two lines appeared at the corners of her mouth, which was painted in a light pink, almost as light as her skin.

"And you waited for me all that time?" he asked.

"Yes."

She filled his glass and hers before the waiter could help.

"How much was between us?" he asked, looking at the bubbles, tiny fountains that burst from the glass and fell back in a parabolic curve.

"You don't remember?" Again she laughed. "Well, we could start right from the beginning—a second honeymoon."

Her dark eyes opened wide in reminiscence. They were very beautiful, the large ebony pupil floating in the clear white of the eye, the lashes very long. They were not even painted. She must have had Armenian blood. Only that race has eyes imbued with such sadness and a life of their own.

"Now I know more." Gabriel drank half of the champagne. "But even that has left my mind."

"Just talking about the past, we will never run out of conversation," she said and her good breeding showed in her gaiety. "I might tell you any kind of lie, just to keep you interested. You see, you're at my mercy!"

"Phyllis will have to verify your stories," he said.

"We won't see much of her," Mercedes said. "We didn't before; why should we now?"

She had laid siege to his life and destroyed his former allies one after the other.

"Yes, I want to live a new life," Gabriel said. "It is the only way to go on living—the only one! I wonder if you will have the strength to live with me."

"I?" She looked astonished. "What a question. Of course I have."

"It won't be easy," he said and beckoned the waiter. He signed the check.

"You live at the hotel?"

"Yes. Shall we go?"

"Are you here alone or with Dr. Cory?" she asked. He had avoided talking about me. His evasiveness disturbed her.

Gabriel got up. Seeing so many eyes turning toward him, she put her hand possessively on his arm.

"I know where he is," Gabriel said ambiguously. "You don't need to be concerned about him. Or are you afraid?"

"Afraid?" she echoed his word—it made her wary. "It is the second time that you have asked me that. Why?"

Gabriel walked closely behind her. The music stopped and their exit was covered by the dancers returning to their tables.

They left the bar. From the small room where the elevators stopped, a corridor ran along the penthouse suites.

"You are in eighteen-two," she said, reading the numbers at the doors. "Your Dr. Cory seems to be in the money."

"He is," Gabriel said. That answer pleased her. She seemed to have earned her living and money impressed her.

"I know that his face was destroyed in an accident," she said. "That's why he is hiding, isn't it? I'm sorry for him."

They had reached the door to the suite.

"You'll get used to him," Gabriel said.

He opened the door. The living room with its flower arrangement was impressive. The French doors were open to the dark terrace. The doors to the bedrooms were closed. Mine was locked.

He closed the door and she watched him as he opened the refrigerator and took out a bottle of champagne, iced glasses, and a tray with petit fours. But she still was pondering his reference to me.

"Why did you say I'll have to get used to him? What do we have to do with him?"

"I could not live without him," Gabriel said and smiled at her to soften the blow. Startled, she stepped closer. He opened the bottle and filled the glasses.

"You can't live without him?" she asked incredulously. He held out the glass, but she did not take it. "Is he going to live with us?"

"You won't see him," Gabriel said. "But without him I couldn't marry you either. I had better tell you now."

"I don't understand what you're saying, Gabriel," she was searching for words. The idea of having another man in the house was preposterous to her. "We would have to live with him—always? What kind of hold has he on you?"

"He is keeping me alive," Gabriel said. "Without him I'd have to go back to Brentwood House."

He drank. His hand shook. His other hand held the glass for her, which she quickly took before it could spill. She put it on a table.

"Gabriel!"

Walking very close to him she looked him searchingly in his eyes, her fear hidden behind the urge to understand. He did not flinch.

"What do you see?" he asked, staring at her.

"Why are you staying with him?" she demanded. "Why?"

His past was a closed book, its pages glued together, its writing illegible to me. I did not know what kind of secrets Mercedes shared with Gabriel. Had he lived with a man before? Was she afraid that past would repeat itself? I began to divine his appeal for men and women alike, the mysterious fluid of sex attraction that cannot be explained, but like ectoplasm surrounds certain persons, all conquering but still evasive.

"I need him to live. I told you before," Gabriel said.

"But you are all right," she cried. "You are able to speak, you make sense, and you will improve more every day . . . ."

"I can never be cured," Gabriel said.

She was standing with her back to the open terrace door. His face was fully lit by a standing lamp. He was like a leopard, graceful but dangerous on its springy limbs with its coiled agility. His beauty was a weapon she could not fight.

"But you are," she exclaimed. "You are!"

She put her arms around him. "Say that you're all right! Could I hold you if you were not?"

She tried to kiss him, but he turned his face away.

"We will always be together, Mercedes," he said, his face close to hers. "Always. Whomever you embrace will be me, me, Gabriel! It is my body, nobody else's!"

She withdrew a few inches. The idea that he was insane must have crossed her mind for the first time. "Of course," she said, her face waxen, agreeing with him to keep him calm.

"My mind is not my own," Gabriel repeated. "If you can accept that, we will never have any difficulty."

She was on her guard, playing his game. It was the safest way for her to react. "Whose is it? Cory's?" she asked.

"Yes."

She stepped back as he came closer. "I want to meet Dr. Cory," she said evenly. "I'm sure he'll give you back your mind."

"Mine has been burned out, Mercedes. But you will have me," Gabriel said. "Me and Cory's mind. Don't think that I'm mad. You must believe what I'm saying, or we can never be together."

"Yes, I do," she said. "Of course I do."

"No, not quite," he opposed her. "It needs more than courage to understand and to accept."

"I'm not a coward. I accept," she said, to get out of this situation. He walked so close that he could feel her breath in his face, haltingly, oppressed by her tension and fear.

"You do love me, don't you? You would make any sacrifice for me?"

Many confusing thoughts must have stumbled through her mind. She had known that docile idiot, and before that the handsome, easily influenced young man. Both had been no problem. Mercedes and Gabriel had played together, enjoyed each other without complications as do young people when life is a ride on a cloud. But she divined a sinister mystery that had to be accepted like faith. She could not guess what he wanted to convey. It was too abstract and too weird for any brain not scientifically trained.

She decided to treat Gabriel as she must have before his illness—as a pliable boy who had been her companion.

"What is it, Gabriel?" she asked. "Let's solve it together, whatever bothers you."

I believe it was the alcohol in his system that threw off my contact with him. He did not speak the exact words I wanted him to say. His gestures were erratic and not controlled by me.

"I'm a shell, Mercedes," he said. "I'm directed by Dr. Cory's thought, here—feel it?" He took her hand and forcibly put it on the base of his skull. "These two little nodules, they receive Cory's commands. Without them I wouldn't be able to move." She pulled her hand away as if she had touched hot iron. Now she was beginning to understand.

"You will always have me, Mercedes, but what you will hear will be Cory's mind, his thoughts, not mine. Mine do not exist anymore. If you love me, you will understand and accept me as I am. What more could you have than my body and his mind? You will never know that he is around.

You will never see him. We will have the means to live in luxury. And I will become the scientist Cory has been and still is. I'll do his research; I'll become famous! I'll have a beautiful wife at my side. The man you hold in your arms will be me, Gabriel, the man you talk to, Cory."

"No!" she screamed. "He is mad! He's put that crazy idea in your mind! I don't know why, but he did!"

"I'm telling you the truth," Gabriel said quietly. "I can prove to you what I still am!"

There was no way out. I had to convince her or lose her. If she loved him she would accept him as he was.

I took off the transducers. Instantly he would revert back to the idiot.

Nobody ever lived a life like the one Mercedes was offered. She would be happy if she had the intelligence to accept that kind of happiness. Soon she would forget that the man who was making love to her was not the shallow, weak Gabriel, the perpetual adolescent she had known before. It was a man with his beauty and my brains!

I heard her scream and quickly put back the transcorders.

Gabriel was standing before her. For the few moments while I had removed the connections he had stood like that, his eyes blank, smiling emptily.

"Now you understand," Gabriel said as he came to life. "I know you're strong enough to accept me as I am. We will be happy, Mercedes!"

"No!" she screamed and stumbled on the terrace. He was trying to hold her back. When he held her and pulled her close, away from the banister, she hit him in the face.

Thinking back I cannot reconstruct the incident. As he had at the police station, he must have gone berserk. I heard the scream that reverberated in my ears becoming fainter and ending in a dull thud.

The terrace, but for Gabriel, was empty.

At once I disconnected the transducers. An accident had happened. I had nothing to do with it. All I could think of at that moment was getting away from this tragedy. My presence would complicate matters in a way that no jury would ever be able to unravel.

I threw my few belongings into a suitcase. Moving with clairvoyant precision I left no trace behind. Nobody had seen me arrive at the hotel. Nobody would see me leave.

I unlocked the door. As I passed the living room Gabriel was standing motionlessly on the terrace. His face was turned toward me, and he was smiling.

Chapter Twenty-Five

The corridor was empty, and the express elevator took me down to the garage. I quickly drove out. I didn't care that my face was only hidden by the green glasses and even took them off as soon as I passed the Golden Gate Bridge. It was after the rush hour and the traffic had thinned out. I passed Oakland and in Manteca I turned onto Highway 99. I was on my way to Desert Rock. To go back to my desert hideout seemed to be the logical choice.

It was almost midnight when I stopped for gas outside of Bakersfield. The attendant who saw me gasped. He must have thought that he had seen a ghost. I paid, and he quickly went into his station and slammed the door. Maybe he telephoned the police to tell them that he had seen that ghoulish-looking scientist who was wanted, as he might have heard on the radio or TV. And to collect the $100,000.

I didn't care if he had recognized me or not. Sooner or later they would find me. They knew where to look for me.

I drove along the dark highway, crowded with giant trucks sporting lights like Christmas trees. The windows of my car were open and the warm desert air desiccated my face. Pains had returned to my life like unwelcomed members of a family coming back for a visit. They had to be accepted since there was no other place to send them to. I suffered the pains as a purification of my aborted desires.

I had made my mistake by believing that other people had developed the same tolerance toward science that I had. Tolerance has to be applied not only to revolutionary thoughts, but also to human emotions.

If Mercedes had possessed more than a shallow mind, she would have accepted a life as Gabriel—or rather as I—had laid out for her. Man tries to kill what is strange and new. If men came from a planet of saints to bring their knowledge to earth—a knowledge man is trying desperately to discover—they would pay with their lives.

I had tried to compress time, shunning the slow process of letting my ideas ripen. Ideas are like wine that has to stay in casks to reach maturity. If left too long or released too early it turns to vinegar. I had released my ideas too early. My impatience was to blame; I had left no time for ripening.

Had Mercedes jumped to her death, or had Gabriel pushed her? I don't believe he even touched her. But I am not certain. Here my memory blurs. She had hit him in the face. Had that blow released in him a sudden outburst of violence? I will never know.

How would the law judge my behavior in such an incident? I had run away. If I had stayed, the situation would not be different. Mercedes was dead. Gabriel would be found on the terrace, a smiling, docile idiot. He could not be blamed for anything and would be sent back to the asylum. I had not been on the terrace. I had not even seen Mercedes, and I had certainly not wished her dead. Whatever the accusation could be against me, no jury would ever agree on a verdict. For this incident new laws would have to be written.

I could have put the transducers on to find out where Gabriel was but I refrained from involving myself in this unfortunate confusion. I could not help him. My duty was to adjust myself to a life without Gabriel. My work had to be continued. Since I had—almost—succeeded, my experiments had to be made accident proof.

I was like a designer who sees his newest plane crash and whose first idea is to go back to the drawing board to remedy his mistakes. He does not think of the pilot. A pilot, like a research animal, is only part of the machinery that the designer has created. Perfection is the goal and not the incident of failure.

I didn't stop except to fill up again in Ludlow, where I found a station open. The reaction from the attendant, a woman this time, was the same. She stared at me with the numbing horror that the man in Bakersfield had shown. I was accustomed to it.

"I once was in a fire," I said, "and travel only at night not to scare people. I know I look awful, but what can I do about it?"

That made her pity me. She offered me some coffee, which I gulped down, and put a box of crackers in the car. She refused to accept money for it.

It was early in the morning when I arrived in Desert Rock. A storm had blown sand against the doors and windows of my house and I had to shovel the front door free. The stale heat inside was like a bodyblow. It must have been 120 degrees in the unaired rooms. I turned on the air-conditioning and put a couple of fans into the doors to suction out that suffocating heat. My clothes were wet through in a few minutes. The refrigerator contained ice, which tasted of an onion Kaweah had left.

Then I went to my lab. Since most of the equipment was at Sumac Drive, it was almost empty. The wind had found an opening and blown fine sand over the circuits and instruments. It was as if nature had tried to bury my tools.

Cans of food were left in the kitchen. Kaweah had cherished them. For her, canned food was a luxury. She might have, as a girl, had to grind corn and bake it in an open oven in the desert heat. Meat would keep fresh only for a few hours. Vegetables were rare except for those that from time to time were brought from Mojave City. But inside those closed containers were all the pleasures she had missed.

I was not hungry. But I took a drink of bourbon, grateful to O'Brian that he liked whiskey, or I wouldn't have had it in the house.

Then I sat outside near the broken lily pool while the fans blew out the heat. I had to gather my ideas, my troops, which had been scattered in the battle I had lost.

Victory had been in my grip, but had escaped me at the last moment. Nobody had won this strange encounter of ideas against convention. Everybody had lost.

Sitting in front of my house and watching the new day sneak over the horizon, the eternal, unchangeable passing of time—I did not know which way to turn.

It is by thought alone that man can pass beyond the false appearances of his senses and arrive at the fundamental truth that in the end all is one. The rising of the sun was the symbol of this old Greek wisdom.

But to reach that knowledge man of my time is cursed to unravel the so-called secrets of nature. At the end, after he has enlightened himself, he will be back at the point where he started.

Gabriel's Body

An antithesis exists between knowledge and life. Science seems to be rarely able to answer the questions life proposes.

Sitting in front of my house I felt empty.

Chapter Twenty-Six

Several times I tried to get in contact with Gabriel. But the transcorders did not respond. I was unable to get in touch with him.

After two days of sleep I started cleaning the house. It was therapeutic. I also made a detailed list of equipment I needed, then made plans for my future. But I knew that I was waiting and that my efforts were only diversions to pass the time.

The little food I needed, cans supplied.

A couple of times the telephone rang, but I did not pick it up. I knew it was O'Brian. On the third day he came.

He wore his old driver's cap, which he threw on a chair with the gesture of abandon. "You've been back for days," he said without preliminaries and with reproach, as if I had the duty to report to him.

"I have," I said. "But so far the police haven't come to look for me."

"They won't," he said.

His statement surprised me, which seemed to have been his intention. We were in the living room and O'Brian sat down heavily.

"Gabriel is back at Brentwood House," he informed me. Since that was the case, then my connection with him was technically interrupted. O'Brian must have found the transcorders in his neck. It was no surprise to me that he took a small container from his pocket and carefully extracted those two tiny instruments.

"The corpus delicti," he said, pushing them toward me.

"Helga must have told you about them," I said.

"When she told me I had already found them," he answered.

When she had run away from Gabriel she must have gone straight to O'Brian to tell him everything she knew. I did not say anything and let O'Brian talk, curious to hear his interpretation of the incidents. It would be quite different from mine. He looked at me as if he expected answers to his unasked questions. We would talk about something that we both knew that did not need any discussion. Except that he cleared up one unknown fact for me.

"I took his encephalograms. Want to see the graphs?"

He took them out of his pocket and unfolded the paper strips.

"Here are his old ones and those are the new. Except perhaps for some further deterioration, your transcorders had no influence on his brain, Patrick. They are no cure, nor do they produce any metastasis. You could have put them in a broomstick and they would have done the same service."

His washed-out eyes looked at me with an unpleasant expression. He seemed to hate me. I did not reply to his silly remark and he corrected himself.

"No. Not a broomstick. A broom doesn't move by itself, nor does it speak. Nor does it have five senses which can be used for an experiment. I'm somehow slow in my mind, but I think I've the secret of Patrick Cory figured out. Correct me if I'm wrong."

"Helga must've helped you," I said.

"Yes, in her own way, she did. She's told me a lot, more than I care to know." Again I saw that coldness in his eyes. He was hurt. How unprecedented my part in her infidelity was— I was in the midst of it and never even touched her hand!

"I'm curious to know what you've found," I said. "I'm at a loss myself."

Methodically he went through the facts. "Kaweah is proof that thought transfer is possible. If from that moment on you'd have worked with collaborators, even if they had not contributed anything positive to your work, they at least would have kept you in check."

"Point number one, dear to your heart!" I said. Since my voice is monotonal, he did not know if I laughed at him, resented him, or accepted his reproach.

"Yes. You also have found a way to transfer the senses of living things to yourself. I deliberately say living things, since you also must have made tests with animals. Right?"

"With a bull and a coyote." His deductions intrigued me and I decided to give him a hand.

"Glad you're telling me," he said. "I can only guess and need confirmation. Now we're coming to the important point: Gabriel."

Like two diplomats who skirt a delicate point, we did not mention Helga. He knew that I had experimented with her at the hospital and that she was deeply involved in Gabriel's case.

"Is that also clear to you?" I asked.

"I should've had more courage and helped you make laboratory tests on humans," he said. "I could have, but I was too cautious. And you were too impatient. We both are at fault."

"Glad you take some of that guilt off my shoulders," I said.

"Everybody is allowed a mistake. Mine was a blockbuster. Knowing you I should've been less conservative, or whatever you may call my stupidity. I should also have considered that the temptation for you to live through Gabriel was tremendous. But that does not absolve you from having committed a crime!"

"I did?" I asked. "Which paragraph of the penal code do you refer to?"

"Manslaughter," he said.

"How did you come to that conclusion?"

"Since Gabriel is unable to act by himself, it was you who pushed Miss Cordoba off the terrace. You, Patrick! Nothing in his brain indicates that he is capable of acting for himself. Nothing! Your thoughts directed him."

"Did I also hit the policeman?"

"Yes," he said drily.

"But why? I'm not crazy!" I said. That word suddenly took on monstrous connotations. We both were aware of it.

"There is a viciousness in you, Patrick. You have the instinct of a murderer. In life that is sublimated. But subconsciously it came out in Gabriel. Of course, you didn't want to hit the policeman. You are too clever for that. Nor did you want to push that poor girl off the terrace."

"I tried to hold Gabriel back. I did—but somehow that picture is blurred in my mind," I said.

Though we had no witnesses to our discussion he could, if he chose, put any confession in my mouth. He could have come to my house to talk about the weather and then invented a whole dialogue between us. The jury would believe him and not me.

"Your subconscious gave the stronger commands to him," the psychiatrist said. "You might have been afraid that Miss Cordoba knew too much and therefore wanted to get rid of her. Maybe she guessed what was the matter with Gabriel. Do you believe she did?"

I did not reply. He interpreted my refusal to answer as confirmation and said slowly, "She rejected not Gabriel, but you. And you, Patrick, couldn't stand that, could you? You killed her." I still did not answer and let him gloat over his irrational theory. He continued: "Here your experiment shows its most dangerous flaw: the subconscious personality traits of the man who is the transmitter might take over. In your case they made you a murderer."

"You love to use strong words," I said, knowing that he was trying to punish me. "If you are so sure why haven't the police picked me up?"

"They won't. You'll have the chance to continue your research. But this time under supervision," he said with relish. "Research was always more important to you than any human relation. Now since you cannot have Gabriel, I think you won't kick up a fuss as you did last time. You need help, Patrick. You are going to accept that help or you'll disappear in a lunatic asylum for the rest of your life."

"Blackmail?" I asked.

"More than that. You've no way out. I've talked to Merriam. He agrees with me. Charges could be brought against you. There is enough evidence. But Merriam is against revealing your methods of thought transfer. He wants to treat them as top secret. But he also wouldn't hesitate to put you in a padded cell and let you rot there just to keep you from talking."

I picked up the transcorders. Those shiny beads were the cause of my difficulties and hopes.

"Why did you give them back to me? You could've turned them over to the government. They could figure out how they work and wouldn't need me."

"You're much too important a scientist to be destroyed by a law which does not take into consideration that men like you by necessity stand outside our ethics." He got up. For him the case was closed. Having won, he didn't even ask me for approval. He picked up his battered cap and turned to me with the kindness that from time to time broke through his thoughness.

"As for your sufferings—accept them as companions. Many great people were racked by pain all their lives and still contributed immeasurably to the progress of mankind."

Chapter Twenty-Seven

At Brentwood House a new bungalow has been built for me. O'Brian does not want me to live alone in Desert Rock and I agree. He seemed to have unlimited funds at his disposal when it came to furnishing my laboratory. The bungalow also has a living room and a bedroom. Food is delivered from the cafeteria or I can go there myself. A couple of young chemists are assigned to me. They are alert, sharp, impersonal—a new breed. They might be working for the CIA or any other government department. We have little contact, though in the evenings they sometimes come to me and we discuss abstract problems as I did with Malcolm. They also write reports about our work but I have never bothered to find out who receives them. One day my work will be used for good or for evil, as I anticipated. But good and evil are only words that change their connotation according to man's need.

When I look out on the lawn that spreads in front of me, I am spared the view of the crowd of inmates. Sometimes I see Helga taking Gabriel for a stroll. They are promenading like two lovers. In her quiet, steely way she has got what she was after, and I assume that she is wishless. But he has lost some of that dancer's spring. It might be that his nervous system is deteriorating. If that is the case I used my discovery on a human too early. What would have happened if my scheme had succeeded, and I had lived through Gabriel with Mercedes—and the slow decay that accompanies encephalitis had set in? I wonder if it is envy that makes me consider that possibility—envy that Helga has won and has back her Kewpie doll? Being human we cannot divorce ourselves from our emotions, however much we try to imprison them with logic.

The soft meat in the hard shell!

I have again adjusted myself to work and therefore to my life. Our social structure is based on belief and trust. Founded on these psychological traits, the social, the judicial, and the political world are essentially mystical. The law, principles, and relationships are not the outcome of observations.

The only world that is founded on empirical proof and therefore contains the truth is that of the scientist. His vitality and power will increase as we become more and more aware that our lives and searches are transitory and apply only to the evaporating moment in which we live. We will have to go on experimenting forever, the way nature changes conditions to make them conform with its laws. Its creations must change or they will die out like the dinosaur. Man is nature's creation.

Not many of the values as we know them today will stay with us. But man will emerge from the state of the cocoon in which he has lived for thousands of years to that of his ultimate shape. Though he might, in the agony of growing, destroy the cocoon and with it his future form.

It is the duty of the scientist to lead man through this dark transitory period into the light of his future existence.

CURT SIODMAK CURRICULUM VITAE

I first saw the light of day at the turn of this century. If I had been asked when and where I wanted to be born, I certainly would have chosen another time, since during my life I have witnessed too many repetitions of the horrible atrocities the human race has inflicted on itself. We learn from history that we don't learn from history.

In 1902, when the state of Saxony still had a king, I was born in Germany to a Jewish family. I would have chosen to be a Greek 2,000 years ago at the time of Aristotle and Plato when thinking was not stymied by government or religious taboos.

I went through the First World War in Germany with its pointless slaughter, tribulations, and hunger. After that harrowing time, inflation wiped out the financial security of my family. That era of national decay was succeeded by an explosive bloom of culture in Berlin and for me six years of success as an author and screenwriter. Being a compulsive writer, I had 14 novels published between 1929 and 1933 and wrote seven motion pictures besides — some of which are still on the screen.

The Nazis stopped me from making a living in Germany. I was forced to emigrate and to learn a new language in order to continue my profession as an author. I went to France, as did many other refugees, then to England, where I found work at the British International Picture Company. After that episode I was under contract at Gaumont British Pictures, where I wrote the script for the motion picture *Transatlantic Tunnel*. It was the first British picture to use an English and American cast — including Walter Huston, Fay Wray, Richard Dix, and George Arliss.

When the British film industry collapsed in 1937, I went to Hollywood. There I wrote and directed about 40 motion pictures for Universal, RKO, and other companies. I even went up the Amazon River for Universal to shoot two motion pictures, which healthwise was not a good idea. During World War II, I was a member of the OSS, the secret service of that time.

After I had to leave Germany, I never again wrote any story in German. English became my treasured mother language. I had many novels published by major American publishing houses.

Among them were *Donovan's Brain* (Knopf), which has not gone out of print for over 40 years; *Hauser's Memory* and *The Third Ear* (G.P. Putnam's Sons); *City in the Sky, Spaceport,* and *For King's Only* (Crown). Besides having written and directed motion pictures in America, England, Germany, France, Italy, and South America, most of my novels were translated into other languages, which has given me the advantage of getting a free lunch from publishers in most European countries.

I had a formal education at the German Universities of Dresden and Stuttgart, as well as the University of Zurich, Switzerland, where I received a degree in mathematics, a discipline that inspired me to write science fiction books. The task of a science-fiction writer is to project the future, as he sees it, on his own time. I predicted the laser beam in 1930, radar and the importance of the aircraft carrier in 1933.

I met my wife, Henrietta Erna de Perrot, while studying at the University of Zurich. We have been together since 1924. I have one son who, instead of choosing the insecurities of being a writer, formed his own industrial company, building exhibitions for corporations like Northrop or for countries like Australia or Sweden. His profession is more financially rewarding than mine.

I am engaged in putting my autobiography, *Unfinished Ruminations*, on paper. It records my connection with the history of European and American literature and motion pictures since 1922 — the year I made my first attempts at writing for films by translating English title cards for Mack Sennett's Keystone Cops comedies into horrible German four-liners.

My autobiography, which I hope to finish this year, is a medley of essays that presents my points of view about life, my personal history, and my memories of the many famous people I have known. Those people were not famous when I met them. Laurence Olivier, Michael Redgrave, and John Huston were beginners struggling to make a living as I was. It took them half of their lifetimes to finally become famous. Some of them I knew well — like Van Karman, the aerodynamic engineer who designed the first American fighter plane used against Hitler.

Van Karman now has his picture engraved on an American postage stamp, as do John Steinbeck, Cole Porter, William Saroyan, and other fleeting acquaintances. By American law, to become officially honored on postage stamps by the government, one has to be dead — a condition that so far I have been able to avoid. A writer is not cursed by the age limitation of our youth-dominated society. He sends his work in by mail, which expands his productive years.

I am often asked which one of my novels or films I like best. I know only one answer: the next one.

Curt Siodmak
Three Rivers, California
1992

September Seventeen

Just before we got to Washington Junction, Donovan reached a crisis. His strong heart had delayed the coma, but it was too late now to send him on to Phoenix. He could not have arrived alive.

I had him carried into my laboratory and put on the operating table. The men looked around curiously. They had not expected such an elaborate lay-out. None of them knew my name or anything about me. But people who live in the desert are not very curious or talkative. The heat which thins the blood makes the brain sluggish, and no one thinks more than is necessary for the primitive functions of life. I lived secludedly;

nobody asked what I was doing. The desert is full of anchorites and lonely people with strange habits.

I sent the men away, then changed to a clean shirt which Janice had left in the laboratory. I found iced coffee on my desk and some food. She was silently waiting in her room for me to call her. The accident had interrupted the monotonous routine of our days and she was hoping I would want to talk to her.

I examined the dying man. His pulse was rapid and his heart-sounds so weak I could hardly hear them with my stethoscope.

I called Janice.

"Where is Schratt?" I asked. I could see she had not slept, waiting for me to return.

"He took the other man to Phoenix," she answered.

"Call up the hospital and tell him to get over here right away. Then come and help me."

She ran out of the room to obey my order.

I had to come to a decision. I had to make up my mind now. At once! Before it was too late. I did not feel exhausted any more. The opportunity was unprecedented. Too tremendous. This man was dying, but his brain was still alive. It was an extraordinary brain, the dome large and of perfect shape, the skull broad, the forehead wide.

I tested its reactions with the encephalograph. It showed strong delta deflections.

An animal's brain has weak reactions and very little resistance. An animal gives up when it is going to die. The brain is a minor organ of its body, less important than the weapons of defense. But the man on my table had exercised his brain all his life, trained it, strengthened it. Here was the perfect specimen a scientist might wish for!

If only Schratt were here!

Donovan's skull was nearly hairless. That made it easier. He was in a coma; it was not necessary to use an anaesthetic.

I switched on the sterilizer and put in a surgical scalpel and a Gigli saw.

When the instruments were ready, I picked out the scalpel and made a semicircular incision in the skin just above the right ear, continuing the incision around the back of the head to the upper surface of the left ear. I pulled the scalpel forward until it completely exposed the top of the calvarium. There was very little bleeding from the exposed surfaces.

Taking the Gigli saw, I made an incision in the bony vault completely around the skull. To leave the brain uninjured, I was very careful not to cut through the dura mater. I then lifted off the entire top of the cranial vault *in toto*.

The glistening surface of the dura mater was still warm to my finger's touch.

I made the same semicircular incision in the dura mater that I had in the outer skin.

I pulled the dura forward, and there lay exposed Donovan's brain!

Donovan's breathing stopped; white asphyxia due to cardiac failure began. There was no time to apply stimulants. That would have taken precious minutes. I had to open his brain while he was still alive. I had made that mistake before with the Capuchin, and I could not take any risk now.

I heard Janice at the phone talking to Phoenix. Schratt was on his way back. She repeated the information loudly so I could hear.

If Schratt's Ford didn't break down!

Janice came in. She stopped, seeing me at work over the body.

"Come here," I ordered gruffly. I wanted to give her no time to think. She had studied medicine to please me and have the chance to be closer to me. Concentrated, cool, precise even in emergencies, she was an ideal nurse. But, like Schratt, she deeply resented the work I was doing, for it took me away from her and she was jealous. I was married to my apparatus and scalpels.

"The Gigli saw! Quick!" I said. I stretched out my hand without looking at her. She hesitated, standing there in the doorway. Then I heard her move. She stepped close behind my shoulder and passed me the instrument. I pressed the Gigli saw to the occipital bone. I was so concentrated on my work I did not hear Schratt enter.

Finally I felt someone watching me. Schratt was standing two yards behind me, staring. His face twisting, he battled with himself, undecided whether to run away or come to my assistance, but finally he overcame the shock of seeing me steal a man's brain.

I lifted up the cranium, severed it by cutting the medulla oblongata just above the foramen magnum.

"We would like to be alone, Janice," I said.

She left at once, relieved to go, I felt, and for a second I regretted having called her to help me. I did not want witnesses!

"Put on those gloves and a smock," I said to Schratt, while I loosened the frontal gyrus with a blunt dissector, carefully feeling my way not to injure the eyes.

Schratt impulsively hid his face in his hands and stood motionless for seconds. When he uncovered his face again, his expression had changed. He had known what I was going to do as soon as he entered the laboratory. I was violating his creed and ethics, but he did not refuse to help me, though I had no power to coerce him.

The frustrated potential Pasteur had broken through and Schratt's vocation was stronger than his conscience. I knew that afterward he would have pangs of remorse, fits of repentance he would try to drown in tequila. He knew it too, but he helped me.

He stepped over to the table and pulled on the gloves. Without waiting to put on a smock, he grabbed the knife. His hands, heavy and coarse-fingered, became subtle. He worked with great speed.

"I'll have to cut here," he muttered, and as I nodded he severed the medulla oblongata.

I took blood serum from the heater, affixed the rubber tube to the rotary pump, and turned on the ultraviolet lights.

"Ready?" Schratt asked.

I nodded, took a steaming towel from the sterilizer, and held it over the brain which Schratt was lifting out of the lower cranium. He carried it over to the glass bowl and submerged it in the serum, fastened the rubber tubes to the vertebral and internal carotid arteries, and set the pump in motion.

"Better hurry," Schratt said, pulling off his gloves. "They may come for the body any minute." His face suddenly looked gray and shriveled. He nodded toward the body. "Better get him in shape. Stuff some cotton in the skull or the eyes might fall in."

I filled the skull cavity with cotton bandages and replaced the cranium, taping it with adhesive. I pulled the scalp back over the calvarium, then I bandaged the head carefully and had foresight enough to soak a few drops of Donovan's blood into the bandages as if a wound from the accident had bled through.

I eagerly turned to see if the brain was still alive, but Schratt stopped me.

"We have done all we can," he said. "Let's get the body out of here. You wouldn't want them to see *that?*" He indicated the brain with a jerky movement of his head. "If we get the body out into the sun, it will decompose fast. I don't want an autopsy."

346

Excitement had fuddled my judgment, and I submitted to Schratt. But he did not seem to enjoy his new authority.

For years Schratt had been inhibited in my presence, I knew that. He had lost his own ambition and drive, and he envied me my persistence in carrying through the researches. But now, though he had the upper hand at last, he did not take advantage of me. Cowardly he walked out on his opportunity to avenge himself for the humiliations I had involuntarily inflicted upon him through all these years.

We put Donovan's body on a stretcher, covered it with a sheet, and carried it outside. The heat would do fast work. We returned to the laboratory and washed up.

"Write the death certificate before the ambulance gets here," I said calmly.

He did not answer and I divined that his remorse had already begun.

Now he must register his crime in black and white, set down evidence that could send him to jail at any time. He was not afraid of the prison so much, but he had lost his last shred of self-respect.

"Sorry. I would write it myself, but I'm not the coroner. Besides, it was your duty to take care of the victims of the crash."

"I'm being blackmailed," he said with a wan smile, but I knew he meant it. He was dangerous. He might give us both away in one of his fits of pathological depression.

"Want a drink?" I asked.

He looked up, astonished, read my thoughts, and shook his head.

"You don't have to get me drunk for me to write the certificate," he muttered, walking over to the desk. "What's the man's name?"

When I told him he paled.

"W. H. Donovan," he repeated, and sat down trembling. I waited for him to recover. "We have stolen Donovan's brain!"

He laughed suddenly, turned to the desk, picked up a pen, and took a blank coroner's report from his pocket.

"I had better leave the name off," he said. "I just hope the heat melts that carcass away before every doctor in the country comes poking his nose into it."

He wrote and passed the paper to me.

"Death due to bleeding and shock preceding amputation of both legs," I read.

"They can see for themselves it's true what I wrote down."

He spoke swaggeringly to hide his uneasiness and walked over to the door. "I'll see that Phoenix collects it."

He put on his big hat and walked away without glancing at me or saying good-by. He was walking out on me again.

He stopped outside for a moment to talk to Janice. They have a curious conspiracy I have never bothered to intrude on and I was not interested now in what they were saying to each other, but I went into my bedroom and called her.

Janice entered at once.

"You ought to sleep a little"; she dropped the suggestion casually. For the first time in years she was telling me what to do. She was tapping hesitantly at the door to my consciousness, timidly trying to remind me of her.

"The ambulance from Phoenix will call for the body. If anyone calls, don't disturb me whoever it is." I sank on the bed. I really needed some sleep.

Even while I was turning to the wall, I could feel sleep blacking out my mind.

September Eighteen

I woke at a very early morning hour. There was food near the bed, where Janice had left it in a thermos to keep warm. I ate hastily and went back to the laboratory. I heard Janice moving in her room, but she did not leave it.

Through the garden window I could see that the body had been taken away. On my desk lay the evening paper and a message. The hospital at Phoenix had phoned for me to come over and report to the coroner. Since Schratt was the coroner in the case, I tossed the paper into the wastebasket.

The Phoenix *Herald* had a big headline:

"Tycoon Dies. W. H. Donovan Killed in Plane. Crash in Snake Mountains."

I put the paper into a drawer of my desk and turned to Donovan's brain.

The pump was faithfully supplying blood to the main artery, and the ultraviolet lights shone through the glass tubes in which the serum circulated.

I wheeled the table with the encephalograph close to the vessel which contained the brain and fastened the five electrodes to the cortical tissue. One near the right ear, two high on the forehead, one above each eye cavity.

The brain of any living creature has an electric beat that is conducted by neurons, not by blood vessels or connecting tissue. All cells show varying degrees of mechanical, thermal, electrical, and chemical activity.

I switched on the current that drove the small motor, which, in turn, drew out a white paper strip an inch per second at a frequency of sixty cycles. A pen scratched a faint line on the moving paper. I amplified the infinitesimally small currents the brain was sending until their power was great enough to move the pen.

On the paper strip the activity of Donovan's thought processes showed in exact, equal curves. The curves repeated themselves; the brain was at rest, not really thinking now. The pen drew smooth alpha curves, concise as breathing.

I tested the occipital lead. The deflections were continuous, ten cycles per second, with very low seven to eight cycles per second waves.

I touched the glass and at once the alpha waves disappeared. The brain in the glass was aware that I was standing there!

Delta waves appeared on the moving strip, a sure indication that the brain was emotionally disturbed.

It seemed fatigued, however, and suddenly it fell asleep again. I saw the repeating pattern reappear. The brain slept deeply, its strength exhausted by the grave operation.

I watched its depthless slumber while the pattern of this sleep, drawn by a pen on white paper, slipped through my fingers.

I watched for hours. I knew I had succeeded.

Donovan's brain would live though his body had died.

And in the same value-packed volume . . .

HAUSER'S MEMORY

"A stunner!"— Cincinnati *Inquirer*

Asked by the CIA to save the secrets of a dying scientist, Dr. Cory unwittingly allows a colleague to transfer the man's memory into his own. And soon Cory has to choose between saving one of the most brilliant minds ever known to man — or destroying his only friend.

SPECIAL BONUS PREVIEW OF *HAUSER'S MEMORY* FOLLOWS.

Picking up trays and cutlery, Cory, Wendtland, Slaughter, and Borg joined a line of students and slowly moved past the food counter of the university cafeteria.

"Be my guest," Cory said, choosing a plate of salads and asking for a slice of roast beef.

"You're ours, of course," Wendtland said. "After all, we're on an expense account."

His smile was strained. The call to Washington had put him in a quandary. He had been told to conduct the Hauser case at his own discretion. He regretted having come West; he should have left the whole affair to Slaughter.

"I'll take you to an expensive restaurant if you insist on picking up the tab," Cory said lightly.

His casualness was a mystery to them all. This man, who was proposing to give himself to a dangerous experiment; showed no signs of apprehension. They expected Cory to be solemn, withdrawn, pensive. His coolness alarmed them.

"What time did you finish last night?" Wendtland asked, as they settled themselves in an island of empty tables.

"About three. We extracted every milligram of RNA."

"When are you going to use it?"

"Tonight. Dr. Queen will be around to observe any pathological changes, I'm going to put a running report of my sensations on tape. Mondoro will be with me constantly."

"What do you mean?" Wendtland was appalled. "Mondoro shouldn't be with you at any time. Look, you don't seem to be fully aware of the importance of the information we might get from you. It certainly mustn't be known to a third party."

"Mondoro isn't a third party," Cory said. "Since I'm conducting the experiment on myself, I'm the sole judge of who will be present and who won't. I've taken rooms in the psychiatric ward. Nobody can get in there without permission. The door's locked."

"But that's impossible!" Borg exclaimed. "That defeats the whole purpose of the idea!"

"Let's assume that the experiment succeeds beyond our expectations. That's possible, isn't it?" Wendtland asked calmly.

"Anything is possible."

"All right then. Queen or Mondoro would learn the information from your newly created memory—the dead man's memory. Those secrets must be safeguarded. How do we know your friends won't pass them on—not maliciously, I'm sure, but out of elation, of joy, of pride? What then? That's why we took a man from Sing Sing. He could be handled. Your men can't, legally. That's why I believe that only Mr. Slaughter or somebody else from our office should be with you. We'll supply an expert in your field if you insist, but our man must be there, day and night. Of course, medical help should be on hand—and we can supply that too. But we can't permit an outsider to hear vital secrets."

"I told you that you'll receive a tape with every word said by me or anybody else. But the experiment will be carried out the way I devise it. My objective is strictly scientific. I certainly am not working for the CIA, and I won't permit any interference from you or anybody else."

"Unbelievable," Borg muttered. The man might siphon off important secrets. He might be in touch with the Russians. No idea was too far-fetched. University people had a history of leftist leanings.

"You forget that you don't own that RNA. It's government property."

"Do you legally own that corpse?" Cory grinned, enjoying the fight. "When you turned it over to the Medical Center, you gave it to us for experimentation—what kind of experimentation

357

was left up to us. You can claim the body, though it's slightly damaged. But Queen could restore it to a reasonably good condition."

Slaughter leaned back in his chair, relieved that he was not involved in the argument. Wendtland and Borg were on the spot, not he.

"All right," Wendtland said amicably. "I can see your point. We won't interfere. By the way, Washington agrees on the fee." Wendtland's Junker face cracked into a smile. "I told them that they might get a bargain."

"Good. Send the check to the Dean."

"Dr. Cory?" A young intern in a white coat was approaching the table, flushed and breathless. "Dr. Queen wants you to phone him right away."

Cory got up, visibly alarmed. "Excuse me."

"I wonder what they're up to now," Borg said, watching Cory cross the room.

"Well, since we've got ourselves involved this far, we'll have to go on," said Wendtland. "I had to give in to Cory. I told you it's no use fighting him. You only make him more stubborn. We'll put a continuous tail on him. Twenty-four hours, reporting every three hours. Also on Mondoro and Queen. And their families. Record their calls. Run a complete dossier check on them. You'll look after that, Slaughter."

"I'll make the necessary local contacts immediately." Slaughter was in his element again.

The three men watched Cory threading his way back through the tables. His face was gray.

His eyes seemed to have sunk deeper into their sockets.

"You'll excuse me," he said hurriedly. "I must go over to the psychiatric ward."

"Anything wrong?" Wendtland asked.

"I should've guessed as much," Cory said in distress. "What a fool I was!"

"What's the matter, Dr. Cory," asked Borg. "Has something happened?"

"It certainly has," said Cory grimly. "Dr. Mondoro has injected the RNA into himself."

It was not the first time Karen had picked up Hillel at the hospital; he often worked there. Every afternoon at four he phoned and told her where to meet him. But this time—and for the first time—Cory had telephoned. So it was with a sigh of relief that she saw Hillel and Cory leave the hospital together. Cory's hand was under Hillel's elbow—only when they came close did she see her husband's deadly pallor. Quickly she pushed the door open and Cory shoved Hillel inside.

Karen touched her husband's cheek. "You're sick."

"Not very," Cory assured her, but he said no more. It frightened her.

Queen had objected to Hillel's leaving the ward, but Cory, an M.D. himself, felt it advisable to let Hillel go home. Not only was he physically able to do so, but it would keep him away from the prying curiosity of the CIA men.

Karen drove slowly, listening to Hillel's labored breathing. "What's the matter with him?" she asked Cory, bulldozing her way through the rush-hour traffic into a side street. Neither answered and her anxiety increased.

"I swallowed the wrong medicine," Hillel finally said jokingly. He coughed and his face contorted.

Karen accelerated. She knew Cory would have made him stay at the hospital if he had been seriously ill, but the strange silence between the two men upset her more and more.

She drove the car jerkily into the garage of their apartment house. Cory helped Hillel out. In the yellow neon of the elevator, Hillel looked older. Fine creases ran from the corner of his eyes to the temples and from mouth to chin. For a moment he looked like his father. And moved like him, stooped, his left shoulder lifted.

"He'll be all right by tomorrow," Cory muttered uncomfortably as they entered the apartment. "Why don't you go to bed and sleep, Hillel?"

Wordlessly he shuffled off, and Karen followed him. Cory took a small tape recorder from his pocket. Knowing how close Hillel and Karen were, he felt sure Hillel would tell her about the injection eventually. But it was essential he gain her confidence at once. He needed her help.

Cory realized with surprise he was proceeding on the supposition that the experiment would succeed.

"Why are you sitting in the dark?" Karen had come in so quietly she startled him. Night had

360

fallen; the room was bathed in shadows.

"No special reason. Sit down."

Her eyes shone luminously, the rest of her features dissolved in semidarkness. "Won't you tell me what happened?"

"Hillel will."

"I tried to talk to him, but he fell asleep."

"He's going to tell you right now," Cory said, and turned on the tape recorder. Hillel's voice emerged:

"In case I become incapacitated, I'm putting down the following information for Dr. Cory. I am injecting the RNA into myself because Dr. Cory has decided to volunteer for the test. Being younger than he, I am in better physical condition, and it is inconceivable that Dr. Cory's work should be endangered. I have decided to inject the full amount of the extracted RNA. The amount is exactly twelve hundred thirty-five milligrams. I have dissolved it in five cc of saline solution and now I shall administer the shot intravenously into my left arm."

For a few seconds the voice stopped. The sound of steel touching glass came from the recorder. Then Hillel's voice returned, matter-of-factly, but with increasing tension.

"The sensation is an extensive burning, and I can trace the solution's progress through my veins into the cavity of my chest muscles. Spasms in the diaphragm start."

Heavy, labored breathing, and then the sound of a telephone dial came from the loudspeaker.

"Dr. Queen's office?" Hillel's voice broke. "This is Mondoro at ten-o-four. Tell Dr. Queen to come over right away—emergency!" A gasp. The sound of the telephone receiver hitting the table. "Cramps. Spasms. My stomach's on fire. Mouth seems to be filled with acid. Vision blurred. I think I'm . . . going to pass out . . ." No more words; only moans. Cory turned off the switch.

"Horrible," Karen said in a dead voice.

"I'd better turn on the light."

Karen's face, always ivory pale, had gone dead white. Her lips, painted stark red, looked like blood.

"There's more on the tape, but this is what I wanted you to know," Cory said levelly. "I'm sure Hillel wouldn't have told it this way."

"No. If he told me at all. He never mentions unhappiness or fears to me. But what's going to happen now?"

"Possibly nothing," Cory said. "He's over the shock now and may have no aftereffects, although RNA ordinarily is given in small doses over an extended period of time. I had no idea he meant to substitute himself for me. If I had, I would have interfered."

"I know you would," Karen said. "He was afraid you might stop him. He talks about you as if he expects you to solve all the world's ills. If I had known that you wanted to go through this test, I'd have guessed what Hillel would do. But what is this stuff he has taken?"

"Hillel will tell you when he's had some rest. But just now we have to make sure he gets better

362

quickly." Cory leaned forward. "I need your help, Karen. We must take all precautions possible, since I can't anticipate what kind of effect this injection will have. I want you to report to me every single change you see in him. In health or behavior."

"Change? You think there'll be a change in him?"

"Now, now, there's no need to get alarmed," he said. "I don't expect any aftereffects, and if there are any, Hillel will tell me. But if by chance something does escape him, please let me know at once."

"I'm terrified."

"There's no reason to be. It's only natural that he will experience some sensations, because his brain has been stimulated. Many drugs, mescaline and LSD for instance, produce pathological reactions of one kind or another. Our imagination responds to all of them. But the aftereffects disappear in a short time."

"My mother warned me not to marry a scientist," she said, confidence returning to her voice. "She said I should marry a shoe clerk, who leaves his troubles behind when he comes home from work. He wouldn't think of shoes, he'd think only of me."

"Doesn't Hillel?"

She nodded, then suddenly stiffened. A moment later Cory heard Hillel's scream. She ran into the bedroom.

Hillel was propped up in bed, his eyes closed, his face distorted with fear. Again he screamed.

"Hillel! Hillel!" Karen shook him violently.

He opened his eyes wide and stared at her. "What happened?"

"You screamed," she said, still shocked.

"Did I?" He slid deeper into the bed. "I didn't know. It must have been a nightmare."

He turned to Cory, his voice sober and controlled. "It was like a nightmare drugs produce— reserpine, amytal, phenobarbital. It was vivid." The color was coming back into his face, but the look of horror was still in his eyes.

"A nightmare?" Cory pulled a chair close to the bed. "Do you remember it?"

"He never dreams," Karen said.

Hillel's long fingers were shaking on the bedsheet. Karen picked up his hand, covering it with both of hers.

"Let me record my dream on tape, Dottore. It might be related to the RNA."

"Why don't you keep quiet," Karen pleaded. "Please, Dottore, tell him not to excite himself."

Hillel threw back at the bedcovers. "I didn't inject that stuff to be treated like a sick man," he said. "Let me record the dream as long as it's fresh in my mind."

"I'll remember it for you. You'd better stay here," Cory said.

Karen gently covered him with the bedclothes.

"A bombing," Hillel said, and collapsed on his pillow.

"A war?" Cory asked.

"Yes, I heard air-raid sirens, and then came the bombs. First from afar, then closer and closer.

They whistled before they hit. There was no place to run or hide."

"You haven't been in a war," Cory said in a neutral voice, "How did you know it was a bombing? From movies, TV?"

Hillel closed his eyes; his face was strained. "I was in a shelter with a lot of people. Some were in uniform." He suddenly laughed, surprised and incredulous. "Nazi uniforms."

"Have you seen a Nazi picture lately, or read a book about them?"

"I have," Karen said. "It's still here next to my bed." She picked up the book; on its cover was a blood-red swastika.

"That's what might have triggered your dream," Cory said.

"I can't remember seeing the book, but how can I be sure?" Hillel said. "I'm absentminded, and I only see what I want to see."

"Try to recall the surroundings of your dream or familiar faces," Cory pressed him gently.

"I didn't know anybody, though the people were strangely familiar to me. But I knew it was I in the shelter. I wore a uniform."

"Are you sure?" Cory asked, trying to be objective and not to connect this to the German whose RNA he had extracted.

"No—I can't say for sure. I watched myself in that dream, and in a detached way, too. It was so vivid that I wasn't sure if I was awake or dreaming. I remember I wore a gold ring with a crest made of a gold deer's head on a blue stone; it was heavy, maybe a fraternity ring."

Hillel looked at his hand. "I can even feel where it made an imprint." He lifted his hand close to his eyes.

"It was a dream, remember," Karen said urgently.

"But why can I still feel the imprint?" Hillel turned to Cory for an answer. "Sometimes one only remembers parts of dreams. I might have dreamed much more and forgotten."

"What else do you remember?" Cory suppressed his eagerness to question Hillel too severely. It was too early to force him to evaluate his nightmare; he was a sick man.

"Every time a bomb hit nearby, things fell down," Hillel said vaguely.

"What kind of things?"

"Instruments slid off tables. Electronic equipment. Radios, vacuum tubes, the kind they used in the thirties, not transistorized. There were inscriptions in German on boxes and on the wall."

"You don't speak German, remember?" Cory had to be cautious, subject evidence to the most stringent tests; dreams have their own logic, a logic that has nothing to do with the logic of scientific research.

"No, I don't, although I know Yiddish. But these were words I had never seen before. Strange, but I still see them now: *Notausgang, Hauptschaltung, Hochspannung.*"

"What makes you sure you've never heard or read them?" Cory pressed on. "You've looked at books written in German—we have a lot in

366

the library. They might have lingered in your subconscious and appeared in your dream."

Exhausted, Hillel closed his eyes. "That attack took the stuffing out of me," he muttered, and instantly fell asleep.

Karen took his lifeless hand. Misery was written in every line of her body, in the bend of her slim back, in the dark hair falling around her thin shoulders. She sat quietly, watching Hillel's waxen face.

Cory nodded to her. Slowly she withdrew her hand from Hillel's and followed Cory out of the bedroom.

"Do you think it was simply a dream?" she whispered. "Something his mind has made up? Or could it be"—she looked at him in fright—"someone else's memory?"